Times and Places

Times and Places

* * *

Gary H. Baker

ISBN: 1984196154
ISBN 13: 9781984196156

Also by Gary H. Baker

The Truck Driver Series:
Rookie Truck Driver
West Bound, Hammer Down, Trouble in Montana
Truck Dreams
If My People

The Big Ride – Short Stories
Sea Patrol – The Perilous Journey Authored by Gary K.
Everist, Produced by Gary H. Baker

Table of Contents

*Denotes a nonfiction story

* * *
Foreword

As the stories were accumulating, I had little foresight as to whether there might be a common theme running through them, a familiar thread of wisdom or insight running through all of them. To the contrary, it was beginning to look like a hodgepodge, helter skelter, jumbled patchwork of stories I was writing and soliciting from my friends. My wife says it remains at that level to this day. God bless her beautiful soul. But let's not be careless and hair-triggered in adopting her critique as our own. Let me, at least, defend my side of the story; let me defend a more mature, a more well-rounded, a more structurally sound foundation upon which rest the stories herein.

In the final editing and selection process of stories to include, I began to realize that indeed there was a common theme running through them. Maybe not a bludgeoning hammer that relentlessly pounded home one central theme; who would want that anyway? I think it is a more subtle thought stream, maybe like a country brook after heavy rains, it begins to rise, and before you know what's happened, it has your attention. It's rising, and still it's rising, and yes, now it definitely has your attention.

The "more subtle thought stream" is the Vietnam generation, the Baby Boomer generation – my generation, Ron Greene's generation, as well as Phillip Ray, J. D. Farmer, Larry Price, Aubrey Goff, Butch Hicks, Danny Arnette, Larry Mc Cubbins, Joe Norris, Dewey Smith, Gerald Callahan, Mike Bond, Rick Shelton, Mike Crabb, , Michael Webb, Dennis Haynes, Tom Crumpton, Barry Lobb, Bradley Nicholson, Bruce Bale, Charles Shuffitt, Dennis DeSpain, Dennis Lawrence, Edward Waugh, Fred Pugh, George Daniels, James Barry Jeffries, James Robert Mitchell, Jerry Blake, Jerry Owen, Jim Burke, Jim Dixon, Jimmy Flener, Joe Fields, Joe Sweeney, Keith Flood, Larry Paul, Larry Rooks, Lawrence Fields, Mark Caulk, Ralph Lawson, Richard (Yogi) Buckley, Robert Mayfield, Steve Miles, Warren Ploetner, William Dewey Mitchell, and Larry Wright. These were all young men from Fairdale High School in Fairdale, Kentucky that served in the armed forces in Vietnam. If I've left out a name, it is by no means intentional. Some never came home. Some perished after coming home. And of course, many are still alive today. My love for each and every one of these, my Fairdale brothers, is deep and abiding, and I truly do look forward to the day we all muster-up in that spectacular company formation in the heavens above.

Of the thirteen stories, I counted at least five of my own stories that make some sort of reference to, flash backs of, or memories of Vietnam.

And then there is Ron Greene's account of his ten-month, in-country, tour of duty. In my opinion it's as good as anyone's Vietnam stories. We lost Ron a few years back. His particular experience is up close and personal with me. This will become evident when you read my introduction to his story, <u>Yea, Though I Walk.</u>

As you read <u>Times and Places</u>, you are likely to recall similar events in your own personal Baby Boomer history. Maybe memories that still resonate, still vibrate; maybe recollections of anti-war protest, or that "Summer of Love" in Haight Ashbury in 1967; or maybe that first week in boot camp when the world you knew before would never return again, ever.

In my case, I still remember vividly the reverse Easy Rider adventure my friend Mike Thompson and I stumbled through in 1972. We went from east to west (Kentucky to Berkley), not west to east (L. A. to New Orleans) like Fonda, Nicholson, and Hopper did in the movie. And we went in a V. W square-back wagon, not on a Harley Davidson motorcycle. We met, travelled with, and lived with hippies, political agitators, and law-dodgers along the way. When we eventually dropped out of the sky in paradise (Hawaii), we loved beautiful women, we fought, we drank, we smoked dope, we experienced death and tragedy, and we came back to the mainland, years later, with Jesus in our hearts.

Go figure.

James Michener, I believe, wrote a pretty good novel about our generation in those days. He called it, <u>The Drifters</u>.

I call some of my recollections <u>Times and Places</u>.

And, it's okay if you end up agreeing with my wife. It's okay. She might be right.

And so, now, the only thing left is to give much credit and thanks to Ron Greene, Jim Harstad, and Harry H. Baker for their contributions to <u>Times and Places</u>. Along with Pete Ray, Phillip Ray, Mike Thompson, George Czarnecki, and Gary Everist, they are the truest and best friends any man could ever have, except of course for Jesus Christ, my all, and my only Savior.

Also, much credit and respect , as well as many thanks goes to Laurie Pooler, another Baby Boomer and Army veteran who did the art work for the cover. Her intuition, skill, and dedication to the task made it possible for the cover to be exactly what I had envisioned.

Gary H. Baker

For The Baby Boomers and The Vets

Two Cases of Beer

* * *

Gary H. Baker

"WHAT ARE YOU doing tomorrow night?"

"I don't know. Maybe go to the ball park."

"I know where we can get some beer."

"Uh, you don't mean Walter do you? I don't trust him."

"No, not Walter."

"Who you talking about?"

"Well, I know where we can get it ourselves."

"Where?"

"Over at Saint Vincent."

"The Catholic Church?"

"Yeah, Saint Vincent. You know, the church, the school, it's all right there together."

"Well yeah, sure, but … but …"

"Hey man, it ain't no big deal. I know right where the cooler is. We slip in, grab a couple of cases, beat feet, and we'll be gone. The nuns will still be sleeping when we hit the road."

"The nuns? Whata' you mean, the nuns?"

1

"Well … you see, that might be the only problem, but I got it figured out."

"You got it figured out?"

"Yeah, sure. Look, Adam told me all about it, but they're all to chicken to do it."

"Let me guess … Adam, Bud, and Mac, they told you about it, but they don't want to do it themselves. Right? They dared you and me to do it. Right?"

"That's exactly what they did. And I bet they think we won't do it. They're probably laughing about it right now. Getting' a good joke out of it."

"Yeah, I can see them now. They're probably out joy-riding with Tommy right now. I bet they got a fifth of V O and a couple of six packs. Who does Tommy get to buy booze for him? He doesn't look old enough, and I've seen that fake I D of his. Nobody would fall for it."

"I don't know about that. All it's gotta' say is you're twenty-one. That's it. You're in business."

"But Tommy doesn't even look like the sixteen he really is. You look older than Tommy, and you're only fourteen."

"I don't know where he gets the booze, but I know one thing."

"What's that?" Truman asked.

"Where we're gonna' get two cases of beer from," Pocket answered.

The following evening was a sweltering Friday night. Truman and Pocket were ganged up with Benny Wilson, Harmon Trindle, and Ted Morris. It was after midnight and they were going over their final plans to steal beer from the Saint Vincent Catholic Church and School.

Pocket had naturally assumed command of the operation, with Truman as his main assistant. Benny, Harmon, and Ted, all three of them thirteen years old, would be look-outs. "After me and Truman do a walk-through of the parking lot, you'll know everything is okay. We'll stop and look to you guys. If the coast is clear, give us a thumbs up. If something is coming, give a thumbs down."

"What if the nuns ain't sleeping?" It was Benny Wilson.

"I done told you. Your brother Bud, and Adam too, they both said the nuns all snore like a hurricane is coming through. If we don't hear them snorin', we won't go in."

"What about the Father?"

"He lives over in the house at the end of the parking lot. What? You think he'd live with the nuns?"

"Why not? They're Catholic ain't they? Who knows what them people do?"

"No way! If the lights stay off in his house, we'll be good." Pocket looked at the four boys, his troops, and gave the command-order from behind a bunch of trees a block down the street from Saint Vincents, "Okay, let's go. Everybody get in position."

A few minutes later Pocket and Truman had returned to the side basement door of the school building, after they had made their test walk-through of the parking lot.

Pocket tiptoed up to the door and opened it right up. "Just like Adam and Bud said," he whispered.

The boys slithered into the building's basement and headed for the beer cooler. The racket created by the four nuns, sleeping and snoring, just one floor above them, was almost riotously comical. Pocket and Truman both had to seriously put a suppression clamp over the guffaws they nearly let escape.

In a moment they were in the walk-in cooler. Pocket shined his flash light around and they didn't waste any time in choosing two cases of Schiltz beer. As soon as each boy picked up a twenty-four-count wooden crate with the glass long necks, a tinkling and rattling of glass on glass occurred. They stepped out of the cooler and the first thing they noticed was the snoring up above them had stopped.

"Oh no!" Pocket hissed lowly.

The next thing they heard was a door open above them and someone scrambling down the steps.

"Drop the beer, let's go!" Truman cried out, not even trying to muffle or tone down his alarm.

"Ain't happening! Don't drop it! Let's go!", and Pocket led them out the door and caught just a glimpse of lights coming on behind him. A nun in a long cream-colored cotton night gown stood at the bottom of the steps with a baseball bat drawn back over her shoulder, scanning the room, looking for a target.

By the time they made it back to their camp site a mile and a half away, back behind the railroad tracks, on the banks of the creek by the cornfield, it was after one in the morning. Benny Wilson and Ted Morris were building a camp fire, Harmon Trindle was looking for an opener to uncap his first beer, and Pocket and Truman were still laughing.

"I wish you'd seen her. I swear 'fore God she'd a' took our heads off!" Pocket had a club of firewood raised back over his shoulder in demonstration.

Truman hastily pronounced, "You were funny, man. You were funny. When I said let's drop the beer, you said, 'Ain't happening, we ain't dropping no beer'. Crazy man, crazy!"

"I didn't say that. I just said, 'Let's go'".

"Whatever. It was crazy! I know that."

Harmon Trindle had his first beer opened and two more ready to go, "Let's chug the first three and then we'll get down to some serious drinking." He didn't look like much of a drinker at all, what with his boyish good looks, his brown hair slightly falling just above his sharp, mysterious eyes, and his innocent ways. But he talked a mean game, and the others all gathered around the burgeoning flickers of the new camp fire.

The first round of chugging was underway. Truman was the first to down all three beers, and a freshly lit Marlboro followed it. Pocket put down the first beer in about seven or eight seconds but cooled off because he loved to smoke while he drank. Benny Wilson would never have been sucked into a chugging contest. He drank slowly and deliberately, enjoying every drop of brew. It was the youngest and the smallest of all five boys, Ted Morris, who lost the chugging contest. He puked up what he'd poured down at the one and a half beer mark. His poor stomach simply would not tolerate such an invasion of poison.

A half mile away from the younger boy's camp site, the older boys were walking along the shiny railroad tracks. The rails were sparkling in the moon light, running off to towns twenty or thirty miles away, who knew? maybe a thousand miles away. To the boys walking the rails, they may as well have been running off to Calcutta, or to Timbuktoo. The boys were only fourteen or fifteen years old. They weren't going anywhere real soon, and they had no way of knowing that in just four more years most of them would either enlist or be drafted in order to march into Vietnam and be cannon fodder for the suppression of The Dominoe Theory. In the early years of the war they would believe their service to be honorable – the defense of freedom and liberty, a deterrent to communist aggression and expansion. They'd all seen their fathers and uncles answer the call in World War Two and Korea, and like it or not, it would soon be their time to step up, their time to go to war.

But tonight, the war they were marching off to was something much different, and in some ways it was brimming over with equally startling realizations about who they were and who they might become. Tonight's war wouldn't even amount to a good scuffle; there were just some young hooligans, even younger than they were, and three of them were their own brothers. The younger ones had been foolish enough to accept the dare, and then, unbelievably, walk right into the Saint Vincent School and run out with two cases of beer. There was no doubt the younger boys would at this very moment be in the early stages of their celebration. But the older boys had every intent to put an end to the celebration. Bud, Adam, Mac, and Squirrel were confident about the beer raid they were about to launch. It was going to be easy – just walk into the younger boy's camp, grab the beer, and head off to their own party – no young punks allowed, thank you very much.

They all knew Bud Wilson's little brother Benny wouldn't fight. He never had before. Adam McAllister's younger brother, Truman, now... he just *might* fight. Truman had an unpredictable and wild streak in him. Still, Adam had whipped him before, and Adam was confident that Truman, and for that matter, the rest of the young ones, would not dare challenge this band of four treacherous rebels. Mac Brown and Squirrel Brown, on the other hand, knew their brother, Pocket, would fight to the death for as little a prize as a cigarette butt. But there was no need to say anything to Bud or Adam. If the two of them together couldn't handle their own brother, it sure didn't say much about their own toughness, and toughness was everything in the neighborhood the boys grew up in. It was working class all the way - redneck crackers in the woods behind you, and rugged Irish Catholics in the city in front of you. But tonight's adventures would be no sweat. It was just five young punks they were about to attack, three of them their own little brothers, and the other two, Harmon Tindle and Ted Morris? Come on, you kidding? Harmon was maybe five foot-five and a hundred and ten pounds dripping wet. Ted Morris? Surely you're joking. Ted didn't play football, didn't smoke cigarettes, and rumor was, he liked poetry.

Be all that as it may, it was the five young boys who had the two cases of beer.

It was Squirrel Brown that spotted the campfire first. "That's them, down by the creek. See the fire?"

"Yeah, that's them. Let's split up," Bud Wilson said, and then he looked at Mac and Adam. "When you guys cross the creek, make a lot of noise, you know, maybe like it's an Indian attack or something. They'll be distracted. Me and Squirrel will come in from the back, grab the beer, and beat feet."

Bud and Squirrel snuck around behind the beer camp while Mac and Adam crept up close, easily hiding in the trees just across the banks of the tiny, shallow creek bed. When the war whoops and screaming exploded from the creek, Benny Wilson, Bud's two-year younger brother at thirteen, the boy who wouldn't fight, grabbed his BB gun and started shooting at the two attackers crossing the creek and starting up the bank on the campsite side just fifteen feet away. At the same time, Pocket Brown found a grapefruit- size rock and with a running thrust, hurled it at his older brother Mac, and caught him flush just above his right eye.

The blow nearly knocked Mac out cold, but not quite. When Mac gathered his senses, and pulled his drenched body up out of the water all he could see out of his right eye was a flood of gooey blackness descending slowly. His left eye didn't help him all that much either. Mac had been legally blind in both eyes since six years old. At almost sixteen, he was also the biggest and strongest of all the boys. He lurched out at the first moving object his senses suggested to him might be the enemy. When he got close enough he engulfed his victim with a bear hug and commenced to beat his catch into the trunk of a sycamore tree.

"Mac, it's me!" screamed Adam. "It was Pocket that caught you with the rock! I seen him!"

On the back side of the camp things were about to proceed a little more closely to the original plan– a quick easy victory for the older boys, culminating with the heist of the two cases of beer, or at least what was left of the two cases.

When the battle at the banks of the creek had begun, Bud and Squirrel made their move. First they went after Bud's little brother Benny and disarmed him. Surprisingly, Benny continued to fight, but he wasn't strong enough to stop the two older boys from beating him up and dropping him down in the mud. It was about then that Bud and Squirrel could see Ted Morris abandoning the battlefield. Ted was running off towards home as quick as his feet would carry him.

Harmon Tindle, they noticed, was running away also, not towards home, but out through the middle of the cornfield, doing the best he could not to lose any of the longneck beers in the wooden case he squeezed in towards his chest.

"He's got the beer!" Squirrel screamed.

"Let's go!" Bud yelped.

The chase didn't take long, and when Bud easily pinned Harmon down on the ground, Bud was kneeling over Harmon, completely astride him with his weight on Harmon's belly. He looked down into the jagged fear escaping the whites of Harmon's frenzied moon-lit eyes, and as he did so, something vile and ugly was erupting in Bud.

"Why were you running from us, boy?"

"Yeah, why'd you run off with the beer, punk?" echoed Squirrel.

"I wasn't running … I was just … uh … just …"

"Looked to me like you was running, boy."

"No, no, I was just …"

"Don't you be lying to us. You know what me and Squirrel does to liars?"

"I ain't lying."

The three of them could hear the noise of battle raging back at the campsite, but here in the cornfield things were getting very still and very quiet. Bud didn't say anything and neither did Squirrel.

Finally, after having taken a count of the long necks in the wooden case, Squirrel said, "It looks like about half the beer is gone."

"Well, well, well," Bud said incredulously, still on top of Harmon, not letting him wriggle around very much. "Half the beer is missing. Do you know why half the beer is missing, boy?"

"Uh, well … we drank some."

"You drank some? That was our beer. Did you know that? It was ours. We told you about it, and it looks like you were going to drink it all."

"But we got it, not you guys."

"Yeah, you got it all right, but I don't believe you drank any of it. I think you hid it. What do you think Squirrel?"

"Yeah, you're right Bud. I think they hid it."

"Where did you hide it Harmon?"

"I didn't hide none." Harmon croaked as if he knew things were about to go downhill.

"You know what we do to liars, Harmon?"

"I ain't lying."

"Squirrel, get down there by his head and hold his arms down."

"Now Harmon, I've always liked you, but when it comes to stealing and hiding *our* beer, I sorta' run out of patience. You know what I mean?"

There was no audible response from Harmon, just a trembling that was running through his skeleton that shook the corn stalks he was laying against enough to rattle their dry husks as if a quick wind had set in.

Bud lifted something from a scabbard he had hanging from his leather belt. He let it catch the moon light just a foot above Harmon's eyes. The silvery moon beams made the object come alive. It danced and sparkled. It flashed and glittered. Its' cold steel blade spoke a language previously unknown to thirteen-year-old Harmon.

"You know what this is boy?" Bud himself became something different – something he didn't recognize. But there was nothing he could do about it, only to go along with whatever this thing was that was becoming himself.

"This is a twelve-inch Bowie Knife. You know what I'm going to do with it? That is, if you don't tell us where you hid the rest of the beer."

Again, there was no audible response from Harmon, that is unless tears made noise. There were some of them by now.

"Pull his head back Squirrel." Bud began lowering the Bowie Knife down towards Harmon's neck.

A few minutes later Bud and Squirrel made their way back to the camp site by the little creek. There was no one with them. Mac and Pocket Brown were wrestling around in the mud, half in the creek and half out. Pocket was a biting, tearing, kicking machine. Every time Mac would try to land a haymaker, Pocket would counter with a club aimed at Mac's groin area or his already bleeding face. The fact that Mac was practically blind rendered his advantages of size and strength totally ineffective. The brothers would continue battling for another five minutes when they would finally collapse from exhaustion.

In the meantime, Adam was experiencing similar problems with his little brother Truman. The difference was, both of these boys could see each other, and they were both landing blows that did terrible damage. Sticks, rocks, tree limbs, and in Adam's case, an old tire carcass laying in the weeds, had been used to wallop Truman with. Still, Truman would not give in, and finally, after both boys experienced broken teeth, they sat in the mud nursing their wounds.

A battle of mostly brother on brother had just ended. As for Bud's younger brother Benny, he'd decided to pretty much become a spectator after he'd been disarmed. He would have been a brother fighter too, but of course Bud had been off in the cornfield when the worst of it was going on in camp.

Adam was making his way towards the still brightly burning camp fire. After spitting out more chips of broken teeth through his bloody lips, he said, "Okay, so where's the beer?"

"Yeah, I sure could use one," muttered Mac Brown.

"I got bad news," said Bud, getting closer to the fire himself and lighting a cigarette. He took a deep drag and let the smoke leak out as he talked, "We took off after Harmon because we thought he was running away with the beer."

"Well, was he?" Adam asked.

"No, he didn't have it. He said he was pretty sure that Ted hid it somewhere. Anyway, we let Harmon go on home too."

Mac wasn't happy at all, "If I wasn't so beat up, I'd chase him down and make him tell us where he hid it."

"Me too," quipped Adam.

Eventually Adam was ready to give up on the night, "Let's play some football tomorrow over in the field."

Everybody thought that sounded good. Adam and his brother Truman were headed home, and Mac and his brother Pocket left also.

Bud said, "I think I'll hang around the camp fire a little while."

"Me too," said Squirrel.

"See you tomorrow," was thrown back by Adam.

"Yeah, see you tomorrow," Buc shouted back to Adam.

The three of them Buc, Squirrel, and Benny were sitting around the camp fire smoking.

"Let me try one of your Salems, Squirrel," Benny said.

"I thought you were hooked on those cancer sticks, Marlboros," Squirrel responded.

"Not when I'm drinking beer, then it becomes Salem time."

"It's beer time. They've been gone ten minutes now. They're not coming back," Buc said.

"I sure hope not. There was enough fighting already tonight," Squirrel said, still remembering the beatings his two brothers had given each other.

Buc got to his feet and hollered out loud, "All right Harmon, come on in. They're gone!"

A minute later a happy looking Harmon Tindle strode into camp, an open beer in one hand and what was left of a case of beer in the other.

"You sure they ain't coming back?"

Harmon looked at Benny, "I guess we better bring out that other case."

While Benny got up and headed off into the woods down on the lower end of the creek, Buc and Squirrel opened themselves a long -neck Schlitz and Squirrel said, "A toast. Here's to all's well that ends well."

A minute later Benny returned with the second case of Schlitz. "I just got one question." He was looking towards Bud and Squirrel. "What happened out there in the cornfield? The look in your eyes ... I thought if you caught Harmon, you'd kill him. I swear. That's what it looked like."

"Well we wanted to, believe me, but I couldn't, I just couldn't." Bud complained.

"What do you mean?" Benny asked.

"Let Harmon tell you. All I want to do is get drunk."

Benny looked at Harmon pleadingly and lit a cigarette and handed it to him, "Here, suck on this while you're telling me what happened."

"Ahhh, they caught me and knocked me down on the ground. Buc became some kind of a vampire or something. I don't know what. He put a Bowie Knife to my neck."

"No! My brother acting like he'd kill somebody?"

"He wasn't acting."

"Come on."

"I'm telling you he meant it. Then he started saying I was lying to him. Well, *of course* I was. I knew you were hiding that second case, but I didn't rat you out."

"All right man, keep talking."

"Well, he kept saying I was lying and did I know what he and Squirrel did to liars? I didn't say anything. He was on top of me with that Bowie Knife, you know? And then he was bringing it down towards my throat, and got it real close, and, and ... I was crying like a baby, and he just kept getting it closer and closer, and, and he asked me if I knew what he was going to do with it, you know? That's what he asked me."

"What did you say?"

"I said, Yeah I know what you're going to do with it. You're going to cut my balls off and stick them down my throat. But you ain't going to find my balls. You know why? I'll tell you why. Because I'm so scared right now they done crawled up inside my body and you'd never find 'em. Trust me. I can't even find them my own self."

All four of them broke out into hooting and laughing so hard they almost cried, just like Buc and Squirrel had done about a half hour ago in the cornfield when they had Harmon pinned on the ground, when Harmon had said the same thing then.

Gonna' Miss Them All

* * *

Gary H. Baker

Isaiah 28: 9-10

"Whom will he teach knowledge?
And whom will he make to
understand the message?
Those just weaned from milk?
Those just drawn from the breasts?

IT WAS COLD, maybe fifteen above. Bubba Shiner looked through his drawer to locate a warm pair of socks. Most of them were thread bare and worn out and inside his tattered two-year-old high-top sneakers, they would not afford him very much warmth on the way to school this morning. He walked out of his room and through the narrow hall that opened up to the front room and the kitchen. The house was quiet except for a little cold wind whistling through door and window frames. His mother had died three years ago when he was twelve, and his father was probably somewhere in Georgia on his way back from delivering a load of hardwood lumber with the flatbed trailer.

"You want some coffee?" his sister asked. She was sitting on the couch in the front room watching the morning news on the old black and white which worked overtime to pull in just enough of a signal from Boone, about forty miles away. The picture was ravaged by what seemed to be a dust storm blowing across the screen, and every few seconds the horizontal bars would twitch up and down at differing rates of speed. The audio began to get scratchy and before it disappeared, Bubba's sister thought the last thing she heard the weatherman say was something about a snow and ice storm heading their way.

She braced herself to make an attempt at rising from the couch, and with a hard, final push-off, she managed to stand up not quite vertical, but close enough. She lifted her swollen belly with her hands and appeared to want to carry the massive load to the kitchen with those same hands, not with her feet and legs.

Bubba asked, "We got any sugar?"

"Sure, but there ain't no milk."

"I'll squeeze some outa' your titties."

"Bubba, if you say anything like that again, I'm gonna' tell daddy when he gets home."

"You do, you'll wish you didn't. Anyway, I ain't worried about him."

Later, outside, walking towards the bus stop, Bubba spotted Casey Horner coming down the road in his direction. Casey was wearing a high school letter jacket with a baseball insignia stitched up at the top of the gold S, which represented Luther H. Sloan High School. Casey's sneakers were almost new, and the baseball cap he wore sported the same golden S.

When they both arrived at the bus stop, Bubba said, "I thought you'd be driving the Plymouth today."

"Yeah. It must be that solenoid again, and I ain't guaranteeing it don't need a couple of plug wires."

"Well, you gonna' get her fixed up?"

"Yeah, Daddy's gonna' get the parts today. He's working over at Star Valley. I'll put 'em in tonight. Pick you up in the mornin'."

"All right, and maybe we can go out the ridge and pick up Darrinda, and you know, take the old log road back, and just happen to get lost for a little while."

"Bubba, I don't know she's puttin' out. Even if she was, I wouldn't be takin' you with me."

"I thought we's buds."

"We ain't buds that much."

The school bus driver's name was John. He'd been driving this same route since 1965, sixteen years ago, and he could tell some breathtaking stories about winter driving in the snow and ice on these back-mountain roads in deep Appalachia in northwest North Carolina. John maneuvered the bus down off Tan Bone Mountain picking up a few more riders along the way. There were three switch-backs and rock outcroppings dripping with huge ice cycles, but the narrow road was clear and dry. At the bottom the road continued northeast for about five miles and they passed the Humphrey's Paper Mill Plant where many of the rider's parents went to work each day. The rank, sour odor discharged from the plant's boilers and evaporators would gag outsiders, but to natives, it had seeped into their skin for as long as any of them could remember, and posed no problems they could recognize.

Continuing to pick up riders every half mile or so, John was now just a couple of miles from Luther H. Sloan High School. The James Brothers Poultry Plant sat over on a side road a half mile away. Whereas the paper mill drew very little objection from the citizenry, the chicken plant was a continual complaint, a severe blemish on the county, a disgrace. The foul odor alone was enough to cause anyone to avoid close proximity to the plant. But there was no escaping it. A cloud of stench from decaying chicken and turkey innards hung over a good piece of the valley a good part of the time. The stench, however, was not the only problem. In the winter, fifty per cent of the labor force at the chicken plant were migratory Mexicans. Many of them would move on to less oppressive field work in the spring and summer, but the cold weather brought them to the little town of Gumtree, North Carolina and the James Brothers Poultry Plant where they bided their time de-heading and de-gutting chickens.

The main problem they presented was the fact they would work hard for anything. This, of course, drove the wages down for everybody, natives included. There wasn't any violence or big trouble most of the time. Occasionally some drunk locals would start a fight, but most of the time the lid was kept on what could have been plenty of trouble.

In the half-hour bus trip to school, Bubba and Casey were talking about what Mr. Lanning might have planned for them today. Will Lanning, thirty-four-years-old was the first and only Alternative education teacher the Wautauga County School System had ever hired. His wife, Emily, was an Anthropology Associate Professor at Appalachian State University in nearby Boone. Will and Emily were most often found mingling in the university social circles in and around Boone as opposed to getting very much involved with the staff of the Luther H. Sloan High School in Gumtree. That fact, in no way, reduced the passion and energy that Will brought to his job – teaching the alternative education program every day.

The program didn't operate on Wautauga County School System funding, but rather, was bankrolled by a federal grant. The county school system had a grant specialist whose primary focus was to go after any free money he could capture. There was a lot of it floating around, and a highly skilled grant specialist was worth his weight in gold to a small, low budget, rural school system.

"I hope we don't go out on the road picking cans today," Bubba said, as the school bus was getting closer to the high school.

"Nah, too cold. I bet we build more paper stands," Casey offered.

"Ya' know, I still ain't too sure about Lanning."

"That's Mr. Lanning." Casey held a healthy regard for the young alternative ed. teacher. Shucks, if it wasn't for Mr. Lanning, Casey would not have maintained his eligibility to play sports. His ninth-grade year he had all F's and D's in the academic subjects. He did great in wood shop, auto shop, and P. E., but to play sports, that wasn't enough. This now, his second year in TAP (Teen Advancement Project), he'd been able to maintain high C's and low B's in enough academic classes to keep him eligible to play sports.

"Whatever. I just think he's a little too smartelicky for his own good."

"Bubba, that's what you've said about every teacher you've ever had."

"No, it ain't."

"Yes, it is. You remember what you did to Mrs. Tetterbone back in the sixth grade?"

"I didn't do nuthin' to her."

"What do you mean, you didn't do nuthin' to her? What was that dirty picture you drew on the blackboard with her on her knees, and that writin' you put under it – Mrs. Tatterbone at work?"

"She was a sorry-ass teacher."

"No, she wasn't."

"Yeah, I think she was."

* * *

As John's school bus was pulling into the Luther Sloan property and nudging its way on up to the loading dock to unload his passengers, other high school students were arriving in other buses and also in automobiles driven by parents, and a good number of student-driven cars and pick-up trucks. A handful of maybe thirty students walked to the school daily as their homes in the small community of Gumtree were very close by.

One student whose home was nearby but who was always driven to school by her mother was almost sixteen-year-old Wanda Oakley. Only on days that one or two of Wanda's friends would pick her up did Mrs. Oakley not perform the morning transportation ritual. She liked to think it was one small way she could build on and bolster the bonds with her daughter who was going through that most difficult year of change – from a girl of fifteen to a girl of sixteen. And it wasn't the physical changes. For

Wanda, that had already happened. With Wanda, there were the emotional and intellectual changes that were proving to be a significant source of worry to her mother. The teachers in the county were apt to use the term cognitive development. Since fourth grade, Wanda had been identified by the school psychologist as border-line special education material. To the professional educators in the field, being labeled a special education student could mean many things – developmentally delayed, learning disabled, dyslexic, language impaired, and a host of other designations. But to the kids her age, it only meant slow, stupid, dumb, and all the other slurs attached to being different.

Little did Mrs. Oakley know that Wanda wasn't very happy with all of her mother's attempts at helping her with all the adjustments she, Wanda, was having difficulty with – the adjustments from middle school to high school, the adjustments from a too skinny eighth-grader to a comely and shapely teenager who was nearing her sixteenth birthday. And, now, this adjustment that Wanda was having to make – her second year in the alternative ed. class, TAP, Teen Advancement Project.

Many of the fourteen students in TAP were like Wanda – they had either been in special ed. most of their first eight or nine years in public schools, or they had been borderline special ed. and barely managed to avoid that dubious distinction. And of course, some TAP students were simply squares trying to fit into a round hole, trying to fit into an educational model of "one size fits all". And then there was the majority of TAP students – the throw away children of Appalachia. Parents giving up on life and thereby giving up on their children, many of them using alcohol as the tool to do so.

You see, Wanda felt like most teenagers do. She wasn't crazy about being seen as dependent on her mother's nurturing. Again, like most teenagers, she wasn't too crazy about simply being seen *with* her mother in public, or her father either for that matter. Wanda might have had real issues with cognitive development, but in the complex arena of parental frictions and problems, Wanda was like every other teenager in North America. She wanted to be in control of her own destiny, regardless of whether or not she had the ability to do so, especially the maturity to do so.

* * *

Will Lanning's day had begun in Tom Norman's office at 7:30 A.M. Setting up an early meeting was sometimes the only way he could get a private audience with the principal. Tom Norman was medium height, lean, a heavy smoker, and kept his salt and pepper crew-cut trimmed low and hard. His football coaching days were ten years behind him, and most educators in the county felt it wouldn't be long before he might be considered for the school board superintendent position.

"What's this I hear about a spring trip to the beach?" Tom Norman was behind his desk looking relaxed and businesslike at the same time. He swiveled his chair away from the window he'd been gazing out as more school buses arrived. "J. P. said something about Nags Head."

"Yes sir. I talked to Mr. Hinkel about it yesterday. You don't see any problems with it do you?" Will knew that just about anything he proposed with the TAP program would be approved by Tom Norman and J. P. Hinkel, the assistant principal. So far, everything he'd thrown on the wall had stuck. The Scared Straight Program went through without a hitch. Will had taken the TAP class to a state maximum security prison down near Charlotte where some hardened convicts talked to the students about why they should never want to end up behind bars. There were over-night camping trips, civil war battlefield trips, outings to the National Mall and the Smithsonian Museum in Washington D. C., tours of factories in Winston Salem. It seemed that TAP, the alternative education program, under Will Lanning's leadership, was working out very nicely, in this, its third year of existence.

And why should it not be working out? The administration and faculty at Luther Sloan now had a place to send its most incorrigible problem students. They had a legitimate alternative ed. program that was pleased to accept any wayward kid the county could throw its way. And at Luther Sloan, the TAP program got plenty of wayward kids. It got some students from juvenile court, it got some who special ed. had never had success with, it got some whose diet had been little more than dog food, and unbelievably, it got a few who had high I Q's, but who had the grace, social skills, and ability to work in a group that you might expect a rhinoceros to have, or maybe a boa constrictor.

Tom Norman's response was what Will Lanning expected, "No, no problems. Just make sure you've got chaperones, and the parent's permission slips signed."

"Yes sir, sure will. And, Mr. Norman, something else I wanted to ask you about."

"Shoot."

"I'm having my students get into a letter writing exercise for English composition. You know my kids, they are way behind grade level on their writing skills. I've been looking at several writing programs for low achievers and one in particular I'm going to give a try. I'm asking them to write personal letters to the faculty and administration here at Sloan. Kind of an ownership thing. Encourage them to be frank, be honest about their life here at school. Maybe even encourage them to make a few suggestions about how we, the faculty and administration might make some improvements on how the school is run. Some alternative ed. programs around the country seem to be getting some favorable results from this approach. I wanted to let you know ahead of time, just to make sure you and the staff were willing to read the letters, maybe even respond to them if you would."

"It sounds pretty good. I don't see a problem. When do you think we might receive the letters? I'll let the staff know what's coming."

"No more than a month from now."

"Good enough. I'm sure our people will be glad to read them."

The TAP classroom was a hundred yards from the rear of the main building. It was a double-wide modular structure. From its two small windows you could look out across the high school's rear parking lot and beyond that to the football field.

It was now 7:50 a. m. and Will Lanning was thinking about putting the new letter writing activity into place as he walked toward the TAP classroom. He knew that most of the fourteen TAP students would be around back of the small modular building smoking cigarettes as if life itself depended on that nasty habit. He also knew they would not come into the classroom until he walked around the corner of the building at exactly 8:00 a. m. and call out loudly, "Okay Tapsters, eight o'clock, let's go!"

Will's master's degree work at the University of North Carolina six years ago had emphasized the fact that Alternative ed. programs had to do just that – provide alternatives to traditional education models – they had to be really different. And no one would ever argue that Will Lanning's TAP program wasn't different.

The way Will saw it, there was no use in attempting to badger his fourteen students into sitting quietly through fifty-minute blocks of time taking notes on lectures, or other activities relevant to the high school credits needed for graduation in the subjects of math, algebra, geography, history, English, business ed., and all the rest. That's why these fourteen were in Will's TAP program – they had all been abject failures in normal classroom educational models, i. e. traditional programs. Why utilize the same models that none of them had ever had success in?

Will Lanning would never be accused of teaching in traditional models.

All of the Tapsters crushed their smokes and saved what was left to be used at the first smoke break which would normally be about 9:15, or 9:30, or whenever Will thought the time was right.

As they trudged into the classroom, Will directed the crowd of young teenagers to a corner of the room he called the "Team Office." The floor was carpeted there with cheap material donated by a local dumpster Will had raided. But the stuff had been scrubbed good by Will and a couple of the boys. It was clean and in fact much better material than many of the TAP students had at home. There were two bean-bag chairs in the corner of the Team Office where two blue-jeaned girls promptly got comfortable in. They were Libby and Teresa Murdock. Their father had burned their house down when the girls were eleven and nine. In the midst of a three-day drunk he'd dropped his cigarette on a pile of newspapers just about the time he'd passed out. It was late at night, the girls and their mother were already in bed and when the smoke finally woke them up, they were lucky to get themselves out alive. The older sister, Libby, went back in with her mother to drag her father out and was struck by a burning door frame as it collapsed. Her pajamas caught fire and by the time she had run outside and had been put down on the ground by a neighbor man, the damage altering the rest of her life had already been done. The scars covering most of her legs and back looked sort of like a barrel of huge spaghetti noodles had been poured on her. Her hands, arms, face, and the front of her upper body had escaped any scar damage, but the innocuous, the innocent, the banal, the painless, these kinds of facial expressions on Libby would never come to be.

Or, would they?

That's what had been going on in Will Lanning's mind for the three years that Libby had been in the TAP program. Will wanted only the very best for all of his students, not just Libby, but with her it was a little more intense.

Will remembered the meeting three years ago, with Nancy Barker, the guidance counselor at Sloan. These meetings were labelled "referral options" but everybody knew that once a student's name got this far, Will would have a new student.

"Yes, she completed ninth grade last year. It's not that she can't do academic work. I think a good deal of it is her stubbornness. She simply will not dress out for P. E., and without the two years of P. E. credit, well, you know, there's no way she'll be able to graduate." Nancy Barker pushed Libby Murdock's school records across the desk. Will picked them up and was scanning them, and after a moment, he said, "I see. Well, as far as academics, you are right, but she *is* two grade levels behind in reading, but that's a lot better than most of my kids. Let's get her started in TAP. I'll work on a solution to the P. E. credits."

That "referral options" meeting with Nancy Barker was three years ago. Now, Libby was a senior and had those two P. E. credits safely put away in her total count of credits needed to graduate this spring. As soon as Will Lanning had discovered the reason Libby refused to dress out for P. E. it didn't take him long to suggest an alternative activity to accommodate the requirements for those two credits. And it was scandalous (he thought), that the P. E. teachers, Mrs. Nancy Barker the guidance counselor, or anyone else in the Sloan Administration had never cared enough to find out what the problem was and work out a solution to it. The problem was, of course, pretty obvious – Libby's embarrassment and refusal to dress out in gym shorts was because of those hideous burn scars. Will immediately knew the solution – have Libby wear sweatpants not shorts in P. E. class. But, oh no! The P. E. teachers wouldn't allow it ... couldn't allow it. It would have led to a breakdown in discipline. If they let one student get away with it, well ... they'd have big trouble. All of the students would start asking for lenience on this rule or that rule.

Will remembered Libby's response to his suggestion to a solution to her problem; it had a lot to do with his own personal interest of the last ten years – distance running.

"Libby, you want to graduate, right?"

"Yes sir."

"Okay, we know you must earn those two P. E. credits, somehow, right?"

"Yes sir."

"Okay, let's just forget about the regular P. E. class at Sloan, okay? Why don't we think about how you can earn those two credits right here at TAP."

Libby didn't say anything; nothing but a blank look on her face.

"Have you ever done any distance running, Libby? A mile or more?"

"You mean like cross country?"

"Yeah, something like that."

"No, and I ain't going to if I gotta' wear shorts."

"What if you didn't have to wear shorts. What if you just wore loose fitting sweats when you're running?"

"I don't know. I ain't never thought about it."

"I know you haven't, but here is what I think we can do. You know, my contract to teach hear at Sloan is an eleven-month contract. Unlike the other teachers, I'm here most of summer vacation. You could come this summer and we would set a goal for you in distance running. If you can reach that goal, then you'll earn a credit in P. E. It would be up to you. You'd have to do a lot of work, a lot of running, but if you achieved your goal, you'd get the P. E. credit. Then the next summer, we'd do it again, but set a little higher goal, and you'd get the second credit you need to graduate."

"How far could I ... uh, I mean, how far would I have to run?" She tried to hide the quick line of hope that had tightened up at the corner of her lips – almost a smile.

"Well, how about four miles the first summer. We'd start you real slow, actually start you walking, but work your way up to the goal – running four miles."

"I'll try."

* * *

Yes, all of that was three years ago, and now, as Will Lanning walked over to the Team Office and sat down in one of the twelve or so chairs loosely forming a semi-circle around that corner of the room, he noticed one of the boys, Terrence Cogburn, giving the finger to Bubba Shiner, who had just settled his two-hundred-and-thirty-pound bulk into a chair he had leaning on one of the walls that formed the corner.

Will thought about whether or not to come down hard on this act. He knew that if he spent much time on it, he would (A) be starting the day off negatively, and (B) he'd be encouraging similar juvenile exploits to take bloom.

"Good morning everybody. It looks like we'll be here all day today. It's too cold to do any can pick-ups after lunch, and the weatherman says there may be some snow and ice. We can build a couple of paper stands this afternoon. Those two over at Rainey's Market are in pretty bad shape." Will used that news as an introduction to a report on the status of TAP's aluminum can recycling project, and on TAP's newspaper and cardboard recycling project. The money the students raised from the two projects is what would pay for the end of year beach trip.

"Let's see," Will said, "our bank account balance is six hundred thirty-four dollars and fifty-nine cents. Not bad at all. I'm very proud of the work you've done so far, but we still need at least five hundred more dollars. With spring getting closer, I'm sure we'll raise what we need. I'll push you hard when the weather gets a little better."

"You ain't pushing me hard. I ain't goin' on no beach trip," Bubba Shiner said in a pretty loud voice.

Wanda Oakley shifted a little in her chair to look over at Bubba, "We know you ain't goin'. You been saying that all year." Wanda was a little more perky today than she normally was. Her boyfriend, L. B. Turner, was sitting next to Wanda, and he threw his head back quickly to toss his long black hair out of his dark, handsome eyes. L. B. was pretty skinny and he normally would avoid trouble with the other boys, but he had to say something now that Wanda had spoken up. "Bubba, you just do what you gotta' do. Okay?"

"I tell you what I'd do, L. B.," but he didn't go on, and nobody else said anything more.

Will continued, "So anyway, we are in pretty good shape on the beach trip to Nags Head."

He scanned the open notebook on his lap, cleared his throat and started again. "It looks like some of you haven't given me a solid date yet to do the field interview with one of your older kin-folk – Wendell, Lucky, Casey, and Sissy. Can you all let me know something on that pretty soon? You know that project goes a long way towards getting you a credit in both History and an elective credit in American Studies."

The field interview with an older relative was one of the more popular activities that Will had sold to the TAP students. For starters, they got to "get out of jail" to work on the project – they piled into Will's V. W. van and left school for the project. Also, they had ownership in the project – it was centered on people in their own family. It wasn't trying to memorize dates and events from Asia Minor, wherever that was, or from the Roman Empire, whatever that was. The genius of the activity was that when the tape-recorded interviews arrived back in the TAP classroom, the Tapsters were eager to get started on transcribing – playing the tape back again and again in order to write down the speech of their kin-folk. Amazing! Young people who had never written much more than the alphabet were decompressing speech patterns and writing it down in an organized manner. Questions began popping up like, "Hey Mr. Lanning, how do you spell *truck*, or, how do you spell *mountain*, or, how do you spell *firewood*?" It didn't take long for Will to realize he was going to have to bring in a bunch of dictionaries.

Will zeroed in on the four again – Wendell, Lucky, Casey, and Sissy, but only Wendell Renfro answered up, "My granddaddy said maybe yal' could come out to his place, Mr. Lanning, but it'd shore be hard 'nough gettin' 'ere."

"Where does he live, Wendell?"

"Ah reckon hits a good piece back in there the other side ah Tan Bone Mountain. Hit might be over in Virginia."

"Well that would be fine. Why don't you see if you could get me some directions, and find out when it would be okay for us to come out?"

"All right," is what Wendell said, but he knew a trip to his granddaddy's place would never happen. His granddaddy might say okay to the visit, but his father never would. Raynor Renfro had worked in the coal mines in southwestern Virginia until the "black lung" had nearly killed him, and he moved his family to the North Carolina mountains to access some state rehab programs he'd heard about but which never materialized. Ever since then, he'd failed at supporting his disabled wife and four children by cutting, splitting, selling, and hauling fire wood. His family was crumbling around him. The two oldest boys were in prison and Wendell and Wendell's younger sister, Elsie, were about to be removed by the state to be placed in the state orphan's home. Raynor would have killed before allowing "them uppity school people" to go off gallivanting around the mountains, dragging his own Wendell and the rest of them alternative school kids to visit his own father. And why in hell was Wendell in the TAP program to begin with? Why in hell was he even in school? If they let him stay at home where he belonged, the whole family would eat a lot better. Wendell was the only one left to actually do the labor to cut and split the wood. And by God, they make him go to that damned school instead of let him take care of his family!

Will felt like it was time to spring the letter writing assignment on his Tapsters, "Later today we're going to spend some time on writing letters. You won't actually write them today. We'll just talk about the assignment a little. I'll have some information for you on a hand-out."

Next, he quickly launched the plans for the next fifty minutes. "Okay, reading first period, everybody except Casey, John, Teresa, and Lucky who will work on your math sets."

As he said this, Mrs. King, Will's teacher's aide walked into the room and deposited her hand bag and winter coat on the chair behind her desk, and walked over towards the Team Office.

Will said, "Here she is everybody, the best math teacher in North Carolina."

The students got along great with sixty-two-year-old Mrs. Rachel King. She brought a friendly, grandmotherly manner to the classroom, and Will knew he'd really be up against a wall without her. In fact, the loose-knit afternoon structure at TAP would be impossible without her. It was always in the afternoons that most of the class would be out collecting aluminum cans from the roadways and picking up the recycled newspaper and cardboard from various collection sites around the county. Mrs. King always stayed in the classroom with any students that couldn't go, or occasionally, wouldn't go. That usually meant Bubba Shiner and Lucky Dirksen.

"Hey Rachel, how you doing?"

"Did you watch Mayberry last night?"

"How's your little puppy? He okay?"

All the girls in the class checked in with Mrs. King every single day. And they were all on a first name basis with her. It was never Mrs. King. Even some of the boys called her Rachel, but most used the more distant, more formal, Mrs. King.

"Good morning everybody. I have a feeling we've got a great day ahead of us." She chatted the group up for a minute or two and then she knew it was time to get started. "Casey, John, Teresa, Lucky, I'll meet you over at the math table."

The rest of the Tapsters searched the book shelves or their personal boxes for something to read. When they found what they wanted they all scattered to a different reading nook. Some to the Team Office, some to chairs at tables, and some on the floor against a wall.

Will Lanning's approach to teaching reading to non-readers began with the simple notion that it would never happen unless you had some kind of reading material that would actually hold the student's interest. For that reason, he made sure that scattered all throughout the bookshelves and the reading table were motorcycle magazines, hunting magazines, comic books and the like for the boys, and girl magazines, romance stories, etc. for the girls. There was plenty of "traditional" reading materials also.

Will only had two rules when the reading hour got started. One, you had to have some sort of reading material in front of your eyes. Two, there was absolutely no talking, horsing around, or sleeping.

After a new student got used to those two rules, Will would add a few more. Eventually you would need to write down five or ten words you didn't understand and Will would help you look them up and also talk about the words with you until you got a pretty good feel for what the words meant.

Also, eventually you would be asked to make a "reading report" on what you had read. It could be verbal or written at first, but eventually it would need to be both.

Will's writing classes worked in a similar fashion. There were no grades given for accuracy, neatness, spelling, punctuation, grammar, sentence construction, or mechanics. The students got credit for their work based on participation, and effort. Just like the reading class, eventually, expectations were raised.

At 9:20 a. m. Will called out, "Ten-minute break." It didn't take long for most of the Tapsters to head around back of the modular classroom building and light up.

A few walked the hundred yards over to the main building where the nearest rest-rooms were. Two of the girls, Wanda Oakley, and Marcy Logan stayed in the room to talk with Rachel King.

Wanda asked, "So, Rachel, what about the letter writing? Who are we supposed to write the letters to?"

"Oh, Mr. Lanning will go over that … next period, I believe. I bet you're going to like the assignment. You know Mr. Lanning though, if it's something you truly don't want to participate in, you can always write up your own assignment."

And it was true. Will Lanning not only *allowed* students to alter an assignment he'd given them, he, many times, *encouraged* it. But only a few of the TAP students went down that road, because it would invariably require more thinking and planning than the original assignment.

While the two girls remained inside talking with Mrs. King, Bubba Shiner, Casey Horner, Lucky Dirksen, L. B. Turner, John Harrington, and three other girls were outside smoking and doing what many teens do – talking about summer, which was only four months away.

But, like usual, the break was too short and all of the TAP students made their way back into the classroom at the call of Will Lanning's voice, "Okay, let's go everybody, back at it."

Bubba Shiner's words were, of course, lost to Will. There was no way Will could have heard them, "Back at it my ass. If he tries any shit on me the rest of the day, I'm gonna' cold-cock him. I'm sick of his crap."

The next period was writing and transcribing. First, Will had all fourteen Tapsters sitting around a huge table, actually two big work tables drawn together. The assignment was for everyone to write a story about their favorite movie. Three or four sentences in, you had to pass your story down one person to your left. Everyone continued writing the same story on the paper passed to them. Each time the paper was passed, it was folded so you couldn't read any prior sections. Eventually you ended up with your original paper, and the class ended up with hilarious stories, completely fragmented, making no sense, all bunched together from thirteen different seed stories.

This was a typical warm-up exercise that Will would use before the harder work of transcribing would begin. Everyone had a lot of fun with it. Everyone except Bubba Shiner.

"What the hell is this crap? I ain't doing this no more." Bubba's outburst surprised no one; nor did Will Lanning's response to it, "Bubba, you are free to remove yourself from the writing table and spend the rest of the period in the Team Office."

"You're right about that. It's the only thing you're right about," and Bubba left the table and sat in one of the bean bags on the floor in the Team Office.

Everybody felt like the worst was over. They knew it would take more than that before a security council meeting would be called. That's when Mr. Lanning would stop everything and herd the entire group over to the team office and encourage the students themselves to handle the problem – not Mr. Lanning.

But they were all wrong. The worst was not over. It took about four minutes for the seething Bubba to explode again. "Yal' a bunch of pussies. You lettin' this phony tell you what to do all the time. He ain't no teacher. He just thinks he is. He don't even teach us nuthin', just does all this stupid shit all the time."

Normally, Will's "security council meetings" were very useful. It was a way for the students to look at themselves in the mirror. If there was trouble in the classroom which threatened total disruption of the teaching process (and there was such trouble on a regular basis), the "security council meeting" afforded them the opportunity at getting real life experience in conflict resolution. The overworked catch phrase of "student government", for the most part, didn't amount to much in most traditional high school settings, but in TAP, it meant a great deal, because in TAP, things could get so tilted, so quickly, that unless the students *did* get very much involved, very quickly, the TAP program never would have lasted three years.

Will wasted no time on arriving at his decision today. "Okay everybody, it looks like we've got a problem to deal with. Security Council in the Team Office."

Bubba Shiner was growling and threatening this and that, and he'd got to his feet as everyone was shuffling over to the corner of the room where the Team Office was. Lucky Dirksen and Terrence Cogburn smiled and chuckled as they got close to Bubba as if to say, "Good job, we had about enough of that writin' crap too."

Most were seated by now, but it was obvious that Bubba was physically staking out his territory by stalking around and looking for more support, or maybe a fight.

"Bubba, why don't you have a seat. We will hear you out. We will sit here until we get to the bottom of it." Will was seated in the semi-circle nearest the main part of the room. Mrs. King was at her desk. Most times she stayed out of security council meetings.

"Ain't no bottom of anything to get to."

"Come on Bubba." It was Libby Murdock. Bubba started to sit down, but didn't.

Will didn't say anything. Nobody did.

"Bubba, just sit down, okay?" It was Casey Horner.

Bubba took a couple of steps towards the last remaining chair and finally sat down.

Will knew what strategy he would use, but as he was thinking about that, he was also wondering how long it would take before Bubba pulled the pin on the next grenade. "Okay, everybody knows the drill. I'm staying out of it unless you get to a log jam." With that, Will folded his arms and sat back in his chair after having pulled it back out of the circle just enough where he made no physical imprint on the group but close enough to hear what was going on.

Nobody said anything for a couple of minutes, then Libby Murdock's younger sister, Teresa (thirteen) said, "This is pretty stupid. Don't yal' know what we ought to do?"

"Yeah, I know what we should do. We ought to trash this stupid room and go home." Bubba was heating up again.

"Sure Bubba. What you gonna' do when you get home? You got a job?" asked Libby.

Then, little sister jumped back in, "Hey, I just asked, don't yal' know what we should do? Forget Bubba, he ain't so bad. Look, we need to vote on it, that's all."

"We ain't votin' on shit," Bubba countered, and giving little Teresa as devilish a scowl as he could.

Finally, Casey Horner felt like it was time to get involved. "Bubba, if we want to take a vote on something, by Gawd, we will. You ain't stoppin' us."

"Yal' a bunch of pussies. You let this phony act like he's some kind of boss."

"Bubba, some of us would be in jail or a state home if it wasn't for Mr. Lanning. Why are you always trying to tear things down?" It was Sissy Darby. She, like most TAP students, had been in a chaotic childhood, tossed here and there as a result of the poverty, the isolation, and the cold reality of life itself. As mountain children, they knew they were different than the kids in some of the valleys down below. They knew they were laughed at and joked about. Even so, they had a stubborn pride about them. Sissy continued, "You want to go home, you go on, but you shouldn't be talkin' the way you are."

Again, nobody said anything for a while, then finally, Wanda Oakley piped up, "What kind of a vote are you talking about, Teresa?"

"I don't know ... I guess ... whether we ought to kick him out of TAP."

"We can't kick him out." Casey felt torn. He didn't want to make things bad for Bubba, but on the other hand, they had to do *something*. But what? He knew the principal at Sloan wouldn't kick Bubba out of school based on a vote by the TAP class. That made very little sense. Or, did it? Casey was thinking about it. *Isn't Mr. Lanning always telling us we have to learn how to make decisions for ourselves? We have to learn how to take chances based on good thinking and good planning? And isn't my friend Bubba threatening to blow up the class? And would I myself be able to stay eligible for baseball if something happened to TAP?*

It was all a moot point because it was now, this instant, that Bubba Shiner decided to detonate not a grenade, but a nuclear explosion.

Bubba stood up, then turned and kicked his chair back against the wall. He walked across the Town Meeting area right past Will Lanning and took aim at a stand-alone book shelf that served double duty as a room divider. He dropped his shoulder into it, knocking it over, books flying in all directions.

Will was up quickly and got between Bubba and the work tables on the other side of the room. "Outside Bubba, right now, get outside!" Will was prepared to fight him if it came to that, and he probably would have won. He wasn't nearly as heavy as Bubba, but his strength and quickness was pretty good.

"Outside I said! Right now! You are not going to tear this room up."

Bubba didn't say anything, and surprisingly, he started walking towards the door.

Will was right behind him, "Go on outside."

Bubba opened the door and walked out on the small wooden platform with a weather awning over it.

Will looked back into the classroom and called back to Rachel King, "Mrs. King, please start a reading period, or if they want to, you can get out the current events trivia questions. I'll be right back." He closed the door behind him and turned to face a boiling Bubba Shiner.

"Bubba, I think you've made it perfectly clear how you feel about the TAP program, but I want to make it perfectly clear to you … I will not give up on you. Now, today, well, we can't just brush this aside. I'm going to take you home right now. I'm not taking you down to Mr. Norman. If you will get in my van, I'll have you home in half an hour. If you won't get in, then I guess we'll go down and see Mr. Norman, and I think you know that he will call the police."

Bubba didn't say anything but he walked out into the big gravel parking area in front of the TAP modular classroom. Will's van was close by and he got in and pulled it over to where Bubba was waiting. He got out and walked over to the passenger door and opened it up. Bubba got in and sat in the middle two-person bench seat. Will closed the door shut, got back in the driver's seat, and drove out of the school grounds heading for Bubba's house on top the mountain.

On the way up the mountain Bubba began thinking about what he would find when he got home. What if his dad had returned from the Georgia trip in the flatbed? He was thinking that nothing good would come from that situation. "Stop the van, I'm getting' out."

"Bubba, I can't stop. I've got to get you home."

"You better stop. I'm jumping out!" He opened the door and was ready to jump even as Will had slowed down to maybe twenty.

Will continued slowing down with intentions to stop, but at about ten miles per hour, Bubba jumped out. Will could see that he rolled on the shoulder of the road, but he got to his feet, and didn't' seem to be hurt. Also, he knew it would be useless to try to get him back in the van, so he turned around and started the drive back to Sloan.

* * *

No one was surprised the next day when Bubba Shiner didn't show up at TAP. In the opening town meeting session, Will had told the students the details of the trip up the mountain and also let them know that he was certain Bubba had not been hurt. Will had gone back up there after school was out and talked with Bubba's sister. She said that he'd come home in the afternoon but didn't stay long and that she didn't know where he'd gone, but that he looked okay to her.

Later in the day, Will rolled out the letter writing assignment. "Okay everybody, the hand-out I'm giving you shows the technical way to write a letter. It shows and describes what each element is and where it is located. The same information, you can see, I've put up on the blackboard. If you keep this hand-out, you'll always be able to write a good letter, whether for business or a personal letter to family and friends." At this point, Will went through the various elements of a letter and asked if there were any questions. There were none. Other than getting through this assignment, most of them probably didn't see themselves as ever writing another letter again in their life.

"Here's the thing on this assignment, Tapsters. Your letters are going to the administration and the staff at Sloan. I want you to pick out a teacher, a coach, a counselor, a lunchroom lady, or even the principal or the assistant principal to write your letter to. I want you to be honest; tell them what you think about school in general; tell them how you really feel, good or bad, I don't care. I think it's good for all of us to vent our feelings, our emotions every now and then."

Wendell Renfro asked, "What's an emotion?" Some of them snickered and laughed, but then, from Teresa Murdock, "What's vent?"

Such was life in the TAP classroom.

"Vent is a way to expose things, to let them be aired out, to show your feelings, your anger, or other personal things on your mind. And emotions are your most personal feelings. The reason I've asked you to write to the teachers and administration here at Sloan, is because I think it would be important for you to examine your true feelings about high school in general – what it was like before you came to TAP, and what it is like now. Is there any difference? And guess what? I'm not going to be reading your letters. I don't want to influence what you have to say. If you've got things you've always wanted to say about school, now you have the opportunity. Be honest, be yourself, step outside of your shell a little, ask tough questions, right a wrong, explore a thing or two, have no fear. You can do all of that and more by simply writing a letter."

Will hadn't thought about adding to his instructions things like you should be polite, you should be respectful, you should not be offensive. And of course, as an encourager, an advocate, a supporter of his TAP letter-writers, he felt like it was important not to read or edit the letters. Just like he'd been reading in some of the models he'd been studying, he wanted to stress the fact that the letters really were the raw, the bare, the true feelings of the students – Oh! The ownership! His training in alternative ed. was support, support, support; encourage, encourage, encourage; never do something to tear a student down, weaken their self-confidence; always give positive reinforcement – never negative.

That afternoon Wanda Oakley and her boyfriend, L. B. Turner, were out in front of Luther H. Sloan High School waiting on Wanda's mother to pick her up.

"I didn't think Bubba would be back today," Wanda said

"No, not today, but I bet we'll see him back soon. I don't know. I hear his old man is mean as a snake. If he ever finds out what happened yesterday, I bet he'd kill both of them, Lanning and Bubba."

"Maybe," and the look on her face changed from indifferent to determined. "Who you gonna' write to?"

"What?"

"Who you gonna' write your letter to?"

"I don't know."

"I know who I'm writing to."

"Coach Walters?"

"No."

"Uh, Mrs. Simpson?"

"No."

"I don't know. Tell me."

"Mr. Norman."

"You're kidding. Why do you want to write to him?"

"Well, I guess 'cause just like Mr. Lanning says, be honest, tell him how I really feel, vent some emotions. I think I understand what he means by that."

"You sure?"

"Yeah, I'm sure."

* * *

It was the middle of March, almost a month after the letter writing assignment had been made. Libby Murdock was on track to be the first high school graduate to come out of the TAP program, and she was a ball of energy, always pushing the other Tapsters to work hard on the recycling project. The project itself had built its bank balance up to eleven hundred dollars – enough to cover the travel, the motel, and the food for the three-day trip to the beach in May.

Bubba Shiner had returned to the TAP program a week after he'd wrecked the classroom. A juvenile court judge had ordered him back and had warned him that if he wasn't on his good behavior this time, his next stop would be a state juvenile detention center. Bubba lasted two weeks before launching a chair through one of the two classroom windows and tearing down, not one, but two bookcases.

Casey Horner and the Luther H. Sloan High School baseball team were enjoying great success in the early part of spring baseball season. The team was ranked second in the region, and Casey himself was considered one of the top utility players in the state. He could do it all – any infield position (including catcher), any outfield position, and occasionally he'd go to the mound as a relief pitcher. But it was in the batter's box where Casey became a high school legend. They said he had the quickest hands ever seen in the valley. Match those hands up with great eyes and you had a long-ball hitting machine.

Wendell Renfro had been right. His father wouldn't allow the TAP class to visit Wendell's granddaddy. Will tried every way he could to help Wendell develop an alternative assignment so that some type of high school credit could be awarded. Nothing came of it, and by the end of the school year, Wendell had been removed from his father's home and placed in a foster-home. To Will Lanning, it was the hardest failure he (Will) had to endure. There were other similar tragedies with his TAP students, but Wendell's case hurt bad.

The weather in the middle of March in the North Carolina Appalachians was always unpredictable. You were as likely to have pleasant conditions in the upper seventies as you were to have violent thunderstorms peppered with half a dozen tornadoes. And then a good ice and snow storm would tumble in when you least expected it. This particular mid-March weather pattern had witnessed unprecedented rain which led to some flooding in Gumtree and other sections of Wautauga County.

On a Wednesday afternoon in the TAP classroom, most of the students were touching up the letters that would be delivered to the staff at Sloan. It was too wet and messy to be outside working on the recycling project.

Will Lanning went around the room collecting the letters and checking the names of the staff in the center of the envelopes and student's names in the upper left-hand corner.

When he had them all gathered up, he said, "Good job everybody. I'm really proud of you. For how many of you was this the first letter you ever wrote?" All of the hands went up.

"Great! Again, I'm very pleased with the effort you've made. Remember, I'm not going to look at them. They will go straight up to Sloan in twenty minutes. I think it was important you all did this first letter on your own. Now, the next letters we write, I will check them closely for form, punctuation, spelling, and all the rest. I believe you'll be ready to clean them up a little, now that this first one is out of the way." He stopped and was looking around the room at the Tapsters scattered about, then,

"Just out of curiosity, how many of you feel good about the letter writing assignment – that you had something important to say, and you said it?"

Most of them responded positively, nodding their heads, a smile here and there, but Will noticed that Wanda Oakley seemed to be beside herself. She was elated! Will could see it in her eyes and in her body language. She really felt good! Evidently, what she felt good about was the letter she had written to Tom Norman.

Two days later, early Friday morning, Will noticed a note in his mail box in the teacher's lounge in the main building at Sloan. He opened it up and read, "In my office, this afternoon – 3:15, Tom Norman." Will laughed to himself and thought back twenty years or so when he was in the ninth grade. This note he just looked at read very much like one he'd received from his principal back in the day. How he managed to graduate high school was anybody's guess. The truth was he needed summer school credits in typing and two years of English. He remembered the big high school on the other end of the county where his parents had to haul him to, for seven weeks for two summers. The third summer Will drove his old 51 Chevy. He remembered the student parking lot in the hot summer afternoons as the teenagers poured out of the building and made a bee-line for their cars. You could almost hear the unspoken words – **Gentlemen Start Your Engines!** These cars awaiting the crazed, unrestrained mob were not like Will's common six-banger, plebian, so unsexy 51 Chevrolet. These buggies were souped-up, customized, bored and stroked, dual four-barrel carbs, mag wheels, and polished and shined to a liquid glimmer. They were, to Will, what being a teenager in the early sixties was supposed to be. Cruising the hamburger stands in one of these chariots meant one thing to the boys of that era – girls. And although Will never quite fit the mold of the true hot-rod fanatic of the sixties, he would fake it every now and then. His dad had a 59 Impala two-door hardtop. It was cream and copper, and Will had stolen four Plymouth Pointer hub caps from the bowling alley one night to dress it up. He'd do a little cruising in it after he'd removed the big round air cleaner from the carburetor to make it sound gnarly, make it hiss, make it sound bad!

Yeah, Will Lanning grew up in much different circumstances than did his poverty-ridden alternative ed. students. His parents provided all the essentials a higher end middle class kid needed. Why Will didn't take advantage of the status, the connections he had access to baffled most of his friends and family. All boiled down, it really wasn't all that different from the Tapsters. He was a square peg trying to fit into a round hole. So, what happened to Will? Where along life's trail did he get studious all of a sudden? Where did he get serious about things? What on God's green earth changed him from a carefree rounder, always looking for a gravy ride or maybe even a con?

Vietnam.

Yeah, that was pretty much the turning point. After two tours as a marine infantryman, he came home and studied the humanities at UNC Chapel Hill on the G. I. Bill. Later he earned his masters in alternative education. From that point on he had been dedicated to working with other square pegs, and trying to help them not make the same mistakes he'd made. He could understand a lot of what they felt. No, he had not been hungry, or cold, or unloved, and that is one of the reasons he cared about them so much. He'd had it all, and squandered it. He was bound and determined to help get them a better shot at things – things he himself had frittered away. He was one hell of a teacher, and his students didn't know what they had in him, but they did know that without him they didn't have a chance.

It was almost 3:15 p. m. and Will had to hustle over to Mr. Norman's office. He'd been over at the baseball field talking with the baseball coach, assuring him that Casey was on track to receive five credits this year – legitimate credits in English, Math, Geography, American Studies, and wood shop (thanks to the newspaper recycling stands that Casey had done a lot of work on).

On his way over, Will had actually thought that this meeting might be about Casey. It was well known that

Tom Norman had played minor league baseball back in his own athletic hay day. *Well, I guess I'll find out*, Will thought for a moment, but as he opened the door to the principal's office, a bolt of cold reality shot through his head and said, *this is not about Casey Horner*, and Will knew it was true.

"Good afternoon Mr. Norman."

"Have a seat Will." Why was it when an authority figure used a casual, even friendly tone of voice, and addressed you by your first name, it signaled something very disturbing just under the surface, something threatening to ruin your whole day, maybe your whole life?

Mr. Norman looked like he always did, like most high school principals always looked like – a smooth and confident exterior that appeared to have some alien thing trying to come out from under their skin. Kind of like a cloud of red pressure always seeking the surface, especially when something had prodded it alive and challenged it.

Mr. Norman had an envelope in his hand and held it up to where Will could see it, "Do you know what this is?"

"Why yes sir, I think so. It looks like one of the letters my kids sent up here the other day."

"That's right. That's exactly what it is. Can you see the name on the front?"

Will looked a little closer, "Yes sir, it looks like it's addressed to you."

"Yes, it is, and can you see whose name is here?" Mr. Norman was indicating the name in the upper left-hand corner, but he didn't give the envelope with the letter in it to Will.

"Yes sir, I believe it's from Wanda Oakley."

Norman didn't say anything. He seemed to be waiting for more from Will.

Finally, Norman said, "Well?" as if an immediate explanation was expected.

"I beg your pardon sir. I don't understand."

When he saw that Will was not responding, he started out again. "Mr. Lanning, I want to ask you a very important question. And, I want you to consider your answer very carefully."

Now Will was thinking that he preferred the first-name relationship. The formalized, *Mr. Lanning*, had him worried. "Yes sir, I understand. What's the question?"

"In your formal teacher preparation and studies at the very highly regarded University of North Carolina, Mr. Lanning, did any of your English professors ever remotely suggest to you the importance of thoroughly editing the content of your English student's work that would be disseminated to the public?"

Ah, thought Will, *I see what's happened here! Wanda's letter is fraught with misspelling, punctuation errors, incorrect format, etc., and Mr. Norman in his role as astute overseer of all things academic is correct in wanting to point these errors out to me as quickly as possible. Well, I suppose I had it coming. I didn't do a good job of explaining to him my reasons for not editing, not even reading the letters my students composed. I brought this on myself. I sure did. A clear explanation of my teaching methods with the Tapsters should clear the air, un-muddy the waters. It should get me and Mr. Norman back on level ground.*

"Okay, yes sir, I see exactly what you mean. I brought this on myself. Let me explain," and with that Will launched a lengthy dissertation on many of the accepted principles of basic teaching methods with previously failing students – alternative ed. students. He talked about ownership, building student's self-confidence, independence, and the necessity to try new things, to do things differently, hence the reason he didn't edit or read the letters prior to delivering them to Sloan's staff, and yes, to the principal himself.

"You mean to tell me, Mr. Lanning, you didn't even read those letters?" A lot of that alien red pressure was now beginning to escape from Mr. Norman's skin.

"No sir, I did not." And then, almost as an afterthought, "I'd be glad to read them now sir. May I see Wanda Oakley's letter?"

"You may not. You will never see it. It will be burned in a heap of trash it is so justly deserving of!"

"Mr. Norman, I beg your pardon sir. I believe you are over-reacting. A few grammatical errors and probably third grade sentence construction, and you want to burn one of my student's letters? I would think sir, that you would be a bit more accommodating, uh, you know, a bit more understanding to students who have had zero success with this sort of thing in the past. I bet you didn't know that this is the first letter Wanda has ever written in her life. I would think, sir, you'd be applauding her effort, that you'd be giving her some positive strokes. Frankly sir, I would think you'd be much bigger than this."

"Mr. Lanning, it is obvious that you fail to see, that as a teacher/employee contracted to this county, that there are minimum professional teaching standards that we require you to uphold. Editing the content of writing assignments that will be exposed to the public by your students is one of those standards. Since you failed to read Wanda Oakley's letter, you would have no idea as to the nature of its crude, slanderous accusations she aimed clearly at me. Mr. Lanning, this letter," he held it up in the air and shook it quite excitedly, "this letter is the foulest, dirtiest, single most filthy communication I have ever read. Sailors on a three- day shore-leave in Okinawa use cleaner language. You and Miss Oakley's family are lucky I don't file a libel lawsuit against you both. Against them as they are her parents and against you as you failed your responsibility as her teacher. But don't feel too lucky, Mr. Lanning, I may change my mind."

Tom Norman slipped back a little in his chair, as now, some of that alien horror, underneath his principal's skin was escaping in a vapor towards the heavens.

"Now, Will," *Oh no! He's gone back to the first name,* "I'm inclined to let this whole sordid affair slide by. I think I could allow it to disappear. Yes, I think I could. There'd be no blemish on your record, no reprimand, no trouble at all, and that means that I'll see to it that funding continues for your position, regardless of whether or not the federal grant comes through for next year. I understand you are still a relatively young teacher, and I know young teachers will make mistakes. But in order for this to happen, I'll need some assurances from you."

"What assurances are those, Mr. Norman?"

"Simple, all I need you to agree to is that you will never again allow unedited, unchecked, unread material written by your students to come out."

Will didn't hesitate, not for a second, "I'm sorry Mr. Norman, I can't do that."

* * *

It was early June. Will was working in the real estate business. The notice about the termination of the federal funds which paid for the TAP program in Wautauga County had appeared in a tiny column on the fifth page in the <u>Community News</u> section of the Boone Sentinel. The article also stated that the Wautauga County Board of Education officials had said that at the present time there were no plans to authorize county funds to continue the program.

Three months earlier, as March died out, and the weather was warming up, Will saw to it that the Tapsters were out of the classroom as much as possible. There were hiking trips, camp outs, movies over in Boone, and of course they all continued working hard on the aluminum can and newspaper recycling projects.

Will had hinted to Wanda Oakley several times that he'd be interested in knowing what it was she had written in her letter to the principal. Wanda always declined any elaboration on the contents of the letter other than it was personal and she didn't want to talk about it.

The big beach trip went off as scheduled. With the additional money the Tapsters had raised, Will expanded the trip to four days and added soaring flights for the kids at Kitty Hawk, and there were fancy dinners at the steak and seafood houses in the evenings. None of the Tapsters had ever seen a shrimp, or a scallop, or a lobster, much less eat one.

After it had all wound down, and Will started his new career as a real estate agent, he was showing a home in a nice area not far from Boone. The potential buyer was a foreman at an electrical parts plant. The two men were getting along splendidly. The property Will was showing seemed to be a perfect match for what the man was looking for, and better yet, the price was well within his range. Will couldn't believe it. He was about to sell his first house. The man was ready to sign a contract and in fact sealed the deal with a check for twenty percent of the asking price as earnest money.

The buyer was very pleased with the house and also with the deal this young real estate agent had just walked him through. "I must say, this could not have worked out better. I bet you've closed plenty of real estate deals."

"Well, no sir, this is my first one," Will said shyly.

"I'll be! You don't say. Well, uh, what were you doing before real estate?"

"Would you believe, teaching school?"

"Really? Where were you teaching at?"

"Over at Sloan High School in Gumtree."

"At Sloan? Then you know all about that scandal the principal over there got caught up in. You know, I still think he should have been nailed to the wall. I mean, you know, he had the inside dope on the thing. He had the names, he had it all, but kept his mouth shut. I guess the good old boy network is what kept him out of jail, you know, greased the rails for him. I always thought that Oakley boy got a raw deal."

Will was listening closely now, but he'd never heard a word of any of this before now. "Must have been before my time. I was only there for three years. I just left a month ago."

The new home owner looked surprised, "You never heard anything about it?"

"No sir, not a thing."

"Well, it *was* five years ago, and I guess when a cover-up gets put in place, it *really* gets put in place. My neighbor, you see, he's a fifteen-year veteran in the state police; been in the drug investigation unit most of that time. He told me all about it. He worked the case."

"I see. What did your neighbor tell you?"

"Well, it was one convoluted mess. That's what it was. It seems that a bunch of druggies got into the crack cocaine craze. You know, it was new then. I guess they were content with pot, and then all this crack business sprung up. And here's the crazy thing – you'd never guess who these druggies were."

"Who were they?"

"Most of them were the teenage children of most of the big education hot shots in the county. The superintendent of schools, the school board chairman, the head of secondary education, the special ed. director, and four of them were principal's kids. It was nuts. That group was not only using crack cocaine, they were bringing it in from dealers in Charlotte, and selling a bunch of it. The drug investigation unit called them the mountain mafia."

After a moment to catch his breath, he noticed that Will was a captive audience, so he continued, "This is where the Oakley boy got involved."

"The Oakley boy?"

"Yeah. His parents weren't big shots, just normal working folks. He was probably a senior at that time and a pretty good football player. Well, he made the mistake of getting involved with the Sloan principal's daughter. She looked like an angel I'm told, but she had the worst addiction to the cocaine of anybody in that crowd. They said the boy, Buck Oakley, was crazy in love with her, and was doing everything he could to get her away from that druggie crowd."

Will stopped him, "Did you know anything more about Buck's family?"

"Like I said, his folks were good people, I think he worked for the Carolina Power Grid, a lineman, and Mrs. Oakley did a little seamstress work."

"That was the whole family?"

"No, Buck's little sister, was probably about fourth or fifth grade. I think her name was Wanda. Why?"

"Nothing."

"So, like I said, if you asked me, that boy, Buck, he drew an awful bad card."

"What happened?"

"The drug investigation unit got leads on who was running the crack over there in Gumtree, and they set up a raid at a cabin in the woods one night. Somehow or other the plans for the raid got leaked to one of the football players on Buck's team. He told Buck about when and where the raid was going to come down." He stopped for a second or two and thought that Will had a strange look in his eyes.

He continued. "Evidently Buck knew that his girlfriend, Melanie Norman, the principal's girl, she was going to be up there at that cabin that night. He drove up there to warn her, but nobody was there. Guess who showed up a couple of minutes later?"

"The drug unit."

"That's right. And guess what they found in that cabin with Buck?"

"I suspect they found cocaine."

"That's right. And guess who they arrested?"

"Buck."

"That's right. And do you want to hear the really crazy part of the story."

"You better believe it!"

"Buck's family did everything they could to keep him out of jail. You see, after he was arrested, Buck's dad came to visit him at the county lock-up. You know, there was no way they could go his bail, you see. Buck told him about the druggie group, you know, all those kids of the school big shots. He told his dad about all of them except one."

"Melanie Norman."

"That's right, but Mr. Oakley, you see, he knew Melanie was involved because that night that Buck went up to the cabin and was arrested, his dad had asked him where he was going and Buck said, 'to see Melanie.'"

"What else happened?" Will asked.

"My neighbor said that Mr. Oakley went straight to Tom Norman and told him that he (Mr. Oakley) knew the names of those kids running the mountain mafia including Melanie, and that his son Buck was totally innocent."

"Don't tell me. I bet you Mr. Norman said something like. 'You could never prove it. It was *your son* Buck who was caught with the drugs, not my daughter. Your son Buck, the one I warned Melanie to stay away from. I knew he was trouble all along.'"

The new home owner was looking closely at Will and said, "I don't think anybody could ever prove it, but what you just said sounds exactly like the same thing my neighbor said, you know the drug investigator."

Later that night Will sat down at home and was thinking about the whole story. He was thinking about Wanda Oakley, and even though he didn't know exactly what she had written in her letter to Tom Norman, he knew it was justified. And he knew he was glad he had taught the Tapsters to be themselves, trust their own judgement, be proud that TAP does things a little differently. Be proud that we try to be honest in everything we do, in everything we write because it is the best way, it is the only way.

And he knew he was going to miss L. B. Turner, he was going to miss Bubba Shiner, he was going to miss Casey Horner, he was going to miss both Libby and Teresa Murdock, he was going to miss Wendell Renfro, and yes, he was going to miss Wanda Oakley, and yes, he was going to miss each and every one of his Tapsters. He was gonna' miss them all.

Rookie Surfer

✳ ✳ ✳

Gary H. Baker

CLINT TROTTER REMEMBERED the first mid-watch he stood at the Naval Communications Station just outside Wahiawa, almost dead center on the Hawaiian Island of Oahu. Honolulu was an hour and twenty minutes away and the north shore was thirty-five minutes away. As a third class CT (Communications Technician) and the new man on the Alpha watch team rotation, he expected a certain amount of hazing and trickery to be aimed at him. The problem was, he didn't know exactly what was coming or when it might come. Still, he had made certain preparations to be ready for the trickery. An old shipmate had been stationed here before and had given him a detailed account of what had happened to him.

The last duty assignment Clint served was fifteen months aboard the USS Green River. Twelve of those months were served patrolling off the coast of Vietnam in the South China Sea. Clint had joined the Navy two years ago and already he'd seen a good deal of the world. He certainly had seen Navy tradition in action as well.

Initiation rituals for new troops varied by command, but you could be certain that brand-new personnel transferring in to a new duty station would be prime targets for some special attention, almost always negative, or maybe better put, attention designed to get a great big laugh out of those designing the chicanery.

As Clint finished his pre-watch meal in the mess-hall, he wasn't worried or even thinking very much about what might take place in the next eight hours. He'd already accepted the fact that his watch team would cook up some kind of nonsense, and he'd have to see it through, and so what? Get it over with and after the necessary hazing and everyone getting their jollies off, he'd begin to blend in and after a reasonable amount of time he'd be in the mix, accepted as just another member of watch team Alpha. No big deal.

He left the mess hall alone, and went outside to the cool Hawaiian night. It was 23:15 hours (11:15 p.m.) and the duty bus was just pulling up to receive passengers to make the short, one-mile trek out to the operations center. Clint's thoughts weren't about the next eight hours. They were about the stories he'd been reading in the surfer magazines about the world famous surfing beaches just twenty miles away, up on the North Shore. Places like Waimea Bay, Sunset Beach, and the Banzai Pipeline, he knew were recognized as perhaps the best surfing breaks on the planet. He couldn't wait until he got a few days off duty and maybe tag along with some of the surfers from here on the Naval base. Maybe they would have an extra surf board for him and teach him how to surf. He knew that surfing was the big rage with young people not only in California and the east coast, but here in Hawaii as well. Duh ... of course Hawaii. It is where surfing was born and then introduced to the rest of the world. For heaven's sake, the Hawaiian kings were the original surfers! Well, Hawaiian kings or not, Clint knew that two days ago as he explored the south shore beaches down at Waikiki, the surfers attracted the most attention from the bikini-clad women.

Clint was just a couple of months shy of twenty-one years old and he was thinking ... why not me? Why shouldn't I be one of those golden tanned, muscular, ocean-gods called surfers that the beach babes seem to drool over? And the truth was, Clint loved the ocean. Ever since a kid in land-locked Missouri, he had loved the water. He loved the lakes, the pools, the creeks, and the rivers. He was a good swimmer, and he loved diving off diving boards and high dive towers. When he was stationed at Pensacola, Florida for the Navy Communications School, he'd been drawn to the beaches, and that's when the surfing bug had bitten him. Of course the Florida surfing was tame compared to the monster waves of Hawaii, but still, when rumors of a four or five-foot swell coming from the Gulf of Mexico began circulating, the excitement in the surfing crowd was electric and palpable. Clint had never

even been on a surfboard in Florida, or anywhere else for
that matter, but that was the reason he declared to himself
that night, on the ride out to the ops-center, that he was
not going to waste the two years he had facing him here
in Hawaii. He was going to learn how to surf. He was going to be a surfer!

The bus pulled up to the ops-center and Clint and fifteen or twenty other sailors got off and walked toward the
Marine security guard at the gate. The marine checked
the photo I.D. of each sailor and admitted them in to the
electronically monitored, fenced-in, ops-center.

As he walked the thirty feet from the Marine sentry
to the entrance to the building, Clint was thinking that
this was not a lot different from the security procedures
on the USS Green River. Inside he was confronted with a
second-class petty officer sitting behind a desk. The second-class had allowed the other men to bypass his desk
and move on into their work place in the building.

Clint could see the second-class stand up and come
his way. "You must be Trotter."

"Yes sir. Third-class Com-Tech Trotter, assigned to
Alpha duty team"

"Alright Trotter, we've been expecting you. Follow
me."

What was it in the second-class petty officer's voice
that sounded just a bit ominous, maybe even treacherous?

They walked back through a long hallway and into a room where there was obviously a lot of Naval communicating taking place. Large, sophisticated radio-receivers were manned by com-techs with earphones on. Several of them were working the transmit key of a Morse code circuit and Clint instantly recognized the dots and dashes of high speed Morse code leaking from several earphones and from a speaker at one of the positions. Specialized direction-finding oscilloscopes resembling radar scopes were in use, as well as four or five teletypes pounding out incoming messages. Encrypted land-line circuits were also manned by several higher ranking enlisted men. Large 16 inch reel to reel recording machines were humming at several locations around the room, and off in a far corner Clint saw the watch-chief's desk. A grizzled Navy vet of at least twenty years' experience sat behind the desk chomping on a two-inch cigar stub. He was reading through a list of medium priority messages that had just been placed on his desk.

Strictly routine. Nothing out of the ordinary for the midnight watch in the middle of the Pacific Ocean.

The second-class petty officer, Reggie Attaberry by name, led Clint all the way across the room to the watch-chief's desk. "Chief, here's your new man, Trotter."

"Welcome aboard Trotter; glad to have you. They said you just came off the Green River. How's Chief Flaherty doing?"

"The last time I saw him he was doing fine. He had a bar girl on his left and another on his right back in Hong Kong."

"Yeah, that sounds like the old sea dog. Okay Trotter, let's see ... tonight you'll man the tsunami teletype for the first four hours, then we'll move you around the room and let you get a little taste of everything we've got. After a couple of weeks, you'll be assigned a permanent work station. Got it?"

"Yes sir."

"Attaberry will fill you in on the tsunami teletype. Good luck."

"Thank you chief." But Clint was thinking ... Good luck? What was that about? Actually, Clint knew what it was about, but for now, he'd play along with the game.

Second-class petty officer Attaberry led Clint through all the squawking radios, Morse code chatter, the clattering teletype equipment, and other assorted electronic gadgetry that supported the U. S. Navy's Seventh Fleet mission all the way from San Francisco to Bangkok, Thailand. They stopped dead in the middle of the room, and Attaberry motioned for Clint to take a seat in the chair in front of the tsunami teletype machine. The machine was bolted to the deck. The keyboard for sending messages was at desk height, or in other words, at the normal typing position any typist would expect. The machine's roller which the print-out tracked over, was wider than a normal typewriter roller by eight inches. The per-forated copy paper on large rolls fed up through guides and then folding on itself, ended up in the copy basket attached to the back of the machine.

A prominent label in fire-engine red letters just below the keyboard, identified this particular teletype as the TSUNAMI WATCH TELETYPE.

Before Clint could ask any question, Attaberry began the standard training spiel, "You are looking at a normal Navy teletype machine, Trotter. I know you've been trained on its function and operation, but on *this* teletype, your operating procedures will be modified. Comprehendo?"

"I'm with you so far." As he said this, Clint thought he caught several other teletype operators near him cast suspicious glances his way.

"Good", Attaberry shot back quickly. "Here's the thing, Trotter. You are sitting at this position for one reason only, and that is to monitor incoming traffic only. You will not be sending any outgoing traffic. Comprehendo?"

"Sure, that sounds easy enough."

"Now, why do you think we call this position the TSUNAMI WATCH TELETYPE?"

"I really don't know."

"Where are we, Trotter?"

"In the operations center."

"No, I mean in the broader sense of things."

"Uh, the broader sense," he paused for a moment, then, "We are on Oahu, in the middle of the Pacific."

"Good! Good, Trotter! Exactly! Correctomundo! We are definitely way out in the middle of the largest ocean on earth. Trotter, the Pacific Ocean is over one hundred and sixty-five million square miles, and if it were the only drinking water available, it would provide every man, woman, child, walking and crawling creature of every stripe and species enough water to last for eighty trillion years. And then some."

Clint was beginning to wonder where this circus was going. Attaberry was good at what he was doing; his timing perfect.

"So, Trotter, what would you think could be the absolute worst thing that could happen to a little island like Oahu, you know, being as it is, way out in the middle of such a body of water?"

"Ummm ... I don't know ... uh, maybe a tidal wave?"

"Absolutely. Trotter, you are sharper than most of the tacks in the box."

"Well, sir, I don't know how sharp I am, but that's got to be it. The worst thing that could happen would be a tidal wave. I think they call them tsunamis ..." Clint looked down in front of him at the red lettered label on the teletype – TSUNAMI WATCH TELETYPE, he looked back up at Attaberry and said in a resolute tone, "Okay, I get it. This teletype has something to do with,

I guess … uh, probably something to do with an early warning system, God forbid, if a tsunami were detected and on the loose somewhere in the Pacific."

"Right, Trotter. You're a quick study. So, here's the deal. We put all new men on this teletype for a very good reason. This teletype is exactly as you say, but it doesn't *just* have *something* to do with a system of quick response warnings which could save thousands of lives. No, Trotter, this teletype is the *only* accurate warning we have – not just for the Naval Communications Station, but for the entire island of Oahu, and the entire state of Hawaii. We put new men on this teletype in order to see how they might react in the event of an actual tsunami emergency. It is set up in such a way that it will print out exact instructions which the operator must follow. These instructions are somewhat random in nature. You might get instructions to make certain entries in the watch log-book. You might get instructions to make emergency phone calls to civilian emergency response teams; you know, firefighters, the red cross, ect.

"Now keep in mind, Trotter," Attaberry tightened-up his most sobering military guise and continued, "that this position is a training position as well as the actual device used to warn the entire state of an actual tsunami alert. In other words, this is the ultimate "on the job training." As you sit here reading off every message coming in, it will, as I said earlier, be giving instructions on what actions you must take. El understando?"

"Yes, I think so." Clint felt as if a hook were sliding down his throat and if he didn't already know what it was all about, he would have been powerless to spit it out.

"Good. Now, normally, the messages coming over will all be training messages, and you will respond to whatever instructions are given. You will do exactly what the instructions say to do, no side-stepping, no variance, no self-interpretation. Just do exactly what it says to do. As I said, normally, everything will be mundane and routine. But if an actual tsunami alert comes through, it will be preceded by FLASH-FLASH TSUNAMI ALERT IN PROGRESS, and this little red light will come on. You will not panic and come running to me or the chief. All the training of following each and every instruction will then make sense. If an actual alert goes off, you will follow each and every instruction to the letter."

As Attaberry walked away, Clint settled in and began reading the incoming messages on the TSUNAMI WATCH TELETYPE in front of him. At first there were several weather reports that concluded with "no action required". The machine was quiet for a few minutes and then it spit out several messages with instructions for Clint to deliver them to several places around the room, which he did. The last went to the watch chief, who looked up from other documents he was scanning and said, "Did Atteberry get you set up okay?"

"Yes sir."

"Good. Carry on, sailor."

Clint was very suspicious of the slightly crooked smile the chief seemed to exhibit. "Yes sir," he said and walked back to the tsunami teletype. The machine sounded like an electric typewriter gone mad – clackity, clackity, clackity, on and on it went for three or four minutes before ceasing the nervous, whining, rattle of its printing cycle.

There were instructions with nearly every message. Clint was charged with delivering more messages around the room, making three "com-check" phone calls, and finally to check the escape route out of the building to make sure he and the others would find no obstacles in their way as they ran from the building to higher ground in the event of an actual alert. As he performed this last instruction, he was certain, this time, many of the twenty or so men in the room were stifling laughter.

The night wore on; it was nearly 03:00. The communication traffic in the ops-center had slowed down considerably. Evidently there were no confrontations bubbling up anywhere in the Pacific between American forces and potential enemies. Much of the traffic was dealing with logistics related to the massive troop build- up in Vietnam, as well as Naval support bases in Japan and the Philippines. Also there was some routine data on satellite telemetry being processed and forwarded on to air force bases on the mainland.

Clint's tsunami alert teletype had not kept him very busy the whole time. He'd made one "head call" (bathroom break), and he'd gone to get some coffee several times. Other than that, all he'd done was process the message traffic from the tsunami alert teletype and followed each and every instruction to the letter.

At 03:25 Attaberry stopped in front of the tsunami alert teletype with a worried look on his face. "Trotter, we just got word there's been an undersea earthquake four hundred miles from here. Your teletype will probably start shooting a lot of traffic. You may or may not get an actual flash alert with the red light. Sometimes these quake reports turn out to be bogus. But if it's the real thing, you know what you are to do, right?"

"Yes sir. Follow the instructions. Do exactly what it says to do."

"Good enough. Just wanted to make sure. Let's hope the report on that undersea quake was bogus so we won't have to worry about anything." As Attaberry walked away, Clint noticed most of the men had been watching and straining to hear what it was Attaberry had said to him. And Clint was thinking, *Okay, now it's about to happen. They're ready to get the show started. Well, let's get it over with. I'm ready if they are!*

It didn't take long. Five minutes later the red light erupted into a pulsating, fearful harbinger of disaster. The machine seemed to jerk to life and the first message rattled, and thundered, and tore its way into print. Clint was reading it as the message was printing and as it concluded, Clint tore it off in a flurry of duty, responsibility, and utter determination to prove to all eyes in the room that were on him (and all eyes *were* on him) that he would carry out the instructions on the Flash Alert to the best of his ability. They were in good hands, the ops-center was in good hands, the state of Hawaii was in good hands, the U. S. Navy was in good hands, Clint Trotter would not fail them!

But first, Clint re-read the message to make sure he knew what he was counted on to do. The message read as follows:

FLASH – FLASH TSUNAMI ALERT IN PROGRESS! This is not a drill. A tidal wave on the tsunami scale of 8 has been detected. The scale range is 0-10. REPEAT - this tidal wave is currently reading a scale 8, travelling at seventy miles an hour, its estimated time of arrival at the Hawaiian Islands is in twenty-three minutes - -3:53 HST.

PRIORITY INSTRUCTIONS FOR TSUNAMI ALERT TELETYPOE OPERATOR:

1. Proceed to center of the main room in the ops-center and follow steps 2 and 3 which await you there.

Clint didn't hesitate a second. He was up and out of his seat and on the way to a table in the middle of the room.

y H. Baker

/

Now the entire ops-center staff, some twenty sailors, were on their feet too and headed for the same place.

And look! There she was! Lulu! She was a life-size figurine, no, a life-size bobble head, gyrating and vibrating to some Hawaiian Hula serenade escaping from a speaker somewhere on her luscious body. Lulu's grass skirt swayed and the flower lei around her neck tickled her exposed breast. Lulu was gorgeous. Lulu was plastic. Lulu represented the Hawaiian Goddess of Hula, as Clint was about to find out.

As Clint approached the scene, he saw the instructions for steps 2 and 3 lying there on the table. He picked up the instructions and began to read: STEP 2 – This is not a joke. It is deadly serious! The lives of hundreds of thousands depend on your discharging your duties. To you, Lulu may look like any ordinary plastic doll dressed up in a traditional hula costume. She is not ordinary. She represents the life force of all Hawaii – the ancients as well as modern day Hawaiians. As in Christianity, the pagan religions of the South Seas have always demanded a blood sacrifice when doom and destruction are at the door step. By fulfilling your duties, you may be able to satisfy the God's demands for a blood sacrifice. You must now drop your pants and lay out your dick on the table. This concludes STEP 2.

Clint dropped his pants and unfurled his ample manliness right on top the table. All of the sailors looking on were very much impressed with the size of what Clint brought to the table. By now of course, the cat was out of the bag. The crowd was roaring with laughter and shouting out, "lay it out there sailor, Lulu is wanting all of it."

Determined to fulfill his duty, Clint picked up the instructions for STEP 3, and read:

You will now remove the machete from the drawer in the table, and whack off your cock at its base. After this has been done, you will pick up your severed cock and present it to Lulu. It is all of our hope that there is enough of it to appease the God's demands and stop the tsunami from wiping out our beloved Hawaii.

Clint opened the drawer and removed the machete and with one last proud glance around the throng of sailors, he said to them, "Let no man say Clint Trotter didn't give all he had to save Hawaii." He raised the machete and brought it up high, trembling there for a moment, all the sailors screaming "cut it off, cut it off!" Not a one of them were thinking he was crazy enough to actually do it.

They were wrong. Clint wrenched up the tension in his shoulders and tightened his grip on the handle of the machete. He slammed the machete down on the base of his dick, severing it cleanly, fake blood spurting everywhere. The howling frenzy of the other men came to a halt. To a man, they seemed to turn to a pale shade of disbelief. Several fainted on the spot. The others, wide-eyed, wild-eyed, locked in mad incredulity.

Clint trussed up his pants, taking his time to zip up and fix his belt correctly. He picked up his severed member and walked the four steps to the end of the table and presented his ample manliness to Lulu, whose spring loaded head was bobbling around excitedly.

* * *

`Three weeks later Clint, Tom, and Randle sat astride their surfboards a hundred and fifty yards off the Waianae coast. The swell was four to five feet and Clint had already caught five or six waves. His riding style was stiff and cautious, unlike Tom and Randle who pulled off stunning kick -backs, nose rides, and tube rides. But now it was between sets and the three of them sat bobbing up and down in the ocean, absorbing the tropical sun, eyes to the northwest awaiting more waves.

After another minute or two a small group of Hawaiians appeared on the beach and three of them began to paddle out towards the young sailors.

"We got company coming," Randle said.

"Yeah. It looks like Aku, Billy, and Mongoose. You know, those guys from Makaha."

"They the guys been asking about the hero that saved the state from the tsunami?"

"Yeah. It's them. Hey Clint, you got some admirers coming out to meet you."

The ocean was still resting before the next set of waves would be coming through. As the three Hawaiians got closer, Clint could see they were the real deal – true Hawaiian watermen. Dark bronzed skin taut over steely, toughened paddling muscles. The effortless, flowing rhythm of their paddling told the story. A gene pool not unlike fish. The pride in their comfort and familiarity with the ocean surrounded them like a halo. No matter what aquatic athletic prowess a white skinned surfer might have had, they would never have the same relationship with the ocean that the Hawaiians had.

The Hawaiians were getting close. They recognized Tom and Randle, but paddled over close to Clint. Aku looked at Clint seriously, "Eh brah! You dah haole cut off his ule and save our islands from dee big wave?"

Clint had no idea of how to react or what to say. Tom and Randle didn't seem to be interested in getting involved. Water slapped against the railing on his surfboard and Clint was thinking maybe he could dive to the bottom and hide in a sea-cave.

Billy, the largest of the three Hawaiians finally broke the tension. He delivered a rugged yet conciliatory ocean smile and laughed like a bull whale being tickled by the tail of a manta ray. "Oh man, we know what happened! Dee story all over dee island by now. We know all about it. The ule you cut off was rubber. A fake ule. Right? What dey call it? A dildo? Yeah! Oh man, I wish I was there. All the sailors teenk it was real! Right Brah? We hear some of them pass right out. Wish I could see that."

All three Hawaiians were now laughing and hollering. You could have heard them a good way off. "You one crazy, crazy haole. But we got one small problem. Dat why we paddle out and talk with you."

Clint had been on the verge of laughing himself, but now all he could do was nervously kick his feet a little in the ocean as he sat astride his board. The sun continued beating down on him. He wished he had some fresh water to drink. He glanced to the outside and noticed some decent lines starting to gather up far out to sea.

Billy, now in a very serious tone, continued, "Yeah, that night all very funny. Big joke, right? You cut off fake ule and take it to plastic hula dancer. Very funny. But you know what? It very disrespectful also. No class. You treat our culture like we some kind caveman. You teenk we have no pride. You teenk we stupid. You teenk U. S. Navy government G.I. pulling bad joke could save our islands. You laugh at our culture by handing fake ule to hula dancer!"

"Look, haole, we sit on beach last half hour and watch you try to surf. You make our ancient sport, our true and righteous marriage with the sea, you make fun of it the way you surf. You surf like you scared. You surf like old maid. We don't like you making fun of surfing."

You gotta be kidding, Clint was thinking. *They've been watching me?*

Mongoose paddled up very close to Clint and removed something attached to the deck of his surfboard. Mongoose looked like maybe he'd escaped from Halawa Prison – scars and tats covered his arms, chest, and back. His eyes were black with ruthlessness and fever. The words he carved out were dripping with tortured promise, "You see this, haole? You know what this is don't you, haole? It one machete, maybe little bigger than the machete you cut off fake ule with. We gonna use it to cut off your real ule. How you like that, haole? But wait, haole. Don't start crying yet. We give you one chance for save your ule. That's right. We righteous Hawaiians. We fair. We give you one chance. You see the swell coming? Yes, good set of waves coming in now. You see them?"

Clint looked outside and yes, a good set of waves was drawing near. He wanted to puke, but heard himself, as if he were far away, say to Mongoose, "Yes, I see the waves coming."

"Okay, haole, I told you. We are righteous, we are proud, but we are fair. We give you chance to save your ule. Ride these waves like we do. Ride with pride, with joy, with fever, with excitement, not like you riding before. You ride like Hawaiians, we no cut off your ule."

The Hawaiians paddled off towards Tom and Randle, and all five of them let the current drag them inside the break where they would have the best vantage point to observe the rookie surfer try to save his ule, his real ule.

As the five settled into viewing range and were all openly chuckling and laughing, Randle asked the Hawaiians, "Did he swallow the hook?"

"I guess so. Look at him paddle to get outside. You should have seen his eyes when I showed him the machete." Mongoose was whooping it up. He hadn't laughed so hard in a good many days.

"There he goes," Aku shouted.

They all watched as the rookie surfer paddled furiously to get into position to catch the first wave of the set. The beautiful aqua wall was swelling up, flashing its sultry smile as a billion sparks of refracted sunlight danced off its face. Clint was in good position. He swung his board back towards the beach and paddled even harder, three, four, five paddle strokes and he was no longer trying to match his speed with mother nature's. He was with her now, trying his best to become a silky smooth, wave streaking, surfing artist, just like the Hawaiians; and trying his very best to keep his ule.

Driving To Mildred Blaney's

* * *

Gary H. Baker

MAPLE VALLEY TENNESSEE wasn't big enough to have a post office or a school. In fact, the only thing that made it any different from twenty thousand other rural cross-roads was that it did, at least, have a stop sign and a few mail boxes, and a hundred yards down the road from the stop sign there was the Maple Valley United Methodist Church.

The time was 2015, the United States was still trying to deal with what appeared to be the ever-growing polar-ization of progressive thought and government policies on the one side, and conservative fundamentalism which those who accepted its maxims desperately hoped would finally knock some sense into the heads of the corrupt politicians, on the other side.

There was little doubt about which side Glenn Tasker was on.

Glenn pulled his pick-up truck up close to the rusty mail box perched on a rickety five-foot-long wood slat supported by a couple of old cedar post in the ground. Four mail boxes dripping with rust and stained by bird droppings clung haphazardly to the rotting wood slat. He was thinking about some of the preliminary duties his wife Sarah had laid out for him today as he rolled the window down and reached to release the catch on his mail box. A church yard-sale, that's what she wants to do. Why not? We had made a few bucks at our personal yard sales years ago. But now, will a church yard sale bring in enough to slow the impending melt down of our little country church's dwindling checking account? Probably not, but just like Sarah said yesterday, "If we can pay a couple of heat and electric bills with it … well that'll make it worth it."

He needed to drive to town and pick up a set of table and chairs that a church member, Mildred Blaney, was donating to the yard sale. Also, Sarah had asked him to stop by the barbecue stand and put up the yard sale sign. The man that owned the barbecue stand was willing to let them use the strip by the highway in front of the business to sell the stuff Sarah and the others helping her hoped to accumulate. He grabbed a hand full of sales promotions and women's clothing catalogues out of the mail box, and he noticed a couple of bills in the collection. He laughed as he noticed one last envelope. The return address was

Midwest Valley Life Insurance, Moline, Illinois. *You're kidding*, Glenn thought. *They have another renewal commission check for me? I know I sent all those companies notification that I forfeited my insurance license at least fifteen years ago.* Still, even after all that time, Glenn would receive an annual residual commission check for perhaps ten or twenty dollars from several of the life insurance companies he had represented years ago as an independent agent. It was a pretty good joke to Glenn.

The day was cool, a mist hung in the fields from a light rain earlier in the morning, fall color in the trees was muted by the moisture and the light gray cloud bank. Glenn turned towards town, and in a couple of miles he pulled off the main road into a little driveway that tracked fifty yards to the tidy little building that was Country Barbecue. There were no signs of anyone around the small, white, red trimmed barbecue cookery. It was early on a Tuesday, and anyway, the owners only opened for the weekend this time of year. He parked and got out of the pick-up and removed the sign from the truck bed:

CHURCH YARD SALE – HERE
SATURDAY 9 A.M. – 2 P.M.

He set the sign up near the main road, angling it to get the most exposure from traffic both ways.

He turned his truck around and slowly pulled up towards the road, sure to look both ways, then he started on out. WHAAAAAAA screamed the air horn of the tractor trailer roaring along at about sixty.

Glenn missed a breath and lurched back in his seat like he'd been hit with a bat. His eyes caught the smoke from the tires on the big truck, now sixty yards on up the road, as the driver must have nearly locked up his air brakes. Then another WHAAAAAAA from the driver's air horn as he wanted to make sure Glenn knew the nature of his thoughts at that particular moment.

Glenn regained his composure to some degree and once again began to ease on out on the main road, this time making sure nothing was coming. *Whew, must be losing more than my hearing*, he was thinking. And he was. His strength and endurance was ebbing; his balance was getting worse as evidenced by a horrendous vertigo episode. He'd had a couple of serious panic attacks, and he was flirting with high blood pressure, probably due to his weight.

Well, he thought, *what's so unusual about an almost seventy year-old starting to show a little wear and tear? I'll outlive most of 'em I'd bet.* He was probably right. Longevity ran on both sides of his family, and until the last twenty years or so Glenn had been a model of pretty good health habits, not perfect, but better than many others.

He glanced down again at the life insurance envelope on the top of the pile, laying there on the seat next to him. He drifted back to the mid-nineties and thought about the industry he had worked in for a total of about fifteen years. It was an industry, like most industries, that had its good side, and its not so good side. The first face that popped up in the old catalogue of personalities was Curtis James, Glenn's old boss from around 1987 to late in 1996, about ten of the fifteen years Glenn had been an insurance salesman and a registered representative in the mutual fund business.

Glenn let the memories roll, and in short order he was zeroed in on a particular day that he'd never forgotten. The memory started with Curtis James. James was fifty years old, an ex-football player, and he had that subtle east Texas drawl that wasn't anything like a true deep south drawl or a true Okie drawl. James was responsible for weekly FYC numbers at his branch office in Germantown, the most well-healed suburb of Memphis. The FYC numbers were the life blood of the industry. He felt confident that the numbers he would report in the next hour or so would take some of the heat off – the pressure the regional manager, Tom Thraxton, placed on him and all the other branch managers to get their sales force to produce higher and higher First Year Commissions. Curtis enjoyed better than average job security, because for the past eight years he always rode his agents relentlessly to bring in ever increasing weekly FYC results. Still, he knew there were young guns, always aggressive, always ready to pull the trigger and try to out-maneuver him in blatant efforts to steal his job.

Tom Thraxton looked on his responsibility as state regional manager to push his branch managers as a general might push his division, regimental, and battalion commanders in the army. Why, it was patriotic to sell life insurance, wasn't it? Of course it was! Life insurance was the very fabric of the American economy, wasn't it? Yes, of course it was! It protects the American family in a way nothing else could do, not to mention that the big insurance companies are the fundamental bedrock foundation of the entire American financial system. That's saying a lot, and Tom Thraxton not only didn't question it, but held those that thought otherwise in serious suspicion of being subversive, even un-American. The fact that he, as a statewide regional manager of one of the largest insurance companies in the land, Fairfield Mutual Life Insurance Company; the fact that he sometimes pushed his team beyond ethical and legal limits in order to achieve sparkling FYC numbers each week, he never worried about.

"Harold had a big week. He said the lawyers downtown ditched Charter Mutual and re-did their buy-sell plan with us." Curtis James waited to see Thraxton nod his approval. He continued looking through his notes for the Memphis area sales meeting that would commence in fifteen minutes at the statewide regional office, also in Germantown, and only a couple of miles from his Germantown branch office. To many of the local life insurance agents, Thraxton's regional office was known as the Command Post, no doubt a reference to Thraxton's illusion he was running a Navy SEAL unit, not a life insurance and securities operation.

James and Thraxton could hear the agents begin to shuffle into the meeting room down the modern and tasteful vestibule just beyond the lobby.

Tom Thraxton, as always, seemed in the middle of a deep meditation, that is, until the meeting got started and he would launch into his rehearsed sales manager sermon and lay on the enthusiasm in his best pep talk that any football coach would have been proud of. "What this region couldn't do with five more agents like Harold", he finally said after looking up from some papers on his desk.

"Amazing isn't it." Curtis James released a little chuckle and shook his head in delight, "Who would have thought an old country boy like Harold would end up being one of the top four or five senior sales executives in the region?"

"I don't know, but I'm glad he's ours and not with the competition," the regional manager replied. He spoke into the intercom on his phone, "Betsy please bring in fresh coffee."

"Yes sir, right away," Betsy Condiff said. She respected her boss as her boss, but she still wasn't sure what she felt about him as a man, even after six years of being his executive secretary. She tried to avoid that kind of thinking as much as she could. She was, for the most part, content with the knowledge that she worked for an insurance regional manager that knew what he was doing, was a tough and thorough professional, and that as far as she could tell, usually treated people fairly. She'd sensed a few things every now and then that detracted from his otherwise appealing personality, but she could see past that. Nobody is perfect. Her job paid well, not great, but certainly well enough to see that she, as a single mom, and her sixteen-year-old son had enough to get them through most of the everyday expenses. Her ex was off in prison somewhere, and even before the split up, he was a deadbeat who occasionally dealt drugs in the north Memphis black ghettos he grew up in.

As Betsy was leaving her desk to get the coffee, she picked up an incoming call and placed it on hold. A minute later she delivered Thraxton and James two piping hot mugs of Costa Rican Terrazu with a little Folgers to cut it – Mr. Thraxton's favorite blend. "Mr. Thraxton there's a call on hold for you." When alone with her boss, it was "Tom", but when other company personell were around, it was "Mr. Thraxton." Both parties were comfortable with the arrangement. As the office door had been open when she entered, so it was left as she departed even as she felt Curtis James' hungry eyes trailing her.

"Tom Thraxton," he said.

"You're about ready to start your sales meeting, right?"

Thraxton immediately recognized the voice of Ronald Zopata, the southeast region honcho out of Atlanta, and felt a shiver run down his back, for what reason, he couldn't identify.

"Yes, that's right, everyone's coming in now." He pushed the hot coffee aside and slid a blank legal pad in front of him. It was a habit he'd developed over the years when Atlanta called.

"Tom, we've got more of a situation bubbling up in Charlotte than we talked about last week. Frankly, we erred in thinking we could just ride it out. There have been new developments and they aren't good."

"Is it Pastriano?" Thraxton asked.

"Yes. But we can't talk about it on the phone. I'm flying in tomorrow morning. I'll be in your office by ten. I'll be seeing all eight state managers in the next three days. You're the first, and you'll know why tomorrow morning. Listen, and this is important. Run your sales meeting today as usual. Be alert for anything suspicious around the building or in your office spaces – strangers, faulty security, and I'd even like you and Curtis to check around quickly for any bugs."

"Bugs? Thraxton asked quickly. "I wouldn't know one if it were sitting on my desk in front of my eyes."

"You've seen and read enough spy thrillers to know what to look for. Tell Betsy and the other girls in the office to help. Tell them it's new security policy that just came down from the home office. You can tell Curtis what I've just told you, but no one else. And when you get the time, that means when the meeting is over, you will hire a local security expert to go over everything thoroughly. You got it?"

"Yes, I've got it. But isn't there anything else you can cut loose?"

"Not until tomorrow. Oh wait a second ... You might sit down with Tasker for a minute or two. See where he's at on all the term he's selling. And keep your eyes and ears open. See if there are any more termites selling that crap."

"Is that all?"

"Until tomorrow morning, that's it. See you at ten sharp."

* * *

Two Fairfield Mutual life insurance salesmen, Will Dorn and Glenn Tasker were settling into the forty-minute drive over to the regional office in Germantown for the sales meeting. They had another buddy to pick up a few miles up the road – Framton Hornacker, who would have made an excellent stand-in for John Goodman if any movies were being shot in the area. Goodman's character in *Oh Brother Where Art Thou* might have been the authentic, nearly identical movie version of the real life Framtom Hornacker who was just now polishing off a monster chocolate eclair as Will Dorn and Glenn Tasker pulled into his thirty-five acre rural man-cave. Tractors, backhoes, bush hogs and other heavy equipment were spread around here and there. A good-looking tree house for his kids, or him, who knew? was twenty feet up in the split of a huge oak tree. As Tasker wheeled his big SUV up towards the modern log home, Hornacker hoisted his golf clubs in one hand and opened the tailgate of the SUV and threw the clubs in the back. By the time he had wrestled his three hundred fifty pounds into the back seat, he already had another éclair in his mouth. He threw the bag, still heavy with more sugar treats, up front and said, "Get into 'em boys. They mighty good!"

"Here's your coffee," Glenn Tasker said as he handed it back to Framtom.

"Fram, I have a question."

"I got a lot of questions," Framton said. "Most of them are why are we wasting our time at a stupid sales meeting when we could be at the golf course in twenty minutes?"

"Good point, but here's mine. How many eclairs have you put away this morning?"

"Glenn, you know I quit drinking. I gotta' replace those calories with something, don't I?"

Will Dorn was much more the financial services type than either Tasker or Hornacker and he had the pedigree to prove it – MBA in finance, ex-securities broker, estate planning credentials, annuity specialist, and on and on. How he ended up selling life insurance would lead one to think his career was running out in reverse order. But, there was money to be made in selling life insurance, and where there was money to be made, you would expect Will Dorn to show up.

Dorn looked over his shoulder and saw Framtom Hornacker's empty hands, "Here, you may need extra calories this afternoon. Tee time is two," and he handed the bag of pastries back.

The SUV was approaching interstate-40 where in ten minutes they'd be turning off toward Germantown. Glenn Tasker scratched his mustache and wondered out loud, "You think Patton will rip who ever sold a term policy this week?"

"Blood and Guts always rips you termites," responded Dorn.

Framtom Hornacker, in a serious tone, shouted out, "Yeah, just like General Patton's troops used to say, 'Our blood, his guts'."

Glenn Tasker shook his head in disbelief. Was another argument with his friend Will Dorn about to get underway? Just crazy! And it wasn't even that Dorn defended or attacked either of the two main types of life insurance policies: term or permanent, the permanent being further divided into Whole Life, Modified Whole Life, Universal Life, Variable Life, and a few other slick tags attached to policies which were five to twenty times more expensive.

No, it was that Dorn, in his smooth and calculating voice, would explain perfectly why the management of big life insurance companies pushed agents to sell permanent policies, regardless of whether it was best for the customer or not. Dorn for sure was good at the explanation, but it really wasn't necessary. It wasn't rocker science. Any fool could see that why companies pushed Whole Life policies over term was because they made a lot more money on it. Simple, not complicated, and that was the reason. It infuriated Glenn Tasker when he thought about it. In just his short eight years in the business, He'd seen it happen again and again. Why, he'd even done it himself. Sell a Whole Life policy to a young family and after some shocking auto accident, drowning, or death from cancer, he, Glenn Tasker would deliver a death benefit of twenty-five thousand dollars to the young widow with two children. He could have delivered her a death benefit of a quarter of a million had he done the right thing and sold the family a term life insurance policy. How long would the twenty-five thousand last for the widow and two kids, now that the main bread winner had been buried?

But, that was in his early days in the late 1980's. Now it was 1996 and he'd gotten away from selling Whole Life, and in fact was selling more term than any other agent for Fairfield Mutual in the state of Tennessee, hence the derogatory "termite" applied to him and a few others by management.

Tasker glanced Dorn's way as he changed lanes on the interstate, "What kind of a week did you have?"

"A couple of small annuities and a good Whole Life. About twelve hundred in FYC. You?"

"Two million in face amount of term. I think the FYC will be about four hundred and fifty bucks."

There it was right there. Glenn Tasker's two million in face amount meant, as the agents were trained to say, "God forbid," if there was a death claim, the death benefit would be two million dollars. The Whole Life Dorn sold would have paid a hundred thousand dollars. The difference in the higher commission Dorn had earned was seven hundred and fifty dollars. Of course, some of his twelve hundred in commission came from the two annuities, but not much, less than two hundred dollars.

For the hundredth time in the last several months Tasker was thinking to himself: *Something's gotta' give. They'll fire me if I don't quit first. Crazy, it's just crazy! I'm selling more coverage than anybody, making less money, and getting the trash dumped all over me by Curtis James and that rattle snake Thraxton.*

From the back seat Framptom Hornacker shouted out, "Hey, you guys don't want to hear about my week?"

"Shoot big guy," Dorn said, "What did you end up with?"

"Zero, but my wife Ellen brought in three grand from her side gig," he said with pride.

Tasker knew Ellen was a special education teacher's assistant, but he was in the dark on the side gig. "How'd she make the three grand? You're with a fine woman is all I got to say. You'll probably eat up that money in a week."

"Not on your life buddy, but I may play a lot of golf," he chuckled. "You didn't know she's a first class landscape artist?"

"No, but that's great. I know you're proud of her," Tasker said enthusiastically.

"You bet'cha! You oughta' seen the job she did - garden walkways in Pennsylvania Bluestone, a lily pond with a water falls, new willow trees, flower beds, the works." Hornacker went to the bottom of the pastry bag where he had a ham and cheese sandwich in reserve.

* * *

Most of the twenty-six Memphis area agents had filtered into the meeting room, many of them packing coffee and donuts from the adjacent break room. The Germantown branch office assistant manager, Travis Kent, was chatting it up with a couple of almost late arrivals. Curtis James and Tom Thraxton would march in soon and things would get rolling.

Harold Tierney, knowing he would receive a lot of attention today, parked himself up front as close as he could to where Thraxton and James would hold court. He glanced around the room waving to a couple of other senior sales executives and fidgeted with his expensive silk tie just enough to see a few folks take notice.

Other sales reps were reviewing life insurance applications they had taken from clients last week, just checking accuracy and numbers. The Monday morning sales meetings put the stamp on the previous weeks FYC numbers, as well as serving as a training session, and of course as a bully pulpit for whatever home office propaganda the branch managers and the state regional manager might unload on the gathering.

The clatter around the meeting room hadn't slowed down much, even as everyone saw James and Thraxton entering from the propped open side door. Tasker, Dorn, and Hornacker were talking about the fourth hole at the Doe Run Golf Course, a par five, over water, with fairway traps, and a big oak tree hiding half the green.

"Do you guys ever work on Monday afternoons?" Katie Larson was asking while trying to muffle the snicker in her voice. Katie loved to joke around with some of the men in her branch office, not all of them. But with these three and a couple more she could relax and be "one of the guys." She would even crack some pretty raunchy dirty jokes now and then.

No one even noticed when after entering the room and closing the door behind them, Tom Thraxton and Curtis James sort of walked around the room checking a few things out. Windows, a couple of air vents, and the thermostat seemed to get James's attention. Meanwhile Thraxton had shown interest in the two phones in the room as well as the microphone on the lectern which normally was not used for sales meetings this size.

In short order both men met at the front of the room and the chit-chat of the assembled sales force died down. Thraxton sat down near the lectern which was the signal for Curtis James to start the meeting.

"Good morning everyone. I can see you've all got caught up on your adventures over the weekend and no doubt are getting fired up for another big sales week." He paused a few seconds to gage the mood of the Germantown, North Mississippi, and Downtown branch office sales teams. Looking around, he took special notice of the new young agent from midtown, but who was assigned to his branch, not to the downtown branch. Penny Ackerman was cute as a button he was thinking, but then he said to himself, no, no she's hot, and he reminded himself that she would probably be receptive to a warm and personal welcoming to the Germantown branch office as soon as the meeting was over. Then again, he reconsidered the thought when he remembered that the mood of Tom Thraxton seemed to go sour just minutes before the meeting got started. Thraxton may put him onto something today. The personal welcome he'd like to offer Penny Ackerman might have to wait for a better time.

"Okay, let's look at FYC from last week. Everyone has the print-out. We'll start at the bottom and work up. Wait, this can't be. Two zeroes? Let's pretend we don't see that! We know both of these guys had good numbers the week before last and we know they will kill it this week. Right guys?"

Hornacker and another agent shook their heads vigorously, and Hornacker piped up, "Yes sir, boss! Just watch me go this week!" There were a couple of muted laughs, but Thraxton wasn't smiling or laughing.

"Okay, let's go on: Peyton Thompson – three hundred and fifty dollars FYC -a new enrollee on a group health plan. I'm sure there will be more next week. Let's hear it for Peyton." A scraggly applause from four or five agents scratched quickly through the room. Finger nails on a chalk board would have sounded better.

"Brent Wilder – Four thirty-five. Brent sold a hundred thousand Universal Life on a twenty-nine-year-old. Let's hear it for Brent." The applause meter rose slightly.

"Glenn Tasker – Two million term. Four fifty FYC" James didn't encourage any applause, still, a reasonable hand clap arose from five or six reps around the room.

Curtis James continued reading the agents' names and their sales results for last week. The higher the FYC rose, the better the applause.

A little over halfway through the twenty-six individual FYC results Will Dorn's twelve hundred first year commissions was reported by Curtis James and he asked Dorn to give the sales team some of the background on the cases.

"Yes sir, be glad to. The annuities were a result of some unexpected cash my clients came into - her mother's estate. I put them in our new variable annuity product. They've been very conservative in their 401-K's and their IRA's, so they were open to a little sexier strategy on the annuities. We went 40, 30, 30. Forty percent small caps, thirty international, and thirty on that fantastic dot com fund our brokers just got their hands on. And the Whole Life? Well what can I say? It sells itself. A fixed premium for around twelve years. Dividends paying it from then on. You can take loans out of it. It has the disability waiver. It annuitizes at age ninety. It's a Cadillac all the way around."

What Dorn didn't say, and forgot to tell his clients as well, is that dividends aren't guaranteed, so it may take a lot longer than twelve years for the policy to "pay up". He also neglected to say that loans against the policy had to be repaid with interest in order not to reduce the death benefit. This effectively charges the client for the use of his own money. But the biggest omission Dorn would not want to discuss is that the actual cost of the life insurance in a Whole Life policy based on actuarial and mortality tables, was at least ten times higher, sometimes twenty times higher or worse, than the actual cost of term life insurance based on those same actuarial and mortality tables. Also, you'd not be likely to get Dorn to discuss what kind of investment return a client might expect on the difference in premium from a Whole Life to a term policy. In fact, an entire industry of term life companies was emerging because it was being proven that "buy term and invest the difference" was providing clients a much better investment return than a Whole Life insurance policy could possibly do. In short, Whole Life insurance was a pure rip-off to the American consumer, but it has been fueling large insurance companies' healthy profits for as long as life insurance has been sold.

Thraxton and James led the vigorous applause as Dorn completed his analysis of his weeks work which resulted in twelve hundred dollars in first year commissions. When the new FYC was combined with renewal commissions, and certain bonuses and overrides, his pool account would increase enough to bump his gross weekly pay-check to about eleven hundred dollars – annual gross income fifty-seven thousand two hundred dollars - not real big money, but pretty darn good for an agent so new to the industry. Yes, Dorn had a boatload of financial services experience, but selling life insurance was different from all the other things he'd done in the past. The hard work of "beating the bushes" was the main difference. Another term used to describe how an agent found customers was "Prospecting". It was the backbone of the industry and there was nothing easy about it. Obviously, Dorn was learning quickly, and if he could become relentless, persistent, and hardnosed in his prospecting, he would soon be a star.

Curtis James moved on up the list. As the FYC totals gradually got higher and higher, he and Thraxton encouraged the agents to give in depth accounts of how each case was developed and how it was "closed" – the actual signing of the application by the customer and of course the collection of the premium. This was better training for the newer reps than any training manual could possibly be.

As the FYC report neared the top of the list, Harold Tierney was practically squirming in his seat with anticipation. This is what he lived for – recognition! Recognition that he was week in and week out one of the top producers in not only the Germantown branch office, but also in the state region, and high up on the list in Fairfield Mutual's national FYC numbers. In short, his success as a top-level insurance senior sales executive was his life. And no one in the industry withheld admiration, homage, and honor from a man like Tierney; not even those that might have been jealous; not even those that understood they didn't possess the same talent, drive, and business acumen that Tierney had worked so hard for over twenty-five years to amass.

Even Glenn Tasker gave rousing applause as Tierney concluded his condensed report on how he earned seventeen thousand dollars FYC by closing a huge "buy-sell" case with an old, established law firm in downtown Memphis. Yes, even Tasker was amazed at the audacious confidence and intrepid nerve Tierney had used in opening and closing the case. Tierney had said, "After getting in the door, which, by the way, took three years, I was able to convince the three controlling partners that the company they had their buy-sell agreement in force with, was under serious investigation by the state insurance commission, and that their bond rating, and A. M. Best ratings were dropping rapidly." Tierney didn't explain any of the technical aspects of what exactly a "buy-sell" agreement was. Everyone in the room, maybe with the exception of the brand-new rep, Penny Ackerman, everyone else understood that life insurance proceeds were used to buy out the interest in the law firm from a deceased partner's estate, God forbid, that partner died. It prevented lengthy and costly disputes over who ended up with the portion of the firm the dead partner had control of.

Life insurance as an estate planning tool and as a business planning tool was legitimate enough, but just like in family and personal life insurance, why not use much less expensive term life insurance as opposed to much more expensive Whole Life? All the big Whole Life companies had, in their view, good reasons, but the good reasons didn't always withstand a fair and thorough analysis. The real reason was they got rich selling a way overpriced product.

"Okay, good job everyone. For all three branches, we've come in at $45,470 for the week. Let's hear it one more time for all the hard-working producers that made it happen." Curtis James started the applause, and when Tom Thraxton got to his feet to join in, everyone in the room did the same.

"We'll break for five minutes," James announced and people started for the restroom and the coffee pot.

A few of the more senior reps slapped Harold Tierney on the back and were giving him the glad hands.

On the way to more coffee and donuts, Framtom Hornacker said to Glenn Tasker, "He didn't jump on you for your term sales."

"Not yet, but we probably have another forty-five minutes to go."

As they left the break room, Tom Thraxton appeared, "Glenn, do you have a minute?"

Thraxton angled off into a side passageway and Glenn knew that even forty-five minutes was too long. He'd been captured. They stood facing off, maintaining maybe a four-foot buffer.

Thraxton's expression wasn't hostile, actually it was a look of deep concern, as if he were about to confront his teenager on the dangers of experimenting with pot. "You know Glenn, when we hired you, we were all elated. I mean what manager wouldn't be? War hero, successful football coach, all the contacts you could and did use in your prospecting. Those first two years, WOW! You were setting the woods ablaze."

He paused, took a deep sigh, and the look on his face turned to complete puzzlement. "What happened Glenn?"

"Sir, I believe I just sold two million dollars in face amount of life insurance." Glenn didn't flinch or move a muscle.

"Glenn ... Glenn, Glenn. You still don't see it do you?"

"Sir, I believe I've written 160 policies in the last twelve months, and I believe the face amount on those policies is in the neighborhood of 60 million. What exactly is it I don't see?" They both knew what the rub was. All those policies were term, not Whole Life.

"Glenn, I got a call from Atlanta this morning. You know who it was?"

"No sir. Sure don't"

"The Southeast Region Vice President. Do you know how close he is to the board room in New York?"

"I guess he's in tight."

"You guessed right. And do you know what he asked me to do?"

"No sir."

"He asked me to talk with you about your refusal to see what the company expects out of you."

Glenn was starting to heat up a considerable amount and was growing tired of this run- around. "Well It seems to me Mr. Thraxton, the real question is, what do *you* expect out of me? If you'd ever look at the policies I write, you'd see that my customers are not wealthy. They are the salt of the Earth, hardworking, family people. You know, the same kind of people that Fairfield Mutual claims on all their nationwide advertising as being their, I guess you would say, corporate image. No, not corporate image, that's not it. I'm not good at PR. What I'm trying to say is the big shots in New York and Atlanta want the image of Fairfield Mutual to be that we serve the working man, the all- American, tax-paying, middle class, ordinary people, and that Fairfield ought to be honored for doing so. It's who Fairfield is – taking care of hardworking Americans.

115

Well, if that's what you want, why won't you allow me to do it?"

"Glenn, I think you ought to …"

"Save it Patton. You know that's what we all call you – Blood and Guts. Look, I've served under real leaders. I've served in the real Army under real commanders. A real commander would never betray his troops by cutting their throats when they're doing their job. Nice chatting with you, sir."

* * *

Glenn's memories of that conversation with Tom Thraxton were as vivid to him now as anything he could think of in the entire universe. Well, maybe not as vivid as that day at Lang Vei in 1967, or maybe not as vivid as that first night with Sarah in 1977, but seeing the look on Thraxton's face as he (Glenn) turned away from him and walked down that hall, back towards the meeting room, … he'd never forget Thraxton's shrunken face and the superior feeling it gave him over Thraxton.

Glenn continued driving in towards Arlington and hoped Mildred Blaney would be home to open her garage so Glenn could pick up the table and chairs. That "superior" feeling might have sustained Glenn back then, but in more recent times, when his mind drifted back to his life insurance days, that "superior" feeling had caused him a considerable amount of self-doubt and guilt. As a serious Christian, he'd come to learn that certainly Jesus would not encourage any kind of superiority of anyone over anyone else. We are all children of God, and certainly no one should be feeling superior to anyone else. It isn't our place to judge. Glenn knew that to be true and when he would occasionally recall that day with Thraxton, that's when a certain wind of self-doubt and guilt would drift by.

He drove on towards town wanting to rid himself of memories of life insurance and Tom Thraxton. He was successful, but unfortunately what took their place was the memory of a jungle trail about 1967. A squad from Glenn's reconnaissance platoon had set a night ambush in hopes of disrupting NVA troops from snooping around the rebuilding of the Lang Vei special forces camp.

It was August, and the monsoon was in full force – some rain most every day, a lot of rain every other day. Enemy contact on these missions had been spotty, but everyone knew that something was stirring. Intel was pointing to the evidence of major NVA troops amassing on the Laotian border, and there was little doubt about where it was they wanted to go - Khe Sanh. Lang Vei was a village they would have to go through to get there.

The eight men Sergeant Tasker was with were hunkered down and dug into fox holes in deep foliage not more than ten feet from the trail. They heard something on the trail coming their way. The NVA trail discipline was pretty good, not as good as Victor Charlie's trail discipline, but still pretty good. For as many soldiers as they turned out to be, they didn't make a lot of noise.

The second lieutenant running the ambush patrol was two men down from Tasker. Glenn could see through the rain and blackness just enough to see the man between them, Sergeant Wombley, hand signaling to him that the second lieutenant was in fact sleeping. That news petrified Glenn. What now? Their leader was asleep at the wheel and the column of NVA getting real close now. Also, Glenn knew that the firing device (the clacker) for the claymore mines set up on the trail was with the second lieutenant.

The NVA point man now was moving right in front of Glenn's concealed hiding spot, and Glenn could see more coming up behind him. Undoubtedly the other men in Glenn's ambush team could also see and hear the NVA troops as they began slithering through their hiding place – that is, the men that were awake.

As Glenn's heart raced and he could feel the throbbing bump, bump, bump of his pulse speeding up. He also knew the adrenaline was being released into his blood stream. By now he had counted seven NVA in the column but could hear more coming. How big an outfit is this? Could it be company size? Two company size, 175 men, or larger? Maybe they were not a small squad only out for a quick recon of Camp Lang Vei. Maybe they were the spear head of a major assault. He could see that nothing to his right had changed. Wombley, he could see, was as aware of the passing NVA column as he was. And yes, Wombley was still signaling that the second lieutenant was still asleep. Glenn could sense Wombley's predicament. If he made the slightest move to wake the second lieutenant, ten feet away from him, he would give up their position and probably get them all killed.

Glenn hand signaled Wombley to try to get down there to the clacker and fire the claymores that were daisy chained nine feet apart and had been directionally set to fire out and down the trail into the direction the NVA were coming from. His hand signaling also told Wombley that Glenn would cover him if he came under fire. That's what Wombley was waiting for. He moved out, crawling as gently as possible. He made it only four feet and then slid in the mud, his weight rattling the underbrush and setting off some noise in his equipment clanging around. Instead of freezing in panic, he lunged the last four feet and grabbed the clacker from the second lieutenant's side. Even before he could detonate the claymores, two NVA were unloading their AK-47's at him. He caught a round in his shoulder and another in his neck. Glenns's M-16 was rocking and rolling on automatic and took those two out. Then he swung his muzzle down trail, sweeping his fire left and right, over and over again. Now Wombley hit the button on the clacker and 700 steel balls out of each claymore ripped the jungle apart in a 60-degree arc aimed down trail with a kill zone of between 55 yards and 110 yards.

As the echoes of the ear-splitting, soul wrenching explosions were dying down, the intensity of small arms fire from both sides was picking up. The bah ba ba ba ba ba ba ba from the ambushers M-60 machine gun was distinctive in the death stream it lashed out. But it was evident before long that the NVA would not choose to extend this battle. They withdrew, dragging with them as many as they could of their dead and wounded.

It was only after things had settled down that Glenn realized he'd taken an AK-47 round that went clean through his left arm, taking with it a good chunk of bone. Two days later the intel team at Lang Vei said they believed the target of the ambush that night was probably at least company strength, 85 men, and maybe larger. Tasker and Wombley were awarded the Silver Star for "Galantry In Action", in addition to Purple Hearts, in Tasker's case, his third Purple Heart. In Womblesy's case, his medals were awarded posthumously.

* * *

Why is it, the older I get, the more my thoughts go back to the past? Glenn had a silent laugh on that. He didn't think it was a healthy thing – living in the past. Yet the explanation for why many folks his age did it, was in Glenn's mind, straight forward, no mystery at all. Pure logic, better yet, simple math. As the years you have in front of you get less and less, the dead weight of all those years in the past simply drag you backwards. Maybe not math. Also, your deteriorating physical and mental conditions are constantly reducing your confidence about your ability to have an effect on what future you've got left.

What dreary thoughts he was having as he drove along, getting closer to Mildred Blaney's house. But if nothing else, Glenn Tasker was usually very honest with himself. *Well, if that's what it is to get old, constantly reliving the past, I reckon I can do it as good as the next one can. Not a big deal. Probably as natural as morning dew on the grass.*

Glenn hit his wiper switch to clean the mist from the windshield, and swerved to miss a deer crossing the road. *Here I am thinking about thinking about the past and I probably won't even make it to Mildred's house alive.* Glenn's laugh this time wasn't silent and introspective. It was spontaneous, and loud, and if you'd been driving behind Glenn's pick-up truck, you would have sworn it swayed left and right.

Even so, as he settled down for the next five miles on into town, his thinking went backwards again, to nineteen years ago. He saw himself turning away from Tom Thraxton and walking back down the hall towards the meeting room.

* * *

As the sales reps from the three Memphis area branch offices were settling back into their seats, Curtis James broke off the adult fantasy he was building in his mind's eye with Penny Ackerman just as Tom Thraxton entered the room. James could see that Thraxton was not a happy man.

James cleared his throat as he stood to get things moving again. "Just a few items I want to touch on, then I believe Mr. Thraxton has a few words for you."

James went through a few trivial house keeping details for his branch, and asked the other branch managers if they had anything for their sales reps. None of them did, so he proceeded on through a few boring articles on some new industry trends, and closed out his remarks with the promise that every rep that finished this new week with fifteen hundred FYC or better would find a complimentary weekend golf package in his or her mail box. He stepped away from the small lectern and Tom Thraxton took his place.

"Good morning everyone."

"Good morning," was returned to him by almost everyone in the room, some more enthusiastically than others, and not returned at all by Glenn Tasker.

Frampton Hornacker was polishing off a jelly- filled donut as he shared a joke with Katie Larson. The scowl on Old Blood and Guts face put an end to the merriment, and all ears in the room tuned in to what they all sensed was going to be a little different kind of pep talk from their regional manager.

"It seems to me, that in a great organization such as ours, all the associates in that organization would benefit greatly if they could demonstrate that they had a solid and thorough understanding of what it was that made that organization great in the first place. Is there anyone here that would disagree?" Thraxton paused and his eyes scanned the room as if he were the commander of a United States battleship and he was perched outside on the flying bridge heroically searching the rolling seas with field glasses daring an evil enemy combatant to appear.

Yes, this was definitely going to be a little different kind of pep talk, or maybe not, as Thraxton had been known to pull off some pretty bizarre speeches when circumstances dictated. His square jaw-line tightened even more than normal, but he was going to take his time with this. Most of the sales reps in the room weren't sure where Thraxton was going, but Glenn Tasker had a pretty good idea.

"Now, most of us in this room understand that there is no better tool in the world than permanent life insurance with which to protect families and businesses from financial loss due to death. An umbrella of protection is what we sell – a plan that insures our customers from youth, through early adulthood, through the family building years, through middle age and retirement, all the way to what we all want – a dignified departure from the planet; dignified because with the death benefit from our Whole Life insurance policy, we can leave something behind for those we love: funds for final expenses, medical bills, college for the grandkids, an endowment for our college alma mater. I could go on and on. You are all professionals. I don't need to give you a lecture on insurance 101.

"As I just said, most of us in this room understand that this principle of protecting our customers for their entire life is what our industry was built on. However, we have a few in our industry that simply choose to ignore what it is that built this institution we call life insurance. They choose to ignore what it is that provides their jobs, and writes their checks."

Thraxton paused and seemed to be searching the rolling seas again. "I won't mention names, and believe me, I hate to admit it, but we actually have such a sales rep right here this morning."

He didn't mention any names, but his eyes had ceased scanning and fell suspiciously in the direction of where Glenn Tasker was sitting.

The eyes of the entire room shifted in the same direction, and everyone wondered what Thraxton would say next.

Framtom Hornacker and Will Dean both noticed that Glenn's carotid pulse was ramping up just above the collar at about mid-neck. They could actually see the bump,

bump, bump throbbing as it simultaneously began turning the color in Glenn's face to a dangerous hue of bluish crimson, and vermillion.

Thraxton also noticed that something was happening to Tasker and knowing now that the entire room was picking up on the escalating confrontation, he found himself wondering if he hadn't pushed a button he shouldn't have pushed. But it was too late now. He'd zeroed in on Tasker to make a point, to teach a lesson. If he continued to let Tasker get away with the term madness, then others might follow. God knows what else could come out of such a scenario. Fairfield already had a scandal of potentially massive proportions brewing in Charlotte. Then, of course, there was always the State of Tennessee itself. Their Insurance Commissioner's Office in Nashville was continually sniffing round, causing trouble, always a thorn in the side of most of the insurance carriers licensed to do business in the state. If they could catch you bending the rules just a little, that would trigger larger and larger investigations into anything coming close to breaking the law. Thraxton knew the way his sales team was pushed to operate, actually to tiptoe right on the edge of legal practices. Thraxton knew that someday a true reckoning of his sales organization might take place. It wasn't something he enjoyed thinking about.

"You hate to admit it! You hate to admit the term I sell protects more customers for more death benefit than any other five agents in this room put together!" Glenn had gotten his six foot three, two hundred and thirty-pound frame to his feet and was marching off towards the front of the room, his body gone rigid, his mind gone to another place – the place it always went when it was time to defend what was right. Most of the other twenty-seven in the room stared in amazement. Their jaws dropped open, as Glenn waded through them, pushing chairs and people out of the way as he stalked Thraxton, still behind the lectern.

Framton Hornacker shouted out quickly, "Glenn don't do it!" He and Will Dorn both lunged forward to get between Tasker and Thraxton.

Thraxton, no puny physical specimen himself, was waiting for Tasker and appeared capable enough of holding his own. Still, he looked at Curtis James, and said loudly, but under control, "Get the building security and call the police."

James got up and was heading to the door. Hornacker looked at Dorn and said, "Stay with Glenn." He also looked at a couple other of the largest and most fit male sales reps and said, "Stay with Glenn. Hold him back."

Hornacker got his three hundred-fifty pounds to the door before Curtis James could get there. Evidently nobody was going to leave the room, not even Framton Hornacker's boss, Curtis James.

For a second or two everything slowed down, just like the stop-frame vision you have during an accident. It took a few more seconds for the new status quo of the sales meeting to sink in: the regional manager was under physical attack by one of his agents; three other agents were doing their best to restrain the attacker; the biggest man in the room was blocking anyone else from escape.

It was the biggest man in the room that finally said something. "All right, everybody chill-out. We got things under control."

Thraxton shouted across the room at Hornacker, "Open that door and sit down."

"No sir Mr. Thraxton. It's not going to happen. We all just witnessed the disrespect you threw on Glenn. It was uncalled for. Look, I know I'm still a pretty new agent for Fairfield; I'm still learning the ropes, but I can spot a snake in the room just as good as anybody. The way you just took aim at Glen wasn't right. You fire me if you want to after this is over, but for now, Glenn is going to have the opportunity to respond to the things you just said. Look, I don't know enough about the argument you and Mr. James are always making about how much better permanent is over term. The stuff I sold before coming here was strictly indemnity plans, accident insurance. We were identified by most as snake oil salesmen. I'm used to getting shots taken at me, but I can tell you this – Glenn

Tasker doesn't deserve it, and nobody is going to leave the room until he gets a chance to respond to what you said."

Now, everyone was completely confused. Could this be happening? An ordinary life insurance agent would have the floor in rebuttal against a regional manager of one of the largest, most powerful insurance companies in the land?

"Glenn, how does that sound to you? You sit down and cool off. Then you say what you want with no interruptions. We'll treat the whole thing like Vegas. What's said and happens in this room, stays in this room. What'ya say?"

Glenn could see maybe that was a good idea. He might still be able to keep his job, and maybe he could feel the room out – gauge all the reps. Maybe there were more like him, more that thought selling term was the right thing to do.

Glenn slowed down on his charge to the front of the room. Will Dorn slid a chair up alongside Glenn and the other three men backed away. Glenn didn't sit down, but he did stop where he was and put a foot up on the chair, as if he might have been squirrel hunting in the woods and hunched a foot up on a stump to take a breather, to look around the forest a little, to assess his situation.

"All right, maybe I will say a few things."

Thraxton was still at the lectern, and he wasn't about to stand down. His face looked like stone and he was wondering how this meeting had gotten away from him. All he could do was stand there, and like everyone else in the room, see what Tasker had to say.

"It's not just the term. Did anybody in here, other than myself, see what Mr. Thraxton and Mr. James were doing right before the meeting started?" He waited, but nobody spoke up.

"They were checking the room for bugs, listening devices. Does that strike anyone as odd?"

"Now wait just a minute!" Thraxton was coming from behind the lectern but the three big guys cut him off.

Hornacker, still guarding the door, said in a hard-boiled and uncompromising manner, "Mr. Thraxton we are going to hear Glenn out, whether you want us to, or not. And I'd bet you there are a bunch of agents in this room that would like to hear where this listening device thing is going. Go ahead Glenn."

Tasker took his foot down off the chair and started loosening his neck tie, and began to unbutton the buttons on his white oxford business dress shirt. Using both hands to open the shirt wide and expose his bare chest, he spoke out towards Tom Thraxton, "I'm saving you the trouble Tom. See, I don't have a bug planted on me. Now the rest of you don't have to prove you don't have a bug on you. It's only us termites they're worried about. Right Mr. Thraxton?"

Tom Thraxton was about to voice a response but the newest agent in the room, Penny Ackerman, piped up first, "I don't get it. What's going on?"

"Penny, I'll answer your question with a question." Glenn began to button up his shirt. "When you were hired, did Mr. Thraxton inform you of the investigation that Fairfield Mutual is the target of in North Carolina?"

"Why no, I don't remember him doing that."

"Of course he didn't, and you know what?" He noticed Thraxton about to cut him off. "I see you Tom. I know you want to stop this, but I'm going to get this out. When I shut up, you can have your meeting back. Do what you want to me and Frampton and anybody else. But I don't think you'll be doing anything. That's the last thing you and Fairfield would want – a bunch of firings that might trigger a rebellion from one of your top producing regions."

Glenn stopped for a moment. Thraxton didn't say a word. Glenn looked over at Penny Ackerman, "You know what Penny? He's never told any of us about it either, although I'm sure I'm not the only one aware of what is going on. Here's the deal: An agent in North Carolina named Rudy Pastriano went to the North Carolina Insurance Commisioner office with the claim that the training he received from Fairfield was misleading to clients, deceitful, and that certain marketing pre-approach letters he sent to perspective customers, and were approved by Fairfield, were in fact distorting the nature of our products, which, in fact, made it illegal to sell them. Rudy Pastriano is what is known as a whistle blower. Most of what I'm telling you, Penny, is public knowledge. You could read most of it in the trade journals like *The National Underwriter*, but not all of it. It doesn't tell you why Mr. Thraxton fears people like me and why he'd be checking this room for bugs. Okay, let's back up a bit. Pastriano not only blew the whistle on unlawful marketing, he also sued Fairfield for five million, claiming his career was ruined, and other legal issues I won't get into. I believe that what has happened here today – Tom Thraxton's off the wall paranoia about listening devices, and making me a target of his frustration is this: I may be wrong, but I would bet that Fairfield has just settled out of court with Pastriano, probably for around two million. That was the figure predicted by *The National Underwriter*. Well now … just think it through. If Fairfield settled for two mil with one whistle blower just in the last couple of days, what do you think would be their next big worry?"

Glenn had the undivided attention of everyone in the room, not just Penny Ackerman, Tom Thraxton, and Curtiss James.

"Here it is Penny, the elephant in the room – what Thraxton and Fairfield are scared of happening next: that other potential whistle-blowers start screaming law suit. What if all of us in this room went to the insurance commissioner in Tennessee? What if agents in Georgia, and Florida did the same? How many out of court settlements would it take to put the lid back on? Penny, look at the agenda for today's meeting, it's printed out, there in front of you. What does it say Mr. Thraxton is going to roll out as the next big sales promotion here in our region?"

Penny picked up the printed agenda and scanned down to the regional manager's presentation. Penny read from the agenda, "Distribution of old books of business – new sales contest - *Making The Old New Again.*"

"Penny, do you know what that means?"

"Uh, no. No I don't."

"It means each of us is going to be given a list of fifty to a hundred old, paid up or in-force life insurance policies of our customers here around the Memphis area. Do you know what Mr. Thraxton wants us to do with them?"

"No."

"He wants us to convert them to brand new policies using the cash value in them to pay the premium on the new one."

"What's wrong with that?"

"Well, for starters, it's illegal. It's called "churning". Fairfield has been investigated on this several times in the past. I'm just guessing there were pay-offs in the past. The investigations, I believe, hit Fairfield with a few small fines, but then, just went away."

"Why is it illegal?"

"Actuarial stuff. I don't know the real math, but my guess is that the new policies will be bigger and more expensive. The chance that these new policies will ever pay a death claim are probably not very good because the money coming out of the old ones really won't be enough to pay the premium on the new larger policies. But this isn't mentioned to the customer when we sit down with them at closing and they sign the new application. Most of these folks are old and by the time they may have realized their mistake – they use all of the cash out of the old policy to try to apply it to the new one – it just isn't enough to keep the new one going. They end up with no policy, no death benefit, and Fairfield ends up with the churned cash value from the old policy. Fairfield gets bigger and richer and the customers end up with nothing."

Harold Tierney was the first of the old school agents to voice his outrage. "Now Glenn, that's all a lie! We have never taken advantage of anyone like you just described."

He realized his mistake too late and Glenn seized on it. "Really Harold. How exactly *did* you take advantage of them?"

There were a few laughs but before Tierney could respond, Glenn continued, "Harold, as I was explaining to Penny, the reason I think Tom was checking the room for bugs is because now that the cat is out of the bag with Pastriano, all of you guys, yes *you* guys, any of you that defend Fairfield's history, all of you guys are in panic mode because Pastriano settling for two mil is just the beginning.

"So, what about us here this morning? Is there one among us who just might be the next whistle blower? Could it be an agent that doesn't sell the rip-off Whole Life products most all the rest of us sell? Could that agent be so far gone as to be capable of planting a listening device in the sales meeting that he knows will be asking the agents to do something called *churning* which is illegal? Could the information on that tap, could the words delivered by no less than the regional manager himself be enough to blow the whistle?"

Tierney was thinking and he wanted to respond, but thought better of it. If there was a still undetected bug somewhere in the room … *Oh my gosh, my voice is already on it, defending Fairfield.*

The room settled back down to an uneasy threat of maybe more fireworks. Thraxton was still standing, albeit on wobbly legs, but before he could say anything, Glenn Tasker fired off one last salvo, "Mr. Thraxton, I know you won't fire me, but I'm going to deny you even the satisfaction of thinking about it. I am right now giving you my two-week notice. And don't worry about me asking for a reference letter. I wouldn't use it to clean my bathroom floor."

* * *

Still three more miles to Mildred Blaney's house. Was there any way for Glenn to turn off the faucet, any way to stop the flow of memories of his past life? He knew the answer was no, but he also knew that the insurance memories had run their course, at least for now. That was the good news. The bad news was that he knew memories from other parts of his life would replace the insurance memories.

He might as well face it. He was a sentimental old man that swam in a deep river of melancholy, it seemed to him like, more and more all the time – the very same thing that he'd been critical of many times with older people he'd known. Even with his own father. Glenn loved his dad but was always very short with him when he would continually revert to talking about nothing other than the "old days", his old friends, his old war stories, his old life. Now, of course, Glenn could see the mistake it was to castigate his father for living in the past. It wasn't the right thing to have done, also, now that he thought about it, that he was just like his father, he let it roll. He opened the floodgate, and the mini-dramas of each major segment of his life took center stage.

As he turned left off the road he was on and was getting closer to Mildred's house, he thought back to his truck driving days, and was there anything he learned in that ten-year period of time that had made him a better man? Were there any activities he'd been a part of as he

135

drove a seventy-two-foot tractor-trailer all over the country that showed he cared about people? Showed he tried to do the right thing?

That was it right there. Trying to do the right thing. Just like that day at the sales meeting with Mr. Thraxton. Was that really the right thing to do? Confront him in front of twenty-eight people and insinuate that he, Thraxton, was a dishonest crook? Had he made similar mistakes in his trucking career? Or was it really a mistake – the confrontation with Thraxton?

So much for the purging of the insurance memories. It looked like here they come again, but maybe not.

What about his coaching days? He felt like he'd been fair to all of his players. He felt like he'd given the best effort he knew how to give. He felt like it had been a worthy profession – teaching young people team play, sportsmanship, and life lessons. It was all an honorable thing to do. But was he doing the right thing when he took pleasure in wielding the iron control that he and most other coaches wielded? Was it the right thing to parade up and down the sideline on game night and on the practice field as well, parade around like a general commanding his troops, asking them to sacrifice for you? Berating them, jumping on their case when they failed? Was that the right thing to do? And when Glenn remembered doing those very things he realized he'd acted very much like Tom Thraxton.

Mildred Blaney's house was just around the next corner. Glenn liked Mildred. She always had a big smile for people, she worked hard at church on various committees, and she happened to be one of Glenn's many distant cousins. She was around seventy-five, lived by herself, and was very independent. She travelled often and recently returned from a two-week trip to England and France where she had toured with a friend from the church.

Glenn pulled in Mildred's driveway, parked, and walked up to the open garage. He saw the table and chairs just as Mildred was coming from the house.

"This is a real nice dining room set, Mildred. You sure you want to let it go?"

"Oh yes. Truth is, I can't use it anymore."

"You been doing okay?"

"Well …" she was going to think about it, but eventually she said, "Yes, I'm fine."

As Glenn began loading the table and chairs into his truck bed, Mildred launched right into something she'd been wanting to tell him for some time now.

"Glenn, I've been meaning to let you know how proud of you we all are. The way you've been pitching in at church these days. You know none of us is getting any younger. Most of the men are gone now. You're about the only one that can get in there and get after it!"

"Mildred, you know I've got a few old skeletons in the closet. Shoot, if I don't start doing some good works for the Lord, why ... you know, I might miss the bus."

"Glenn Tasker! Don't be talking like that. You know we're saved by grace, not by works."

"Yeah, but still, them old skeletons haven't left that closet. Why just on the way up here I was thinking about all the times in my life I didn't do the right thing. Believe me, I've got a lot of stuff in the past I'm not proud of."

"I'm not believing that for a minute. You've always been too hard on yourself. Look, none of us are perfect."

"I know that's right, but still, I find myself wondering an awful lot about how many times I had an opportunity to do the right thing, and as many times as not, I did the wrong thing."

After Glenn had loaded everything and was on his way back home, more of the skeletons escaped from the closet and wondered around in his mind.

There was the time in Junior High School he'd clobbered a defenseless boy at the bus stop. There was no good reason for it. Bullying, pure and simple.

He remembered another time he had not done the right thing. It was the one-sided love affair he'd been in. The girl loved Glenn and Glenn knew it, but he only used her for the sex she gave him. When she told him one night that she had aborted the child she was carrying it shook him up a good deal, and he realized that if he'd done the right thing to begin with (cutting off the one-sided affair) an innocent life would not have been taken.

All the way on the drive back home he'd let all his past mistakes come out of the closet and do their best to tear him down. He was certainly not in a good mood. He was beginning to wonder if he'd ever done anything worthwhile in his life, anything that was genuine and unselfish.

He was getting close to the Country Barbecue stand and decided he'd pull in and see if the owner, Ray Whitaker, was around. If so, he'd drop the table and chairs off in Ray's back shed to await the upcoming yard sale. After he parked, he saw Ray around back working on his pile of hickory slab, getting the wood ready to burn and produce coals for the slow cooking and smoking of five pork shoulders. Ray was working a lot harder these days. His wife and co-worker, Juanita, had passed away from cancer four months ago. She'd really been the backbone of the business, doing all the books, ordering, food prep, counter work, clean-up, you name it. Ray, of course, was the barbecue master. He handled the many tedious duties of actually cooking all the meat, and he handled those chores with pride and great skill. The recipes he used and the grilling, slow cooking, and smoking of the tasty products, he did with great enjoyment, and satisfaction, knowing that all of his customers really enjoyed the finished creation.

But it had been a tough go ever since Juanita's death. There were many, many thousands of dollars in unpaid medical bills, and of course all the expenses of the funeral and burial, not to mention the fact that now Ray was *paying* a couple of folks to try their best to do the same amount of work that Juanita had been doing. The future of the business was on very shaky financial ground.

"Hey Ray."

"Glenn, I'm glad you stopped by. I want to thank you."

"Thank me? What for?"

"You don't remember do you?"

"I guess not."

"That life insurance policy you sold us on Juanita. I forgot all about it myself."

Glenn noticed Ray's eyes were filming up just a bit, and he tried to think back twenty-three or twenty-four years. *Did I sell a policy on Juanita back then?*

It took him a moment or so to pull it back out of the time machine. *Yes, yes, I think I remember talking with them about policies on the both of them, but I can't remember if we actually closed the deal.*

Glenn asked Ray, "Did we actually get the policies set up and in force?"

"Yeah we did …. uh, you did. The premium came out on a monthly bank draft, and it wasn't very much. I think you said it was term insurance and we'd never even know we were paying for it. You were right. That premium's been coming out on a bank draft every month for twenty something years. I had forgotten all about it." Ray's eyes were wet now, and Glenn could see it.

Isn't it strange, Glenn thought, *half the morning I've been thinking back to those days I fought tooth and nail with Curtis James, Tom Thraxton, and Harold Tierney about doing the right thing – selling term, not Whole Life.*

Glenn was looking at Ray and he couldn't help seeing the gratitude and thankfulness in his eyes. "Ray, you don't know how good this makes me feel. You know, when we lost Juanita, I should have checked on that policy to have seen if it was still in force. I'm sorry. I hope you'll forgive me. What made you think of it?"

"I was going through all of Juanita's papers. There it was. I called the company, and they said the death benefit of a hundred and fifty thousand would be paid as soon as I filled out a claim form and got it to them." He stopped for a moment with eyes showing even more gratitude than a minute ago. "Forgive you? Are you kidding? A lot of problems can be dealt with now. I got the check two weeks ago. Glenn it's all because you sold us the term policy. You remember that other agent wanted to sell us a much smaller Whole Life policy, but you explained the difference to us."

This time it was Glenn's eyes that were not just getting a little wet. There was a river of tears flowing out of them.

Ray looked at him in surprise, "Glenn, are you all right?"

Glenn was only thinking about James, Thraxton, and Tierney. He wondered what they would say about his tears?

"Yes Ray, I'm fine."

Always Quiet,
Always Reflective

* * *

Henry Bellar

Harry Baker

Always Quiet,
Always Reflective

* * *

Harry H. Baker

HE LEANED FORWARD in the rocker, aimed a stream of tobacco juice at the front of the wood stove, straightened up
and resumed his story, his old eyes piercing the sixty odd
years separating him from the hell of World War I and
the Argonne Offensive that ended it:

"Harry, I was scared to death. We was laying behind a road embankment. Huey James started across
and I run right behind him. A German machine gun
just stitched James right under the shoulder blades.
Nearly cut him in two. I drug him out of the road, and
that same gun laid in on me. I fell flat and I guess they
thought they got me because they lifted the fire over
me. In a few minutes a tank come down the road and
laid a shell in the machine gun nest. Nothing left but
scraps of men and guns."

I had driven down from Louisville that evening to
get my mother, who lives with my uncle and aunt in

Edgewood, a hamlet just off the Yellow Creek Road. Uncle Henry was showing me his copy of the history of the 117th Infantry Division in World War I. Browsing through the book which he had received recently, I could not resist the temptation to draw Uncle Henry into recalling for the thousandth time, it seemed, some of his battle experiences.

Since my earliest recollection as a boy living in a sharecropper's shack on the banks of Yellow Creek, one of the greatest joys of my life has been reading and hearing stories of war, battles, and military combat. Over the years, up to the present, Uncle Henry's colorful reminiscences of his battle experiences have held me spellbound on many memorable occasions. A Dickson County native, he was an infantryman of the 117th Division which was heavily involved in the great allied offensive which broke the Hindenburg Line in 1918. Truly he is one of the last surviving veterans of the outfit.

Let me emphasize that when Uncle Henry talks of his battle experiences it is not boastful. Uncle Henry seldom even mentions his battle experiences, and then only when some special circumstance prompts him. Such as the adroit suggestion of his cousin and nephew, Harry. Never boastful or glory seeking. Always quiet, always reflective.

Dad and Uncle Henry grew up almost as brothers. Thus, it was no surprise when they began courting two of the attractive girls in a family which had moved into the Yellow Creek community from Clarksville. And just before America's entry into World War I, they married the sisters.

In those days the life of a dirt farmer or a share cropper was anything but easy. The Yellow Creek community contained two distinct levels of farming: the good farms located in the rich bottom land along the creek, and the red-clay hills, rocky, red-clay land lying back in the hills. Families worked brutally hard to eke out an existence in many of these marginal small farms. For many, especially young married couples, the only employment available was share cropping for one of the prosperous farmers along Yellow Creek. A share cropper could invest a year's hard labor, and at the end find himself in debt at the "country store."

Many young married couples took their scanty belongings and made for the big city. Industrial centers such as Detroit with it burgeoning automobile industry, Chicago, and others offered employment for country folk. But Uncle Henry and Dad decided on Louisville, Kentucky as a reasonable alternative to share cropper living.

They moved to Louisville in the early twenties, and lived there until they retired in 1955. My father did return to the Yellow Creek community for three years but went back to Louisville in 1930, at the beginning of the great depression.

Editor's Notes

My father, Harry Baker, wrote this little piece on his uncle, Henry Bellar, sometimes around 1980. He also took the photograph of Uncle Henry, probably a few years prior to writing the story. The old World War II navy photo of my dad happened to turn up about the time I considered including this piece in <u>Times and Places.</u>

The pictures are extremely accurate in their visual descriptions of the two men:

Uncle Henry, always quiet, always reflective.

Harry H. Baker, always possessing a confident intellectual curiosity about the existence we find ourselves in. And, most of the time, he was quick to flash a winning smile.

In thinking about these two men, I am fighting a strong compulsion to write at length about other ex-military men in my family. There is, as I'm sure with many other American families, a long history of service, valor, and tragedy running through my extended family's history of military service. I could start with Civil War amputees, and without a doubt, go back to earlier wars. I could continue on up to more modern engagements involving nuclear submarines, destroyers, F-4 Phantoms, helicopters, para- trooping, spy-work, POW experiences, and I could go on. But I won't. There will be more military stuff coming up in the next story in <u>Times and Places,</u> this time written by my old high school buddy, Ron Greene.

What I *will do* is tell an "Uncle Henry story". It is a story I recall quite well. The year was 1975 and the season was late spring. The thirteen-mile drive from the little town of Dickson, Tennessee out the country road to Edgewood was quiet and slow. You see, Uncle Henry was a slow driver. Dad told me that as a much younger man in Louisville, Uncle Henry would come to an intersection and seemingly take all day to mount the decisive action required to cross the intersection. It got to be a joke. If you were going with Uncle Henry, you best bring a lunch. It would take a while.

The day he had picked me up in Dickson, I had just travelled cross-country from Los Angeles. I was twenty-nine and had just left Hawaii for one of my occasional forays into adventure on the mainland.

We eventually made it to Edgewood and Uncle Henry and I were sitting on the big front porch of the old farmhouse. My grandmother, Laura Baker, and my great aunt, Henry's wife, Lizzie Bellar were in the house probably cooking up something they often cooked up - ham, white beans, and corn bread. My grandfather, Marvin Baker, who had lived here with them had passed away about nine years prior to this time.

It was quiet on the front porch and indeed it was quiet in the small hamlet of Edgewood, Tennessee. It was just the kind of place Uncle Henry was comfortable in.

"Well, what's been going on around Edgewood, Uncle Henry? Dick and Nannie doing okay?"

Then I asked him about two of his other brothers and their wives, "How's Emmet and Bessie doing? Benny and Ila?"

"Holding pretty good, I reckon."

"That's good. You see much of Troy and Odelia? How about Melvin and Ila?"

"About the same."

"I see." I was wondering what I might say to get him opened up a little. I decided to try Frances and Earl Jordan. They were his daughter and son-in-law who still lived in Louisville. "Frankie and Earl been down lately?"

"Oh, a little while back."

All right! Maybe this was going somewhere! I quickly followed up with, "Did Wayne or Jimmy come?"

"Nope."

Wayne and Jimmy are his grandsons from Frankie and Earl. But nothing followed the "Nope". I was back to square one.

I kept trying. "They still playing horse shoes down at crossroads on Saturdays?"

He gave me a nod in the affirmative, but no words. I gave up and decided that maybe some of my Hawaiian adventures would somehow coax him into, if not conversation, then maybe some curiosity and questions about the 50th state. I knew he'd never been there.

"Uncle Henry, I wish you could see some of the islands. It's a beautiful place." I noticed another low-key nod. "The Big Island, they call Hawaii, its's got an active volcano on it. It's over thirteen thousand feet above sea level, and about the same below sea level, making it the tallest mountain in the world." Another cool nod.

"And the beaches! I wish you could see some of the beaches! I've surfed off many of them. It's just beautiful!" I wasn't sure he knew what a surfboard was.

I talked about some of the mountain trails I'd hiked, and about some of the old Hawaiian stories I'd heard, but none of it got him talking back. There were a few times maybe his eyes twinkled a bit, but not enough to get him saying much of anything.

So, finally I had to give up. "Come on Uncle Henry. I think Granny's got food on the table."

You know, Uncle Henry was a good man. A country man. A man of slow ways. I remember a few years after he had passed away, I was out in one of the sheds that sat on the old farm property at Edgewood. In fact, it's where I live today. I was going through a lot of old stuff that Granddaddy and Uncle Henry had stored up over the many years. There was an old harness and other horse tack, an old tool box, tobacco drying equipment, a corn planter, an old pot-bellied stove, and then I came across a couple of old army pieces – a pair of leggings, I believe sometimes called spats, or gaiters, and an army tie clip. These items were very old. In fact, they almost looked ancient to me.

I knew as soon as I saw them they were a part of (maybe all that was left of) Uncle Henry's old WW I army uniforms. It meant a lot to me to hold these items in my hands.

I thought back to the day on the front porch of the old farmhouse at Edgewood and I thought maybe, here in my hands, these old spats, and this old army tie clip, maybe they are part of the reason our cherished great uncle, Henry Bellar, had been so quiet and reflective for so long. And if that's the case, is it any different from other vets from more recent wars that I've attempted to drag out of their shell of shutting out the memories? The closed-in life they've led for how many years? Lives where opening the door to old war memories is too painful.

In Uncle Henry's case, sixty years. Could it have been that long? Sixty years? That's a long time for quiet reflection.

But the more I thought about it, the more sense it made. That day back on the front porch, I remember that even though he seemed unresponsive, uninterested in my queries into the activities of close relatives and friends, it was when I began telling him about Hawaii that he seemed to recede further back into a pensive fog of days gone by. That's it! Faraway places, far away over the vast oceans. This, I was sure, was the kind of trigger that would send him back – back to the Argonne Forest and only God knows what pain and misery awaited him there.

Just like my Grandad, and my Father, and the Son I lost, Uncle Henry was a good man. He was a really good man.

Gary H. Baker

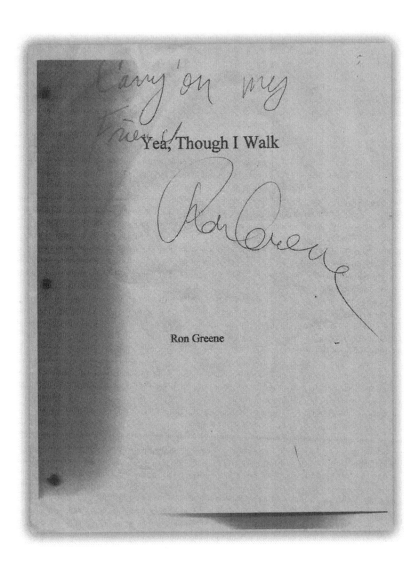

Introduction to <u>Yea, Though I Walk</u>

* * *

THE COVER PAGE of Ron Greene's manuscript, as you can see, is signed by him under the salutation, "Carry on My Friend". He gave me the manuscript a few years back, before his death, but due to one setback or another, I was not able to get it into a book until now. As I think about the salutation now, some six or seven years later, I recognize in it a noble and big-hearted sentiment even as it carried a darker foreboding of what Ron might have felt was his eminent death. The "carry on" indicates to me that Ron may have felt he would not be with us much longer, but that his directive was for us to continue the struggle. Getting his Vietnam story "out there" is, for me personally, what I believe to be my part of "continuing the struggle".

For all of those that love Ron, starting first with his wife, Wanda, and all the rest of us, including Mike and Linda,

Pete, Phillip, Jimmy, and many more, I offer below the only way I know to introduce <u>Yea, Though I Walk:</u>

"Hey Gary, you want to double date Friday night?" Ron Greene asked me.

"I guess so, but I don't have a date."

"No problem, Melanie has a friend."

"Really? What's her name?"

"Lana, and Melanie says she's real cute."

"It sounds good to me. You driving? I don't think I can get Pop's car." This of course was before I graduated in the spring of '64, and my dad, Pop, gave me a 1951 Chevy for my graduation present. I think he paid $260 for it, and I remember putting a quart of oil in it every three or four days.

Ron's car was nice, a '54 Chevy, a beautiful deep forest green, cherry clean inside and out, and it sparkled and shined like a show car. You could tell he took good care of it and was proud of it.

I went on a couple of double dates with Ron and his girlfriend. Mostly we either went to the drive-in movie or to the park to "Watch the submarine races". That's sixties shoptalk for heavy petting, or, if you were lucky … more.

Me, I mostly wrestled around in the backseat with one or two girls and if the truth were to be known, I got very little accomplished in my backseat maneuvering.

Ron, on the other hand, I always thought was a good-looking guy who had a pretty smooth touch with the girls. Although I was a year older and a class ahead of him at Fairdale High School, just thirteen miles south of downtown Louisville, Kentucky, Ron was my mentor when it came to relations with the fairer sex. Not only that, he was just a good guy.

In his story you are about to read, I believe he comes across as a pretty tough character. But in my mind, he wasn't like that in high school. War changes men, and it changes boys. Ron was certainly changed by his Vietnam experience. Likewise, Phillip Ray was also changed by his Vietnam experience. Phillip was one of our best buddies, and like Ron, Phillip was in combat in Vietnam. They both survived the war and came home to live for many years before dying in that all too familiar place of lost hope, lost youth, and the sheer madness of a jungle nightmare that probably trailed them to their last days.

Unlike many Vietnam veterans, Ron Greene didn't return home from the war with missing limbs, deposits of shrapnel scattered throughout his body, nor did he have a drug monkey on his back. What he did have was a desire to put into words what his Vietnam experience was like. As a friend and coming from the fact that I haven't actually been around him very much in the last fifty-three years, I would surmise that Ron also possessed many of the not so obvious monkeys on his back that almost all Vietnam veterans have endured over the years, myself included. For combat veterans, these problems include nightmares, flash backs, paranoia, depression, suicidal thoughts, etc. For noncombat Vietnam veterans like myself, these problems include a sense of confusion about the war, family and friend issues related to the entire Vietnam experience, a sense of abandonment, etc. Ron, I'm fairly sure, experienced all of these kinds of problems, and maybe others I'm not aware of.

But we are not want to shed tears for Ron Greene, Phillip Ray or any other Vietnam vets. We are to honor them. They did what they had to do. From boys, they became men, and from men, they became warriors.

Ron's chronicle of his time in Vietnam is as good as any I've ever read, and I've read most of them. Fill up your ruck-pack, tighten your web gear, lock 'n load, here we go.

Enjoy, but most of all, be honorable.

Gary H. Baker

Yea, Though I Walk

* * *

Ron Greene

Thanks to Wanda, Duane, Mike and Keith
for their support, critique and contributions.

This is neither documentary nor history.
It is but art from half lost, long ago, memories.

Yea, Though I Walk

* * *

A POWERFULLY BUILT black sergeant stepped up to the platform and said, "There are two hundred species of snakes in this country. One hundred and ninety-eight of 'em, if they bite you, you're gonna' die. The other two will squeeze you to death, Leave 'em alone."

Welcome to Vietnam, Cam Ran Bay. This was the beginning of orientation – 1970.

I had just left Seattle in September. The temperature was now 115 degrees. I couldn't get enough to drink. From the plane, we were transported by small bus to our barracks for a week or so of orientation. The bus windows were covered with heavy metal mesh. I didn't know if it was to keep me in, or keep "them" out. But, of course, it was to keep someone from throwing in an explosive.

About the third day, a beautiful day as I remember, they marched us to some bleachers to explain how the enemy attacked us on our bases.

"Sappers," the sergeant said, "They would send in the sappers."

Now a sapper was someone who would sneak in on you. They would get inside your perimeter at night. He told us they were the little people of the little people. They might carry a pistol or small carbine, or nothing but satchel charges.

The sapper kept a piece of straw in their mouths they used to probe for trip wires to our mines and illumination. They would disarm them. They also carried a small pouch of staples. They would pull back the razored concertina wire and use the staples to hold it back just enough to squeeze through. Probing with the straw, they would also turn around your claymore mines so they would discharge on us.

Once the sappers were in place, the mortar barrage began, trying of course to get you in your hole. When the mortars ceased fire, the sappers quickly went to work. The satchel charges they carried were percussion explosives. No shrapnel. They threw the charges in your holes. I believe an instructor said it was like hitting a tomato with a sledgehammer. Just exploded you. They even had ex-sappers, who now worked for us, tell of some of their experiences. As the sappers did their job, the main force would attack.

The next day they took a large group of us to this room. A staff sergeant entered and said, "Raise your hand if your mother, father, uncles or any close relatives are the mayor of a major city, a governor, congressman, or have a position with a large newspaper or magazine like an editor or something."

No hands were raised.

I was brought up by my grandma and grandpa, or "pap". That's what all the kids called him. He worked in a candy factory. Pap did some hard time in a federal prison and numerous stints at the workhouse and the jail. That was before him and grandma decided to raise me and he quit drinking whiskey. They were fifty years old. I was just five.

A day in Nam didn't go by that I didn't think about them. I still do. Pap was tough, but good as gold. I remember the day I told him I planned on attending college. I was a junior in high school.

He said, "You don't know nothing about no Goddamned college. You get that Goddamn college stuff out of your head. Besides, you ain't got no Goddamn money anyway."

I didn't mention it anymore. I was fortunate to have some relatives in the trades. I worked construction as a journeyman sheet metal worker on permit from the union. Made top wages. I didn't know a kid from my end of town that made more.

I was twenty-three when I went to Vietnam. A graduate of a small teachers college in Eastern Kentucky with history and sociology majors and a teaching certificate. I was substitute teaching when I got my greetings. I would have had a permanent position if not for my draft status.

Our education continued.

The sergeant addressing us stressed, "Never set a pattern, that's the number one rule." He gave us several tragic examples of people who became lax.

"Keep your curiosity to yourself," he went on, "remember, curiosity killed the cat. Never pick up anything on the trail. It could be booby-trapped. If you want a souvenir, buy it. Hell, they've booby- trapped dogs and children. And if you step on a punji stick or you trip a rack of them on the trail, you're history for a while. You're out of commission."

Now, punji sticks were sharpened bamboo spikes, simple booby-traps, dipped in human feces. They would set up an infection that needed immediate hospitalization. Even the slightest wound would put you out of action for a while.

* * *

At the end of orientation, I was assigned to an artillery unit with the 101st Airborne.

"Do you understand how to place these positions on the map now?" asked the major, the commanding officer.

"I'm not sure sir. I think so. I don't know why they put me in artillery anyway, sir," I said. "I'm a social science and humanities man. I was always poor at math and the physical sciences." I told the major that I had only made a 78 in artillery school. That's the lowest passing score. They had math majors and one guy with a masters in physics in the class. They had a quick understanding of the instruction. I was mostly lost. However, there were those who failed, including an officer candidate.

The smart ones were National Guard and Army Reservists. They were going back home. The dummies like me got the tour.

I spent a week or so at our base camp – Camp Evans. This was battalion headquarters, a fairly large compound of hooch's with tin roofs covered with sandbags. There were bars, crude warm showers and hot meals in a mess hall.

About the second night I had guard duty on the perimeter. The young lieutenant gave me the password and my orders. "Anyone who comes down this road and doesn't know it, shoot them," he told me.

It was a dark night, but the helicopters with their searchlights and the periodic burst of illumination allowed for some vigilance. Several times I thought I saw something. This was the lowlands, on the coast, and the mosquitoes ate me up, even with the insect repellent.

It was early in the morning, maybe three o'clock when I thought I saw something. A figure coming down the road. It *was* a figure. I got out of the hole, knelt down on one knee, and pointed my weapon at this ghostly figure coming through the morning mist. "Password," I said. No response. "Password," again. Nothing. I took off the safety and had pressure on the trigger. One last time, "The password," I ordered. Hesitation. Then came, "Don't shoot, don't shoot."

It's the Lieutenant, and he gave the password.

I can't tell you how close I was to killing this young man. Even today, some thirty years later, I cringe and am so thankful.

When he reached me, he said, "Good job, good job, soldier."

I said, "Sir, you don't know how close I was to shooting you."

He didn't say anymore and was on his way.

A day later we went on patrol. Everyone now knew what the point meant and as luck would have it, they chose me to walk it. Looking back, this was a fairly secure area, however anything can happen.

We walked around the rice paddies. The natives were busy in their fields with the work animals, their buffaloes. By now, everybody knew nothing would get you more hassled than to shoot one of their buffaloes.

I did not know if I would do much patrolling. It would depend on my assignments with the artillery. I might draw a radioman's slot with a forward observer, who would be a young lieutenant. We were told about that position. The life expectancy for a radioman and the forward observer, in a firefight, was about fourteen seconds. It might have been eleven seconds, I don't remember exactly.

They were going to shut down your communications. Knocking out any additional firepower, primarily artillery and gunships.

One day we were filling up sand bags outside the base near the coast. There were several of us. We had only one M-16 between us. We took turns while one watched and the others worked. We noticed a native, at a distance, coming toward us riding a moped. He had it wide-open and we could see he had one arm raised above his head and something in his hand.

We were all cherries. That is what they called us – the new guys. You guys will get your cherries busted, the veterans would tell us, then laugh. Well, we were concerned. Did he have a grenade in his hand? The man with the weapon positioned himself. When the Vietnamese man got in sight we saw he had a little bird in his hand. A wounded little bird.

I knew then how dangerous cherries could be, just like the night with the lieutenant.

The major was the commanding officer. There was also another major, the X. O. (executive officer) and a Lt. Colonel over the battalion. The battalion consisted of three batteries, Alpha, Bravo, and Charlie. A captain ran a battery. Each battery had six guns. They were especially designed 105's, called one O' deuces, with 360 degrees capability without having to reset the guns when you turned them around.

In the previous conventional wars there were front lines. The old artillery pieces had to be reset, data changed when turned around. Precious minutes that could not be tolerated in guerilla war, when they were all around you.

These guns were much lighter than older 105's. This was an airmobile unit – what they call now, air assault. The guns could be carried by a Huey, the same light helicopter that delivered men into combat.

The major, the C. O., had spent a goodly amount of time on me before he made my assignment. He seemed a fine man. Looked as if he could have played football for Army – over 6 foot and 200 lbs., not fat.

The major made his decision. I was to be assigned to one of the batteries. Bravo battery located on a firebase called Rakkasan. I was to report to their F.D.C. (Fire Direction Control). The only way to Rakkasan, a mountain top in the jungle, was by chopper. It was the outpost, the point.

When I arrived, there was also a 155 battery, heavier artillery, at the location. I went to the wrong F.D.C. The 155-people seemed genuinely happy to have me. Seems they were shorthanded. I think they were disappointed when they got a call from the one O' deuces looking for me.

Once I found my home the education began. Fire Direction Control ran the guns. It was the hot seat. The chief and assistant chief immediately began to school me. They made frankly known that they were "very" short-timers, and I needed to catch on quick. I don't think either had a month left.

F.D.C. was like a platoon in size, about ten people and a lieutenant, on two twelve-hour shifts. Some of the men were old hands. As I found out, some were in Charlie Battery on Firebase Ripcord. Ripcord had undergone a thirty-day siege. The N.V.A. (North Vietnamese Army) had even shot down a big Chinook chopper on top of the ammo dump setting off everything. In the end, there was nothing left standing on the hill, but one broken down one O' deuce Howitzer. These men told me they lost an entire infantry battalion the last day, just getting them off the hill.

Some carried a picture of it in their wallets that was on the cover of Life, or Look magazine, I don't remember which. It showed the one broken down Howitzer among all the rubble, on a hill in the morning fog. I've been told it was up for the picture of the decade. I don't know what it lost to.

I'd been around some hard people in my life, but none hardened by war. I swear I was afraid to look at some of these men. They had scattered the men from Charlie battery throughout Alpha, Charlie, and Bravo Batteries. I guess they didn't think it wise to keep them together.

They were angry about not getting some kind of commendation. They said that some colonel flew over Ripcord the day after and got a Bronze Star and we get some kind of funky ass ribbon.

Well, knowing the 191ˢᵗ as I do now, they're not going to give you much for losing a hill. I was new at this Army business, but morale was not what one would expect.

New Jersey, that's what they called him. He said that Alpha Battery had it worse. New Jersey was one of the men in Charlie Battery that took the beating on Ripcord. He said, "Alpha Battery was killed to the last man, no survivors, on a firebase called The Eagle's Nest." He continued, "They sent a diversionary force up one side of the hill and when everyone went over there to defend that side of the hill, the main force came up the other and wiped them out."

One of the other Ripcord men added, "That's why we are so happy to be here."

"What do you mean?" I asked.

New Jersey interrupted, "You've got a lot learn, cherry. They have to share the wealth. You know Alpha and

Charlie have taken their hit. The hardest assignments will now go to Bravo."

I learned.

* * *

Rakkasan sat on a mountaintop just inside the highlands. To the west were lush green mountains and on the eastern horizon, the coastal plain. Looking west one could see the mountain ranges leading to the enemy's supply lines and Laos. It was a grand view, much like the Eastern Kentucky Mountains where I went to school. This was I Core – the northern part of South Vietnam. The only ugliness was the steep slopes that ran down the sides of the mountain. Most of the trees had been blown away. They lay all twisted and broken into piles. They had lowered the artillery pieces to clear the killing fields. There were rolls and rolls of concertina wire with mines and illumination canisters to deter and notify of attack.

We worked and slept in bunkers, nothing more than nasty holes in the ground with roofs of sandbags. I remember my first night. I'd been working in the F.D.C. bunker under a Coleman lantern. The battery had a generator, but it was not working which was often the case. I could see we needed a mechanic in the worst way.

I stepped out to relieve myself. It was so dark I had to inch my way around the bunker. It was scary. Then they let off a battery six – all the guns. I must have jumped three feet in the air. They're loud, especially at low-angle fire. It was amusing to watch the cherries when the guns went off. They'd jump straight up even in the daylight. I don't care who it was and the condition lasted several days.

I hadn't been on the firebase a week when New Jersey came into the F.D.C. to relay a story he had just heard from an infantry patrol. New Jersey was a small, sharp featured man. He said, in his no-nonsense demeanor, "An infantry patrol just found a recently abandoned underground 150 bed NVA hospital, just a click and a half, (1500 meters) down the hill. And that's not all, they found a basic training camp nearby. Right under our noses. Can you believe that?", he asked.

"No, I can't", I said, "Why would they be so close?"

One of the old hands from Charlie Battery and Ripcord said, "It's simple. They're smart little devils. They don't have to worry about our artillery. We can't shoot that close. All they have to worry about is the mortar men. And that's no problem."

All the old timers shook their heads in agreement.

We were not dealing with the Viet Cong. There were no villages here. Nothing but jungle. We shot at anything that moved that wasn't us.

The army had even recently employed sensors, listening devices. Sensor targets we called them. They had dropped them all through the jungle around us. These devices were the state of the art then. They resembled the foliage, as not to be detected. They were monitored from another location in the rear somewhere. They were given target numbers. We had the targets mapped and the data already computed. Once they gave us the target number to fire on, we would have rounds out in a few seconds. The joke was, what kind of monkey did we kill this time.

The chiefs were going home even sooner than I had expected. The education was intense.

The chief told Savoy and myself to go down to the landing pad and get some gas for the generator. Savoy was a likable young man, a graduate of Boston College. He was an enlisted man with a three-year hitch, a specialist 4th class, same rank as a corporal. We walked down the path, making small talk, to the tiny landing pad.

I carried a spigot that you attached to a large blivet to draw gas or water. A blivet was a huge, round and oblong, rubber container that weighed several thousand pounds. They were so large they had to be carried by Chinook choppers, or "shit hooks" as all the men called them.

We got to the pad and started to get the gas. A buck sergeant told us we would have to get the gas from one of the blivets down the hill. The pad was so small that many of the blivits had rolled down the hill when the choppers dropped them.

The hill was steep and we had to climb over or go around the trees that had been downed. We got to one of the blivets and went to work. A Chinook was coming in to drop another blivet on the pad. The twin rotors were throwing debris all over us. We had to get down behind a small tree to keep the wood chunks and small limbs from pounding us.

I looked up. The chopper had dropped the blivet, missing the pad. It was headed straight toward us. I got up to run, but it was too late. It ran clean over me. In shock, I jumped up immediately.

I heard Savoy, screaming.

They were hovering directly over us now. I looked up. The door gunner's face was absolute horror.

Then I became conscious again of Savoy's screaming. The blivet had him pinned against the stump of a remaining tree. His arms were swinging wildly. I grabbed the strap attached to the blivet trying to pull it off of him. The men came running down the hill. When enough men arrived, we got it off of him.

Savoy was pretty shook up. We helped him get up the hill to the F.D.C. We had a medic fly out to look at him. Amazingly, he was only a little sore and stoned up. But from then on, he always tried to get back to the rear.

I looked at myself. I was half mud. It had buried me in the mud. Thank God it was the start of the monsoons or that I didn't get caught on a stub. I thought we would get a lot of ribbing. But Savoy was so shook up, I guess they saw it as serious and that some cherries were busted that day.

* * *

"He buried his kills with their hands sticking out of the ground and then he'd put a 101st flag in the gook's hand," New Jersey said. "The guy came to Nam as a private. Hell, they'd be in a firefight, and he'd just charge them. He did five consecutive tours of duty. He was a legend. He was given a battlefield commission to officer. He made Captain before he left. He spoke fluent Vietnamese and would taunt them under fire. He was a most feared man. They say, the NVA had a reward of ten bags of rice and furlough home on his head. I can't remember all the stories about this man. But I do know they had to send him home. He tied a dead Vietnamese to the front of his jeep and paraded it around the city of Hue."

I'd gotten quite an education. I had been in Vietnam just over a month. The two Chiefs of F.D.C. had gone home. They had crossed the big pond and were back in the "world" as we used to say. I was running the guns on one of the shifts.

Benji was running the other shift. Benji had a degree in hotel management. He looked like a hotel manager. He was a small man with a penciled mustache. There was no athleticism here, but he would prove to be one hell of a soldier.

Benji had arrived at the battery a couple of weeks before me. I don't know exactly why him and I got the hot seat. We were both still privates. The old-timers, some of them with higher ranks didn't seem interested or maybe command made a decision.

Savoy, as good a man as he was, didn't handle the pressure of running the guns. He'd get rattled. But he wanted to make Sergeant, so when he went home he would have all the benefits for him and his wife.

One day Savoy asked me if he could run the missions that night for me. I said, "Sure."

Well, we had a green lieutenant on duty. A fine man with a master's degree in psychology. But he knew nothing about Fire Direction Control at the time. He would become a damn good artilleryman once he learned the ropes.

I was in and out of F.D.C. keeping an eye on things. Savoy and the lieutenant were conducting a mission. They had fired several marking rounds, a couple hundred feet above the position, a safety precaution before bringing in the high explosives.

I became a little suspicious, so I checked the data. I won't get technical, but they were shooting in the opposite direction.

The lieutenant went frantic, "My career, that's my career!" he screamed.

I said, "Maybe not." I quickly checked the map for all infantry positions. There was nothing close to where the rounds were fired. I recomputed the data and sent it to the guns.

Right on target.

The day after, the chief of guns caught me on the hill, "You shot out last night, didn't you?"

"Naw, naw, un- ugh," I said.

It wasn't a week later, I was given a special allocation to E-4, same as a corporal. It had nothing to do with this incident, but there is a code until they need a scapegoat.

The chief of F.D.C. was normally a specialist 5th or 6th class, the same rank as a buck or staff sergeant. At least I had as high of rank now as anyone in the group, and it helped.

We had a new captain, Captain John Bishop. It was his second tour. He was 23 years old. We'd both turn 24 in Nam.

I asked the new chief of guns how he could be so young a captain. He replied, "Battlefield commission my first tour." It didn't take long for me to find out why he was the captain. They'd sent the best.

After a few days, I went to the captain. " Sir," I said, "I need to go back to Camp Evans and get my pay straightened out. I've got a problem."

They sent a chopper out to pick me up. When I got to Evans, my base camp, they didn't take up my weapon. I was surprised, because you didn't carry a weapon on Evans unless you were on perimeter duty. I was heavily armed. I was packing five bandoleers, about 1,000 rounds.

I got my pay problem solved, then headed for a bar. I needed some whiskey.

I ordered a Scotch and water. They even had ice. I learned to drink Scotch when I was nineteen. I'd worked some weekends when home from college at the local pizza joint. When we'd close, the owner would pull out the Scotch bottle. I acquired the taste early. I liked Kentucky Bourbon, too. There wasn't much I didn't like. I could drink with the construction workers and did. A Scotch and water was 20 or 25 cents. I'm not sure, but I got into it.

At closing, I picked up my gun and walked out the door. I spun around a couple of times and fell flat on my ass. Well, by the time I found my barracks, I was in fair shape. It was the quarters for the transients. There were two other men staying in the hooch. We got to talking and one thing led to another. Then one of them asked, "Do you want to smoke some reefer?"

I said I've never smoked any pot. Well, I smoked, but it didn't seem to do anything to me.

I was taking hot showers, eating in a mess hall, watching movies at night and drinking. The third day headquarters wanted to see me. A captain, believe me, I knew who he was, wanted to see me. If he wasn't the most decorated soldier in the division, he was one of them. The men had given me the story on him. Another battle commissioned field officer, serving his 5th straight year in Nam. He'd go home each year for 30 days. They said he saved the same major's life twice by falling on him and taking the shrapnel and fire. He had been the Commander of Ripcord when under siege. That was just a few things I recall.

I went into his office, "Spec. 4th Class, Greene, reporting, sir."

He was a very thin man. He didn't look like a Hollywood hero. He said, "Greene, they need you back out there. We've got a chopper. If we can get it running to take you back, if it starts, you're gone."

I said, "Sir, I would appreciate you having it running properly before you put me on it."

He looked me in the eye and said, "Greene, they can't kill you and they can't kill me. It's the only attitude to take."

I replied, "Just the same, sir, I hope it's running properly."

They got it started. I was headed back to the Rock.

I was sitting with my legs dangling out of the door of the Huey. You wouldn't fall out, because of the centrifugal force. When the chopper reached Rakkasan, it suddenly turned its nose up and began to climb. I thought what the hell is the pilot doing? He climbed so high in the clouds that the firebase went out of sight. Then the engine quit. The chopper went into a spiraling nosedive. It's called a stall, but I didn't catch it at first. I was still pretty green.

The base finally came back in view and the motor started. I thought why did he do that? The pilot, I mean. It was bad enough being on this outpost without this shit. It was a while before it hit me. The captain must have told the pilot that I was nervous about the chopper's mechanical status.

Take him for a ride, he must have said.

* * *

We were conducting three missions at the same time. Two guns on each mission. The radio crackled, "Contact fire mission, contact fire mission, a voice cried!" I could hear the fire in the background. He gave me his quadrants, ALPHA, DELTA, FOXTROT … you had to decode their position – can't give your position away.

I contacted the guns. Abort missions. Contact fire mission. Standby. Battery six. My men sent the data, which I quickly computed. Then I called battalion for check data – always had to have check data. Battalion computed the data also. When we were in approximate agreement we could fire.

The forward observer was back on the air, "We need that artillery. Get us some gunships!" He was frightened. One of the battalion officers told him not to panic. He screamed, "Don't panic? God damned, we are dying out here!"

The gunships were already on their way. I gave the data to the guns. A battery six – that's six rounds apiece. Commence firing. Fire at will.

We adjusted the artillery in close to our patrol. On top of the enemy. I can't remember all the circumstances of this mission. They all ran together after a while. There has been some current controversy on the body counts after the Tet Offensive. But I can say this. They were correct on our level. In the field, in order to have a confirmed kill, you had to find matching arms or legs, a torso, or a head. The enemy would do anything possible to carry off their dead. But sometimes they couldn't.

The monsoon rains had set in on the mountain. It was either misting or drizzling rain. And it was cold. You had to wear your field jacket.

I got up one morning, stepped out of my hole and stretched my hand out in front of my face. I could barely make it out. It was too cold to shower – what shower there was. You'd get enough water about every two weeks to fill up a canvas Australian shower bag. By the time you soaped up, you were out of water.

At one point I went over thirty days without any shower. In the morning you would just use your helmet to wash, shave and brush your teeth. We ate C-rations. You took a short can and punched holes at the bottom with the sharp end of a can opener. This was our stove. We put, or were supposed to put, a heat tab under it for cooking our meals. The holes at the bottom of our stove can, allowed in the air. What we usually cooked with though, was C-4, a plastic explosive. C-4 is set off with an electric charge. We would take apart a claymore mine for the C-4. I've never seen anything that burned so hot. Just a little piece of it and your C-rations were ready in three or four seconds.

A new man was assigned to F.D.C. – Pockets. He'd been a radioman for an F. O. (forward observer). He was happy to get rid of that job.

Everyone called him Pockets. If you asked him for a light or something he would start searching the many pockets of his jungle fatigues. After a while, he'd usually find it in the first pocket he checked. It was a ritual.

Another thing about Pockets, he was scared to death of the rats. We had some rats on Rakkasan. You could hear them scratchin' and scuryin' around the bunker walls. Sometimes even during the day they'd come out. We'd stomped a few. I eventually didn't pay much attention to them, but an infantry patrol that had just recently come in did not share my tolerance. They killed seventy rats their first night on the Rock.

One day one of the men on the guns came running up the hill. He'd been down at the dump. "We killed a Cobra, you want to go down and see it?" he asked me.

"Naw, not me. Thanks anyway."

By now, I gave snakes little thought. I had more on my mind. Oh, every once in a while, at night, when I put my feet down in my sleeping gear, I'd get a little shiver.

Two or three days after Pockets joined us we got another man. He was from one of the Dakota's. I called him Dakota, a tall' lanky boy who had that no hurry cowboy about him. He immediately proved valuable. The generator was down again on our shift. I said to the men, "My kingdom for a mechanic", or something to that effect.

He said, in his draw, "I know a little about engines. You want me to take a look at it?"

Yeah now! In just a few minutes he had it running.

"Good job," I thanked him. "Dakota, your main job from now on is to keep that God damn generator running! You understand?" I asked.

"No problem," he replied. "I've been working on engines since I was a kid."

I had me a generator man.

We were going a day or so here and there without any supply choppers. The Monsoons kept them from flying.

That meant no mail or beer. They never sent out a supply chopper that I didn't ask for beer. It was one of our few luxuries. Even though we mostly had to drink it hot. Sometimes they would send out small blocks of ice for the men. F.D.C. would get one of the blocks. We' lay the can on its side and spin it on the ice. Once the block of ice got a groove we could chill a beer in a minute.

They assigned a new lieutenant to the F.D.C. He didn't have a clue. He was there to be educated. He was not West Point – fresh out of ROTC and college, I suspected. He didn't last long.

One night things were slow. The new lieutenant and a couple of my men began to cut-up on the radio making sound effects like choppers and calling in crazy fire missions. The major was on-duty. He seemed at first a little amused, but ordered the young lieutenant to stop it.

The lieutenant continued. The major came back on the radio, commanded him to stop and wanted to see him in the morning. "There will be a chopper to pick you up in the morning," he said.

I do believe that was the last I saw of that lieutenant, but we soon got another lieutenant.

Dakota and I were out sitting on a bunker. It was a dark, but unusually clear night for the monsoons. Dakota lit a cigarette, taking a long puff. I asked, "They didn't tell you about that, did they?"

"About what?" he asked.

"You need to cup that cigarette." I lit up one and cupped it in my hand for an example. "A sniper can see that light for a mile and shoot you at over 1,000 meters. Always cup your cigarette."

We had our own sniper. I never saw him during the day. He'd stay in his hole until dusk to get his night vision. He'd walk down the hill every night, not looking at or speaking to anyone. I was getting harder, but he was a scary figure.

All movement, even the NVA's was slow during Monsoons. Some days we didn't fire over 300 rounds. You had to be careful firing. All infantry patrols were supposed to move a click a day (1,000 meters), but they would get settled in against the rain and report false movements. Once an infantry unit bedded down for the night, we would fire defensive targets all around their position. These targets, with data computed, were assigned target numbers. All the infantry had to do was to call in the target number and we'd have rounds out in seconds. These D.T.'s (delta tango's) were supposed to be no closer than 600 meters from their location. If they were hit, then we would walk in the rounds. But they kept fudging on their movement. You never knew exactly where they were.

The new lieutenant who replaced the comedian, was pretty gung-ho. He would stay with Bravo Battery for the rest of my tour. He had already been on the guns and had some experience. He was learning quickly as the Fire Direction Control Officer.

I had a really strange mission during this time. I was on duty when a whisper came over the radio.

"Fire mission," came the whisper, "Fire mission." I acknowledged quietly. He said, "I've got a position of NVA that are partying, smoking dope, laughing, having a good time."

We crashed their party.

* * *

A young black soldier came running and stumbling into our F.D.C. bunker. A black sergeant was hot on his heels. The sergeant hit him several times knocking him to the floor. He then kicked him violently all over the room. A couple of more gunnery sergeants showed up and they dragged him off.

We were changing shifts. All the F.D.C. was there. Benji, who was running the other shift asked, "What the hell did he do?"

New Jersey answered, "He must have had a bad attitude. On a place like the Rock, they don't tolerate a bad attitude from anyone."

Now, New Jersey, though a small man was not a man that would take any disrespect and his word was right. He said, "It doesn't make any difference who you are. If you want to be a punk, then you'll pay the price, out here."

I'd already learned that. I thought this place was like the Wild West. Everybody was armed.

I had already become the chief and was up for another promotion. The old men like New Jersey had even accepted it. But I knew how sensitive it all was. There were plenty of stories about fragging (taking one of your own out of the picture, if he were a real jerk-off). It's a hard thing for people to believe, but they would send you a message if you had your head on wrong.

The captain of Alpha Battery, recently, had a claymore mine set off in his bunker. Miraculously, it didn't kill him, but I would say it got his attention.

Benji was running the second twelve-hour shift. I could see why he was in hotel management. He was organized and detailed. He ran as good a shift as me. I felt a little bad that I was getting the promotions.

Savoy was still trying to get back to the rear. It wouldn't do him any good. He was on the rock to stay.

Pockets carried a small tape player besides his ear all day long, when he wasn't on duty. He only had one tape, a <u>Three Dog Night</u>, that's all. He still couldn't find his lighter or cigarettes.

The lieutenant, whose shoulders were too narrow, or his butt too wide, was still anticipating some real air assault missions when the dry season came.

I did not look forward to the dry season.

One day, one of the men got a "Dear John" letter. His wife wanted a divorce. He was sent home for thirty days to resolve the matter. A lot of that went on. I was married, too. She was a tall, pretty girl, who had the distinction of having the highest I.Q. at our rural high school. I had some awful thoughts about what she was doing. Then one day I said to myself, I'll never worry about this again. And I really didn't. That's all I have to say about this situation now. It didn't last a year when I got back, anyway.

We had a computer of 1960's vintage. That's why I hate them now. When it worked, the generator was down. When the generator was up, well you know. I could compute stick data, manually, much quicker than that 250-pound monstrosity, anyway. I kept Savoy, Pockets, New Jersey, and Dakota on my shift. We were good with the computer or stick data under a Coleman lantern. We were a team.

The weather broke. Captain Bishop came to me and said, "They want you back at Division to straighten out some paper work."

I had never been to Camp Eagle, but I had a buddy back there. I flew back to Camp Evans, our base camp, and they drove me by truck to Camp Eagle. One of the gunnery sergeants, an E-5, from my battery was travelling with me. He was a big black man and I thought awfully old to be just an E-5. I was about to make that rank. We sat in the bed of the truck with our weapons locked and loaded, across our laps.

I'd been two months on Rakkasan, and I don't think I had ever really spoken to him, except over the radio.

We were going through Hue, an ancient, once imperial city, that sat on the coast. The classic buildings were surrounded by concertina wire and their walls were bullet riddled. Even so, they were majestic.

The black sergeant sat with his arms over the rail of the truck. The streets were busy with mopeds, old Citrons and bicycles. The black sergeant said, "They can take your watch off of your wrist before you can say shit. If they try, I'm gonna' kill ..., but before he had got out another word, two Vietnamese, on a moped, had his watch.

I didn't even look at him. I never spoke. I don't think we spoke the rest of the trip.

I came up to the guard shack. I took my magazine out of my M-16 and opened the breech. That's how you did it at a large base. He didn't take up my gun. Nobody carried weapons here, unless they were patrolling.

My meeting about my records was the next day. So, I headed for the nearest watering hole.

As I walked in, I noticed a full table of tough looking Marines. I laid my gun up against the table, went to the bar, and ordered a Scotch and water. I waited until the Marines were not talking and asked if they knew a Sam Frazier?

"Yeah," they all said, "He'll be off and in here in a few minutes."

"Well, he usually does," one Marine added.

Sam was from Eastern Kentucky. All the way to the West Virginia line. I told them I was a friend of his from Kentucky. We had met during basic training. He had gone a year at the same college I attended. He had a football scholarship. He was an all-state lineman.

Sam was so modest and had no reason to be. I've taught and coached, for nearly thirty years, and I don't believe I ever saw a more physical man. He was a Mountain man. He'd tear the stuffing out of the dummies during hand-to-hand training.

One day, our company was training with pugil sticks. They are a broom handle with hard pads on the ends. You were supposed to be simulating using your rifle to knock somebody's head off.

A couple of sergeants and a lieutenant came up. They were from another company. They had a big trainee with them. One of the sergeants said, "You think you have anyone here that can handle our boy? He was Chicago's Heavy Weight Golden Gloves Champ ."

We let them know real quick, Sam Frazier. Let their boy try Sam.

I'm not exaggerating. Sam had him flat on his back, in the dust, in three seconds.

Sam and I had made friends.

The next day, we were at the firing range. Mr. Chicago came up to Sam. I was standing behind him.

Chicago said, "You got lucky yesterday, Frazier."

Sam said softly, "I reckon I did."

I stepped out from behind him and said, "He can whip your ass anytime you want it."

"Who asked you Greene?" Chicago replied.

"Nobody," I came back, "I just volunteered it for your own safety."

I got me another Scotch. I hadn't had three sips when Sam came in. He was both surprised and happy to see me. We began to drink and talk.

"Where they goin' to put you up?" Sam asked.

"I don't know where I'm going to sleep. They didn't tell me anything."

"Well, you're gonna' stay with me. We've got an extra bunk or two in our barracks."

"Good, I appreciate it Sam." We took a few beers back to the barracks. I met the guys and settled in.

"I've got some white bread," Sam said, "Two loafs, just got 'em from home."

I told him I couldn't remember the last time I had any white bread. If I had any bread at all, it was that old rice bread. It'd crumble to pieces in your hand when you tried to butter it.

We got some butter, and ate pretty much a whole loaf.

The next day, I got my business conducted and was headed back to Camp Evans and the Rock.

* * *

A Cobra jet gunship was working out at the bottom of our hill. Everyone was out watching, sitting on the bunkers or anywhere they could find a good seat. We had called in the gunship when one of our patrols made the contact. The enemy was so close the mortars or our artillery couldn't fire on them.

Dakota, who was sitting next to me on some sandbags, said, "This is better than the picture shows on Saturday night."

I agreed. We were amazed, even the old veterans.

The Cobra cockpit is only three feet wide. Not a whole lot of room to work with when diving at over 2oo mph. This was the most dreaded helicopter in my part of Vietnam. It was state of the art. The pilot could just look at the target and the gun would adjust accordingly. Then he would just fire. The electric mini-gun that sounded like a chain saw could cover a football field, every square inch, in seconds. I don't remember exactly, but it put out several thousand rounds a minute.

The Cobra dived again and released it rockets. I thought how could anything survive this.

We had called in many missions for Cobra jets but none so close.

There had been another break in the weather and everyone was making their moves. The enemy was smart and moved inside our firepower, but got caught.

The 155 battery, the one I had gone to by mistake my first day on the Rock, was gone. The only ones left on the hill were us, a mortar team, and a small company of infantry. Maybe a hundred men. But another 155 battery had recently set up close, on a hill next to us.

The only officers I recall seeing besides the captain and our two lieutenants were the colonel and our major. They would fly in occasionally and talk to the captain. The colonel, a full bird, was the commander of all artillery for the 101st. He looked the part. I guess he was in his 40's. He looked and commanded authority. The major, our C.O., who trained me watched over us. There wasn't a place we went that he and the colonel didn't go.

Somebody sent us a copy of the <u>Godfather</u>. I don't remember where we got the book, but it was a hit. We didn't let it leave the F.D.C. Our shift drew straws to see who would read it first. I don't remember who got first dibs. But he read and read, when we were not occupied. Finally, after a few days, we asked where are you in the book?

"Chapter three", he replied.

"Chapter three?" we asked.

I told him, "We are going to have to do something here boy. We all want to read that book." We made the best of a bad situation. I think we had to end up reading some of the book together and out loud. It was our conversation and entertainment for the time.

New Jersey, who was Italian, delighted in the book. He even taught me some Italian, at my insistence. The first thing he taught me and the only thing I remember to this day was how to say Buff Fan Goo. That's fuck you, in his language. You can see, I still don't know how to spell it. He told me it might come in handy one day.

Pockets was spacey as ever, but so likeable. He was still walking around listening to that same tape.

Savoy was the radioman, I mean radio Vietnam. He always had the best equipment available. He had the sounds, even on the outpost. Savoy's bunker was the hub for music. He was the music man and he had a following. I don't know to this day where he got all his equipment and tapes. But if you wanted to jam, his hole was the place to go.

Dakota was very crafty. The infantry always had the best generator. I'd always send Dakota on a covert operation to hook into their lines.

Sometimes they would find out and cut our line. But Dakota would just do it again somewhere else. He was good at it. They couldn't stop us for long.

The rains would come, days at a time, and then it would clear. During a stretch of good weather, the cooks would fly out and cook us a hot breakfast. This was good for morale. The army does run on it stomach. But somebody always tries to screw up a good thing. The captain was going through the chow line one morning and a soldier reached into his pocket and pulled out a handful of drugs and threw them on the captain's breakfast tray. "Have a good day captain", the young man said.

Well, again, several sergeants whipped his ass good. He was gone. I've never to this day figured out what happened to those people they drug off. We were so isolated we didn't know anything.

The captain was making his mark. He was the kind of leader that never looked over your shoulder. But he'd let you know if anything wasn't right. He seldom came into the F.D.C.

The lieutenant was becoming an expert at this F.D.C. thing. He usually worked with Benji on the other shift. However, he was still a little too gung ho for me.

One day the captain came to me when I was off duty. "Greene, let's go down the hill and shoot." He was talking about our M-16s. I kept my gun clean, but I had enough of shooting. I said, "No sir, not today." I think I disappointed him. What I wanted was some peace and quiet. I grew up with guns. I could shoot.

I was up for promotion to E-5. That's Specialist Fifth Class. Same rank as Buck Sergeant – the rank appropriate for the Chief of F.D.C.

It was November. I had been "in country" less than three months, in the army for only seven months. I was to report to the board for what they told me was an oral examination to see if I was fit for advancement.

I never made it in November. The weather did not permit choppers in at that particular time. In early December, I went before the board. There was a chair in the middle of the room. I knew enough to march in, salute and give the proper greetings.

I sat down and they began to grill me.

There were several officers and sergeants on the board. Nixon was the president and one of the first questions they asked me was when the next presidential election would be held.

That was easy.

Another one of the things they asked was what I would do if my battery was under attack and a soldier would not get out of his hole to do his duty. I said, "Gentlemen, I'd tell him I don't want to be here either, but you get your ass out of that hole and defend this hill and all our poor asses."

They seemed impressed that I was a college graduate and was attempting to teach before I was drafted. But I failed on one of the questions. "Who is the commander of the 101st Airborne?" one of the majors asked.

I told them I didn't know, that I had been isolated on Rakkassan and that I had never seen him out there.

I was told I made the second highest score of those who were interviewed. I made E-5, officially, in the middle of December.

* * *

I heard the machine gun. I was off-duty, just walking around the hill drinking a hot beer. It was coming from the next hill where the 155 battery had set up. I could see the men running and jumping behind things and into their holes. Then I saw him, one of their own men was spraying the hill with an M-60. That's our standard issued machine gun.

It went on for a while. Later, we got word that no one was hurt. I guess he didn't mean to kill anyone. He just wanted out.

As you can imagine, it was the buzz of the hill. New Jersey said, "Some of them shot their big toes off. You want to go home? There's a way."

Thirty years later, I was sitting in a bar with an old friend. He told me one of the neighborhood kids had shot his big toe off to get out of Nam. This kid, that same man was my worst enemy. Back before Vietnam, we had a brutal fight. Two of them as a matter of fact. I was nineteen. He was a couple of years older. We were both big middleweights. He lost some teeth and I scarred him up pretty good. I was beat up too and had to have some stitches.

My friend who was telling me the story was there at the fight.

"He hated you, Greene," said my friend.

"I know, I know," I concurred.

My old buddy went on, "Every time I saw him he'd tell me, 'you tell that Greene, I'm gonna' get him.' I'd say to him, 'Tell him yourself. You know where he hangs out.'"

After Vietnam, he'd become a heavy in a tough motorcycle gang. I rode a motorcycle too. I had concern about running into him and some of his acquaintances. You can imagine my relief when I picked up the paper one morning before school and saw where my nemesis was shot and killed in a big shoot out. Some of the gang had got into it with a few other men in a bar near their clubhouse. There were several men killed.

I had wished him no harm, but I was relieved.

Nam just made crazy people crazier.

I was getting letters from home when the choppers could get in - from my grandma, mom, wife, sister, brothers and friends. They meant a lot to me. I was getting care packages, too. Especially from mom - cheese and cookies, fancy breads and puddings. When we got a care package everybody was happy. That's what we called them – care packages. We'd share them with everybody.

We were still reading <u>The Godfather</u>. Damn it was good! A lot of nights we read by Coleman lantern.

Things were slow. The monsoon had really set in. There were days we didn't fire 200 rounds. I had to put Pockets on shit burning detail. I hated to do it. I'd done it once. It was no pleasure. Our toilet was a box with a hole in it. Half of a 55- gallon drum was the reservoir. We'd pull out the drum, saturate it with diesel fuel, then burn and stir the waste until it was eliminated.

I told Pockets, "It could be worse. You could still be out there with that forward observer."

It was wet and cold. The infantry would come dragging in, their feet rotting from the exposure and the jungle rot. It was like a bad boil. An infection to the bone. Some men got it bad. My worst case was on my neck where my collar rubbed. You couldn't wear underwear. You had to be able to breathe. We didn't want anything rotting down there.

We were on duty one day, Savoy said, "I've got the peaches."

Then from Pockets, "I've got a pound cake."

Peaches and pound cake were the highlight of our dining experience on the Rock. The problem was they never came in the same c-rations. We all thought it was some kind of army trick. You had to find a buddy with the peaches if you had the pound cake. Well, you get the picture. It was quite comical.

And the beans and franks, they were to kill for. If you got the ham and eggs, you'd just throw them away.

Life was simple.

They had cigarettes in those c-rations also – five in the pack. If you got Lucky's or Camel's, we'd claim WWII vintage. If I got menthols, I could trade. Marlboro's were my favorite.

We wouldn't drink the water. It sometimes made you sick. I guess bacteria built up in those blivets. I drank hot coke or beer. Sometimes a beer in the morning. We did what we had to do.

Occasionally, when the weather was good, they flew out a PX. That's where you could buy what you needed. We'd stock up. Beef jerky, razorblades, Marlboros, as I remember.

Christmas was coming, and we had gone days and days without any supplies. By Christmas Eve, it was eleven days. Eleven days without anything. No care packages, or letters, or beer. We were down to drinking the water.

But there was to be a cease-fire beginning at 6:00 PM on Christmas Eve and lasting through Christmas.

All batteries in our area were firing until 6:00 PM, thus securing our positions just in case. Shortly after the cease-fire we got a communication that one of our sister batteries, a 155 unit, had fired out on an infantry position. I can't remember exactly, it was maybe 45, maybe 60 men. No survivors.

It seems that a green lieutenant, a forward observer, called in high explosives on their position. He had lost radio contact with the infantry. The marking round had evidently been on top of them.

You never fired H. E. rounds until you had the authority from the infantry. It was a precaution to prevent errant rounds. It happened just 10 minutes before the cease-fire.

I hesitate to bring it up. I doubt their families even know. And maybe that's best.

The captain came around and wished everyone a merry Christmas. He gave every man a rusty can of coke and a beer. It was all he had. I quickly traded my coke for a beer. I could've drunk a case.

Then, to my surprise, the black sergeant who had his watch snatched off his wrist, came to me, "I've got some whiskey. How about some whiskey?"

"Sure," I said.

I had told no one about the watch incident. We went to his hole and drank whiskey and talked of home.

* * *

It was Christmas on the Rock. There wasn't anything to do. The word was that we were the only base in Nam without a Christmas dinner. But at least it was quiet. I thought about family and friends, past Christmases, and I wondered what they were all doing. I was wishing I was there, but I couldn't dwell on it. But I did think about grandma and growing up. I could see grandma in her garden, and I still do. The first few rows were always flowers. She'd be hoeing and hear the rain crow. Grandma would say, "Hear the rain crow, boy? I hear the rain crow. It's gonna' rain. The garden needs it." I never hear a rain crow that I don't think of Grandma. She kept a fine garden.

We had chickens, too. I had to water and feed them. I hated it. The roosters were always after me until I got bigger. As I've said, I was five when I went to live with Pap and Grandma. My father drowned in a fishing accident when I was two. My mother had remarried. There was my older sister, my half-brother, and me.

I couldn't get along with my stepfather. So, I went to live with my grandparents. My mother didn't want it, but it couldn't be avoided.

When grandma and Pap took me in, we lived downtown in a pretty rough neighborhood. But he had already started building a house at the edge of town. Just over the city limit. He had bought a large lot for $122 and an old army barracks for $75. When he got done he had $2,000 in our home. The reason I remember the numbers is he reminded me of it all the time. Pap had cleared the trees with an ax. There were stumps everywhere. But we still had plenty of shade. Except for the garden.

It was a dead-end street. If you walked three houses up you were in the city, on the bus line, or you could go down to the end of the road to the railroad tracks and it was all farmland. It was an ideal place to grow up. You really did have the best of both worlds.

Grandma sold eggs. Sometimes she sewed for people and she canned much of what we ate.

Pap worked in the candy factory. I always had lots of candy.

My grandmother truly was a southern cook. We ate well. Sometimes we ate our own chickens. Pap had a civil way of cutting the chicken's heads off. He'd tie a string around their neck and tied them to the close line, then with a sharp butcher knife, he'd cut their heads off. When he'd tell me I was running around like a chicken with its head cut off, I knew exactly what he meant.

Now, Mr. Vittitoe, down the road, had a different method. He'd just grab two of 'em up by the head (he had a big family), swing them around real good and then just pop their heads off. We kids on the road tried never to miss that event.

Our end of town was mostly working class, but there was a middle class, especially on the hill. We thought they were rich. We didn't have much, but there were some on our road that had less.

When I started to school, I caught the bus on the corner in front Joker Joes, a bar that was kind of like a hilarity hall. It had a coffin on the roof and one inside too, where they said they'd put you if you got drunk and passed out. They also had a jail cell where they'd lock you up. I was told there was money on the floor and if you tried to pick it up, you'd get shocked. That was just a few of the things I remember about Joker Joes. I was amazed. All of us kids would peak in the windows to see what we could see.

My school was an old red schoolhouse with portables (unattached classrooms) I can remember the day we got inside plumbing. I was in the second grade.

I almost flunked the third grade. Ms. Skaggs called in those who were on the line. She decided to pass me on. She said I was bigger than Johnny Downs, who she flunked. I couldn't figure out what she was talking about. Johnny Downs was nearly twice my size. I was in high school before I realized she was talking about our IQ's.

When I was twelve, I went to Fairdale High School. We didn't have junior high then. I was in the seventh grade. The school was five miles out into the country. Fairdale was mostly farmers and hill people then. There was one valley they called Hungry Holler. They used to make moonshine in those hollows. There wasn't even a stop light in the town of Fairdale, just a couple of caution lights.

They were good people, hardworking and tough. But you could get your chimes rung real quick if you ran your mouth too much. I can personally testify to that. I was an outsider and learned that quickly.

I weighed 99 pounds. I remember because you had to weigh 100 pounds before you could play football. They wouldn't let me go out. Baseball was my game anyway, or so I thought. I played a lot of baseball. Our end of town had as good of a baseball program as there was around. I started playing as soon as I could. I also played in high school. There would be summer days we'd play all day long. I caught and played outfield. I played enough to reach my potential, which sadly to say, was not nearly enough.

We had our gang. A lot of parents wouldn't allow their kids to run with us. We weren't bad kids nor disrespectful, but we were a rough lot. We had some pretty bad BB-gun battles in the woods near the tracks.

The initiation into our club was fairly scary. There was a train trestle that spanned what everyone called the big ditch. It was about thirty feet above the shallow water.

If you wanted to be one of us, you had to crawl under the tracks and crouch down on the pillar and I do mean crouch. The train would go over the top of you. If you stood up any at all the train would have taken your head off. We all did it. We did it several times. You just wouldn't believe how loud it was.

I had a fight in front of the school in the spring of my junior year. It was with a senior who called me a chicken shit. I won't go into it all but I never had to fight anymore at school. I'd grown up. I was 5' 11" and 170 pounds.

Mr. Hardin, our principal, told me one day in the gym. "If I had arms on me like you, I wouldn't be afraid of anybody."I knew better. One hundred and seventy pounds will only go so far in this world.

I had a customized, forest green, 54 Chevy. I drove it to school and we'd cruise looking for girls.

I was out on the baseball field for spring practice one day when the head football coach approached. He said, "Greene, I expect to see you out on the football field this season."

I said, "I've never played any organized football."

"I'll see you in August," he said and walked away.

Well, I went out for football. I had a lot to learn. However, by the third game I was starting both ways. I played offensive and defensive end. I made a lot of mistakes at first, but by the end of the season it was mostly instinct. I think I had more potential in football than I did in baseball. Of course, that's not saying much.

In my senior year, all the guys in advanced art class got locked up on a field trip for drinking beer. We were going to the newspaper downtown. It was one of our stops for the art field trips. We had three cars. I wasn't driving. We had girls with us too. We pulled into an empty lot and pulled out a couple of cases of beer. It wasn't a matter of seconds before we were surrounded. The A.B.C., that's our state Alcohol and Beverage Control Agency and the city police were making a raid on a tavern directly across the street.

They let the girls go and took us boys to jail. That included Stewart Chinn, a Chinese immigrant. We all told him this would get him deported for sure and his whole family. He was real nervous, and he didn't even drink any beer. They were going to lock up all the drivers. One of the driver's dad was dying of cancer. I called over a detective and told him about it. He let him go. This was Friday. I didn't look forward to seeing Mr. Hardin on Monday.

Monday came too soon. They were calling names, one at a time, to the office over the P.A. system. I thought they would never get to me, but they did. I walked into Mr. Hardin's office. They were all there, our two assistant principals, and our two counselors. And, of course, Mr. Hardin.

Mr. Hardin did the questioning, "Greene, did you drink any beer?"

"No sir," I responded.

He shot back, "If you lie to me again, Greene, you won't graduate.

"Yes sir, I did have some beer," I quickly confessed.

"How many?"

"Oh, a couple."

"Who gave them to you?" he asked.

"Nobody in particular, they were just being passed around."

"Linda Caulk, was she drinking?' he continued.

"No sir. I didn't see her."

"Yeah, right," he said.

"We already know Greene. I'm going to call your parents. Then I'll let you know what I'm going to do with you. Now, get the hell out of here."

"Yes sir," I said.

Oh boy, I didn't want him to call grandma. Pap would drive us to church every Sunday. I even had a five-year pin. I hadn't missed Sunday school in five years. Now, that's when I was younger. But, we went every Sunday, except for Pap. Grandma was born in 1900. She was sixty-five. I didn't want to worry her.

That afternoon, I went to Mr. Hardin's office. I got in to see him.

"What is it Greene?" he asked.

"Mr. Hardin, I'm 18 years old. I'll take the punishment. My grandmother doesn't have anything to do with this. Besides, she has heart trouble." Well, she didn't have heart trouble and I didn't want her to.

As far as I know, he called everybody's parents but mine. He helped me out big time in college too, but that's another story.

* * *

"You just go in a room and pick out the one you want," said New Jersey. "It'll cost you $25 a day. If you got the money you can get two if you want."

Dakota asked, "What if you don't like her?"

"Just take her back," replied New Jersey. "They'll give you another one. It doesn't hurt to buy her a couple of new dresses either."

One of the veterans interjected, "Hell, you can get anything you want in Bang Kok, if you got the money."

"I've got the money," said Pockets. "Plenty of money."

"Then, if you don't have a good time, it's your own fault." New Jersey emphasized.

"I've got to go to Hawaii and see my wife," said Savoy.

"Well that's too bad," New Jersey replied.

I thought to myself. That's what I'm going to do. But Bang Kok was intriguing.

Dakota said, "I'm going to Australia. They say the women are two to one. Some guys say they're so happy to have a man, that they'll pay the way."

"Where are you going, Benji?" I asked.

"I don't know yet. I haven't decided," he said.

New Jersey said, "The reason you're getting your R&R early (rest and recuperation) is because they want everyone here when the shit starts. The dry season will be here soon." New Jersey added. "Hopefully I'll be back in the world before that."

New Jersey was a short timer. He had already started coloring in his naked woman. That's what we did. The woman's body was divided into sixty parts. You'd start coloring in the sections when you had just sixty days left on your tour. The last few days you colored in the parts of a woman that most interested men.

Now, being a short timer was a very anxious time. You were concerned about returning home in a body bag with so little time left. There were horrible stories told about just such situations. The one I remember most was a plane loaded with soldiers returning home that got mortared on the runway. That's the sort of thing we all feared.

"Anyone know what day it is?" Pocket abruptly asked.

No one knew. Every day was the same now. It was probably best. Oh, at first, you kept up, but it was too painful. You'd think its Friday night and wonder what everyone was doing at home.

Of course, we knew the date. You had to do reports and change codes, but there were no Sundays, or Fridays, or Mondays. Just days.

One of the gunnery sergeants stepped into the F.D.C., "The captain wants to see you, Greene," he said.

I walked out with him.

"Captain, you wanted to see me?" I asked.

"We're moving back while the weather is good. The choppers will be here tomorrow morning. We'll be at Camp Evans for a while. Tell your men to get everything ready," he ordered.

"Yes sir."

I went back to F.D.C. and relayed the message.

New Jersey said, "They're going to give us a little break before the missions start."

"Hot meals," Savoy said.

"And cold beer," added Pockets.

I'd been on the Rock for over three months. It was early January. I was looking forward to the break, too. Just to live halfway like a human again.

* * *

"Greene, did you tear up my shower?" the captain asked.

"Yes sir," I said. "But I didn't know it was your shower captain. It wasn't personal, sir. I like you." And I did. I continued, "I was running down the narrow path behind the hooches to get a cold beer, and I hit the water spigot with my leg. I just reached down and twisted it off, sir."

He gave me a little look but he didn't say anything else.

Camp Evans was the staging area, battalion head-quarters for the units that served on the front. You had all the amenities, but they were a bit rough. We had cots, electricity and there weren't many rats. The hooches had tin roofs covered with sandbags. From the dirt floor you had sandbags and then screen. The mess hall looked the same as our quarters, just a bigger hooch. I think we even had cold milk.

We set up our guns. Our F.D.C. was in a more secure bunker. It was not a tin roofed structure.

The lieutenant with the master's degree in psychology had returned as our F.D.C. officer. The gung-ho lieuten-ant was off in a field hospital with a bad case of jungle rot in his groin area.

But all in all, everyone seemed in good spirits. Savoy, Benji, Dakota, Pockets and me were up for R&R. They had scheduled our leaves so we'd not be all gone at the same time.

I was on my way to the communications center to call home. I had my date for R&R and was calling my wife to get it all set up. You had to go through ham radio operators who made contact with the phone companies. I'd been told how it worked.

Suddenly, a voice got my attention.

"Soldier, come back here." He was talking to me. It was a sergeant major and his colonel. The sergeant major addressed me, "You got your head in your ass or what, Mr.? You walked by a colonel and did not salute."

It was a full bird colonel and his sergeant I'd run into.

"What's your name. What unit are you in?" the colonel asked.

I told him my unit, and continued, "No disrespect intended sir. I was headed to make a phone call home. I wasn't thinking, sir. I've been in the field for over three months. You know you don't salute in the field, sir," I said.

He knew it. No officer wanted to draw attention to himself in the field.

They chewed on me a good while but seemed satisfied in the end. This was a different place, I thought, and went on and made my phone call.

The next day we had a mission to fire on a village. We never fired on a village before. All artillery batteries that were in range were involved. I can say it was done properly. They had dropped leaflets and used a loudspeaker system to warn the natives. All they had to do was come out with the proper identification. If they weren't V.C. or N.V.A., or had a card, no one was harmed.

Duty on camp Evans was pretty routine. We'd fire defensive targets for the infantry patrols before they bedded down, and landing zone targets. All the batteries in the area would fire on an L.Z. before the infantry landed. Sometimes they also used gunships. But as I've said, duty on Evans was mostly uneventful. We pitched baseball and played football. There were no all-Americans here, but we had fun. Yet, we all knew this wouldn't last much longer. There were rumors of an offensive coming.

Some men from the guns came into F.D.C one day carrying a bunch of boxes of lurp rations. I don't exactly remember what LURP stood for, but they were used for long-range-reconnaissance patrols. They were the best food in the field. Our men had broken into a warehouse and stolen them. It was dehydrated food. All you did was add hot water and you had spaghetti, chili, or stew – stuff like that.

The men said they had been shot at, probably over their heads and had to hide them in a ditch. After things cooled off, they went back and got them. We were awful thankful and let them know it. There were enough lurps for everyman for nearly three months. We didn't know where we were going, but at least we were going to have the best food.

Our old lieutenant with the jungle rot had returned. They had cut him to the bone in several places. He could have gone home but he came back.

We had a couple of new men in F.D.C. They were fine young men. You could tell they were from good families. They had gone through artillery school and were quick learners. I assigned them Benji's shift. I would say we were a tough 45 men.

I asked New Jersey to get the F.D.C. together to distribute the lurps. They all knew they were getting the best field rations for a reason. We figured the captain even had a part in it. We handed out the lurps.

New Jersey said, "You guys better know, something big is coming down. I'm real sorry I won't be here for it."

"What's happening?" Savoy asked.

New Jersey replied, "All I can get out of them is they're going to open it up to the Laotian border. Maybe the ARVN's going in to cut their supply lines. I think they're already moving," he said.

"It's been busy around here," Dakota added.

"Where we goin'?" asked Pockets.

"God damn it man, they're going to open up Khe San, the whole area, all the way into Laos," New Jersey answered.

Benji said, "I thought it was occupied."

"Yeah, it's occupied all right," New Jersey answered. "But we haven't been there since TET."

Hell, I didn't know either, that was nearly three years ago. A stupid ass in the field didn't know anything.

That I knew.

New Jersey said, "This is supposed to be a surprise attack, but I guess I won't be here for the surprise, you know, being the short-timer I am."

It was a Sunday. I was on duty, but nothing was happening. I could hear the men cheering and yelling outside. The whole battalion was gathered. They were having boxing matches and drinking cold beer, while the cook's grilled steaks.

I stepped out of the F.D.C. bunker to get a cold beer.

The other lieutenant, the officer on the guns, had just hit the mess sergeant a good one in the stomach. The cook was mad and giving him hell.

The captain spotted me, "Get over here, Greene. You're going to fight him."

"Sir, I'm on duty."

"You're not doing anything. You are going to fight him," he ordered, pointing to a man.

I knew the man, a cowboy. He was in supply. I was told he was an all -state rodeo star in high school, back in Wyoming.

Before they told me, I'd never heard of rodeo at the high school level.

He was about 5' 9" and the same weight as me – just shorter and stockier. I didn't look forward to providing the entertainment that Sunday afternoon, but there was no way out of it.

We went at it!

He was powerful and came at me hard. There was no science to him. He was just a bull. We pounded each other for several minutes.

Then the captain yelled, "End of round one."

"Come here Greene," the captain said. He began to coach me, "You can take him Greene. You're bigger than him. You can get him. Go get him!"

I wasn't bigger than him. The cowboy charged at me again. We exchanged blows for some time. Then he caught me with a good one and I went down. It kind of made me mad.

The crowd had taken sides, you know. The captain called me over again for some instructions.

He hadn't hurt me; I just walked into a good one. I knew what I had to do. I was quicker and had better skills. I put 'em to work. He bullied his way as far as he was going to with me. I started to dance around him real good. I got my jab going. I rocked him a couple of times. I think I was getting the best of him and the crowd knew it.

Finally, we broke. I think we both had had enough. I know I was ready for some beer and steak.

* * *

The first thing I noticed when I jumped out of the helicopter were the rolls of body bags. More than I'd ever seen. I thought about the song, <u>The Green Green Grass Of</u>

<u>Home</u>. That song had an effect on me. It still does. They're going to the green, green grass of home in body bags.

I had just returned to Camp Evans from Hawaii. It was early February. After I checked in I headed for F.D.C. I saw all the guys. We talked about R&R's for a while. Then New Jersey said, "Things are hot around here Greene."

"What's going on?" I asked.

New Jersey answered, "The ARVN's are into Laos to cut enemy supply lines. The word is the whole God damn N.V.A. Army is on their way, or already there. You'll be moving soon."

New Jersey would be leaving in a couple of days. He'd be back in the world soon.

Several days had passed. The captain wanted to see me. "Greene, we're going to move tomorrow morning to a place called Mai Loc. We'll be replacing the ARVN's that were there. We're moving by truck. There's a Montagnard village there. Get your men and equipment ready."

"Yes sir," I said, and went about it.

I saw Pockets. "Pockets, we are going to move. Will you get everybody together?" I asked.

After the men were assembled, I told them of the move.

Benji asked, "We're moving by truck?"

"That's right," I answered.

"We are an air assault unit and we are moving by truck?" asked Dakota disappointedly." Some of the other

217

men seemed just as disappointed. It kind of surprised me. Looking back on it now, I see where the men were coming from. We'd be sitting ducks on the trucks.

The next morning, we were headed north on Highway 1 along the coast, then west on a dirt road. It was a gorgeous day. As we approached Mai Loc, I could see villagers lined up on both sides of the road. Some were waving little American flags, but most seemed to be vendors. Some of them were selling those sandals made of old tires, others were selling cokes and even liquor. One old man was peddling these miniature bows and arrows.

The village was straight out of National Geographic. Thatch roofed structures that sat on a hill above a small river. The Montagnards were not Vietnamese. Their different culture was readily evident. I could see French blood in many. Some were strikingly tall. Just on the other side of the village was the compound. The base had your standard perimeter – wire and all. The quarters were hooches like on Camp Evans. They assigned us our sleeping quarters. When we entered the hooch, there were several rats scurrying around. With rats running about in the middle of the day, we knew this place was really infested.

We were setting up the guns. It was hectic. We hadn't even made contact with battalion when we got our first fire mission. We stopped everything and computed the mission. We were unable to reach battalion for the check data. I explained all this over the radio to the colonel conducting the operation.

His order was to fire. We fired.

He was back on the horn immediately, "This is Red Dog 69er. You fired out," the colonel said.

I told him, "You know the regulations. We told you we hadn't even made contact with our battalion, and had no check data."

Well, here come the captain, "What the hell was that all about?" he asked.

I apprised him of the situation. He didn't say a word. He just left as quickly as he had come in. We didn't hear any more about it. It was just good we hadn't hurt anyone.

I was off-duty. I saw Pockets coming down a path, his arms full with wood and chicken wire.

"What are you doing,?" I asked.

"I'm going to build me a rat- proof bed," he said. He'd gone and traded a bunch of C-rations with the natives for the materials, and he went to work making his rat-proof bed. When he had finished, he had chicken wire on three sides, and had taken his mosquito net and stapled it down on the fourth side, except for a little space where he could crawl in and tie it down tight.

That night, rats were crawling all over us. But, wouldn't you know it, the only one that got bit was Pockets. One got inside his rat proof bed and bit him on the end of a finger.

Later that morning, he came to me, "Greene, I gotta' go back to the rear and get me some rabies shots."

I called for a chopper and sent him back.

They didn't give them to him and sent him back to Mai Loc in a couple of days. I guess they didn't think it serious enough. One thing for sure, it proves that old adage, never corner a rat. You have to leave an exit.

We were bathing regularly. We were going down to the river next to the village every couple of days. They'd mine sweep the road to the village every morning and we'd pile up on a mule and ride down to the river. Now, a mule was a four-wheeled flatbed vehicle with one seat and a steering wheel. We used it to haul ammunition on mostly.

When we bathed, all the Montagnards, kids and all, would come down the hill from the village. It was kind of festive. They would want to bathe you just for your bar of soap. I never had them bathe me, but I always gave them my soap anyway.

They were an industrious people. They'd work all day for a dollar. The natives filled sandbags and washed our clothes among other things. One of the men left his wallet in a pair of pants they were washing. There was over a hundred dollars in that wallet and they brought his money back.

I don't believe I've ever met a finer people.

* * *

We were moving west toward the front. Our chopper was the advance party. It included the captain, the chief of guns, a couple of gunnery sergeants and several of their men. You had to split up your officers and sergeants, to make sure they all didn't go down on one chopper.

Some of the men on our chopper were taking pictures. Stay alert, I thought. But I didn't say anything. It didn't really matter anyway. If you're going to get shot down, you're going to get shot down.

We were deep in the jungle, headed for Firebase Sarge. Our chopper approached the hill. The landing pad was so little it barely accommodated our Huey. They brought in the rest of the men and dropped the guns. We set up. The hill was so small we couldn't turn all the guns at the same time. The barrels would hit.

It was a mountain. On one side there were sheer cliffs overlooking the valley. Vandergrift and a dirt road they called a highway lay far below. Vandergrift was the staging area for the front.

We were assigned a bunker. It included F.D.C. operations and our sleeping quarters. It was a most depressing place. I didn't know that it hadn't been occupied since the Tet Offensive. I don't think any of the area had been. From, what I gathered, we had been withdrawn from Khe San for over two years.

Our bunker had three rooms. The main room we used for operations. A second room had two bunks. I took one and gave Pockets the other. Pockets knew the radio. The last room had a low ceiling. You had to stoop. It had one wooden platform for the rest of the men to sleep on.

Outside the bunker, it was about as scenic a place as I ever saw. A river surrounded by green hills ran through the valley.

I had worked the day shift. It was evening. The sun had not set. I fixed a lurp, got a hot beer and found me a seat on top a bunker overlooking the valley. Some of the men joined me. We hadn't finished eating when Vandergrift came under heavy fire from the surrounding mountains. We had fired into those mountains all day long. Our guns hadn't let up yet. There were all types of light armored vehicles surrounding Vandergrift. They opened up!

Dakota said something, but before we could talk, the quad-fifty next to us drowned him out. A quad-fifty is four synchronized, 50 caliber machine guns mounted on a turret. This guy was really working it. It's a bad machine! The firing continued into the dark, when the tracers added to the show.

Vandergrift got hit every night. We'd sit up there at nights drinking and watching the show when we weren't on duty and firing. We wondered why the enemy didn't turn their guns on us. We decided their priority was Vandergrift and the supply line. Armor, transportation, and choppers were refueled and supplied for the front there. They didn't keep any helicopters there though. They would have been blow up.

It was time to lie down. I took my Coleman lantern into the F.D.C. said my goodbyes and headed for my bunk. I laid down and turned out the lantern.

They came out of the walls, what seemed like hundreds of them. The rats were all over me. I got up and lit the lantern. I put my boots back on and covered my ears with my gear and went to sleep.

The next morning, I saw where the rats had eaten into my mom's care package. I just pinched off a little bit and went on with it. They had eaten half of it. I ate the rest.

The lieutenant, Benji, and Savoy ran the other shift. Occasionally the lieutenant would work with us, he'd gotten over his jungle rot and was on the kind of mission he wanted. Savoy had mostly given up on getting back to the rear. The new men on both shifts were good soldiers. They had adjusted quickly to the adverse conditions. They amazed me.

The major had flown out several times to check on us, and the colonel over the artillery had been there also.

It was in the middle of the day and I was off-duty. An ARVN major accompanied by some of his men had flown onto the hill. He was tall for a Vietnamese. I struck up a conversation with him. I asked him what the situation was with the N.V.A. in Laos? He eluded the question and said he had no problem with the N.V.A., or for that matter, with the Viet Cong.

That was the end of our conversation. I walked over to the captain. "Captain," I said, "See that major over there, he says he has no problem with the N.V.A. or the Viet Cong." There was nothing else said. It was one of those understandings that needed no further comment.

They brought us out a hot meal. There was a 155 battery on the hill next to us. We had to scurry down one side of the hill between us to get fed. As I remember, we had roast beef, gravy, mashed potatoes and some green beans. The mashed potatoes were stuffed into 155 canisters. That was pretty ingenious, I thought, using empty shell casings. One of the cooks was using his dirty hands to serve the potatoes. Some of the men were a little finicky over it and wouldn't eat the potatoes. I appreciated it myself. I thought these men risked their lives to bring us a hot meal. You could get shot down around here real quick.

A couple of nights later, I heard Pockets screaming. It woke me up. I really couldn't see him, but I knew he was jumping around. I lit the lantern. There was blood on the floor and he was hopping around, holding his foot.

"God damn rat got me," he said.

He was bleeding a good bit. I helped him hobble from our quarters to the F.D.C.

"What the hell happened?" Benji asked.

"Pockets been bit again," I answered.

The commotion had woken up the rest of the men not on-duty. We examined him. The rat had bitten him between his big toe and the next one. It took out a fleshy piece of meat as big as my thumbnail.

We doctored him up as best we could. There was no more sleep that night. It was close to morning anyway.

Dakota asked me, "Why did he have his boots off?"

"I don't know," I said.

As soon as it was daylight, we called the battalion and requested a chopper for Pockets. He might really need rabies shots this time, I told them. I also requested some rat poison – a lot of it! They sent three large cans of poison and took Pockets back. They kept him this time for the shots.

That day, anytime we had a break from firing, I spread that poison. I used all three cans.

After a couple of days, the captain came to me, "Greene, you did a good job on the rats. Now get rid of the smell." Honestly, I hadn't paid much attention, but it must have been getting to some of the men.

I made a token response when I got off-duty. I got a five-gallon can of gasoline and a stick. I went around prying up sandbags with a stick. Where there are rats, there's snakes, you know. I gassed 'em and burned 'em. It seemed to satisfy most everyone.

* * *

Our lead chopper was flying so low over the jungle to avoid fire, that at times we topped the trees. We had been assigned to an armored division on the Laotian border. We approached the L.Z. under red smoke, which meant it was hot. However, we were taking no fire. The captain and the other men jumped out. As I struggled with the computer, the door gunner panicked and kicked me out of the chopper, throwing my gear on top of me and dumping the computer, it rolled down into a bomb crater and broke apart.

I talked to the captain about it. He said he'd report it, but I thought if I see that door gunner again, I'd take care of it myself.

The following wave of choppers was causing such a dust storm that I had to drop into a bomb crater to ready the charts and maps for firing. When I got out of that hole and looked around, it looked like the moon. We were on a small plain surrounded by mountainous jungle. But there wasn't a blade of grass to be seen.

We had to dig in and cover up, especially the ammo. It was a physical chore. We filled the wooden boxes of our ammo cases in with dirt and used them for frames. For the roofs, we used a half of those large galvanized culverts that can be bolted together for drainage. We topped it with three layers of sandbags.

We were missing half of our men. They hadn't showed up. We had our guns, equipment and ammo, but a little less than half our men. We figured they'd show up soon. When they did, all they would have to do is secure their own hole.

The captain, chief of guns and I had walked out a ways from our position and were discussing our situation. A mortar barrage began to fall across the plains in front of us. They seemed pretty close to me, maybe only one or two adjustments away. I mean the next rounds could be on top of you.

The captain said, "Do you think those rounds are intended for us?"

Well, that set me off. I jumped six feet backwards and landed in a hole. I shot up peering over the hole with my weapon ready. They hadn't moved. I felt so stupid. I crawled out of the hole, went immediately and stood beside them. I don't think they even noticed. If they did, they didn't say anything. I didn't know this was not their first tour.

We fired all day, but something was wrong. Our forward observers were having major problems spotting and adjusting our rounds. We even fired on an enemy artillery position, but it too was inaccurate. We tried everything. We even talked about sending a small party out as forward observers to try and adjust our fire. Finally, command told us just not to fire any precision missions, just blanket rounds.

We had been firing all day when the radio crackled with the voice of an N.V.A. He was close and had better diction than this southern boy. Maybe he was a Harvard man or something. He told me, "Tonight G.I. Joe, I'm going to slit your throat!"

I said. "You dirty gook motherfucker, I'll cut your dick off and make you eat it. I'll meet you on the plains right now, you son of a bitch."

Well, here come a colonel over the radio advising me of my improper radio protocol or something like that. I acknowledged. But I didn't hear from Mr. Harvard anymore.

Except for an occasional armored vehicle passing by our position, we were alone. We were notified that the rest of our men had gotten lost and had returned to Camp Evans and would be here in the morning.

Night was coming and things didn't look good. We were surrounded by the enemy, with only twenty men, one machine gun, no perimeter defense and we could only operate two of our artillery pieces. Even the captain was nervous. He'd come in the F.D.C. several times to assess our situation and ask for support.

Finally, at dusk, two small armored vehicles showed up to cover our perimeter. I don't remember what you called them, but they had two small guns on them looked like a turtle on big rubber wheels. We let them know we were glad to have them.

The F.D.C was operating out of one of those P.X. boxes they used to bring out merchandise to the field. It was bullet riddled, with the 101st insignia and a skull and cross bones painted on it. It was a death trap for sure. I bet, from the mountains, you could see light escaping from the bullet holes for miles.

I worked the night shift. I was working with Benji's new men. Pockets was still in the rear, most of my shift were back at Evans and I sure missed New Jersey.

I'd been up for two days and nights. Late that night I got a little punchy. I was dropping some numbers and my computations weren't sharp. The new men understood and carried me. When you've been up like that, it was always worse late into the night. Toward morning, I'd gotten a second wind. The rest of our men arrived in the morning. I could get some sleep now. I talked to my men for a few minutes and headed for my hole to sleep.

I hadn't even fallen asleep when Savoy, who had arrived that morning, came to my hole. He said, apologetically, "Greene, you got to get up. We're moving."

* * *

We moved only a click and a half (1500 meters) to an armored position. They had quite an arsenal there including 155 self-propelled howitzers.

I went to the captain for our quadrants. I said, "Captain, I need our position." He gave it to me. It was the same position we'd just left. That explained everything. They had set us down in the wrong place with the right quadrants. That's why we were shooting out and the rest of the men didn't make it. No wonder we were alone.

We were digging in and covering up again when we weren't firing. Our rounds were now on the money.

There wasn't any perimeter security. No wire, nothing. I guess the armor figured they didn't need it. They could always button up, but we were vulnerable.

Later that day two young lieutenant colonels flew in, seemingly, just to talk. They brought us a case of tuna fish. We talked for some time. They were a pair of fine young men.

They hadn't been gone from our position a couple of minutes when it was reported they'd been downed and killed.

You couldn't look up anytime that there wasn't a chopper being hauled back by a Shinook or crane. I don't know how many choppers went down on this mission, but it had to be substantial.

There were rumors about what all the N.V.A. had up there, including tanks, heat seeking missiles and Migs. We even questioned where we were. But I don't think we were in Laos, just on the border. We fired at N.V.A. positions all day.

Evening came and Dakota, Savoy and I were sitting on some ammo boxes. The talk was we were likely to get hit tonight. Dakota said the armored thought so too.

One of the young men came up to me. He said, "Chief, the captain wants to talk to you before you sleep." I went to see the captain.

"Greene," he said, "before you go to sleep, tell all your men to fire all night long. Set no pattern. Fire a clip, then wait a minute and fire a couple of rounds. Just mix it up. We've got plenty of grenades. Do the same with them."

I went around to all the men, to the F.D.C. and those off duty. A couple of the men were working on their little bunker. When I told them their orders they replied that they would try, but were fixing up their quarters. There was emptiness in their eyes. It scared me.

I snapped at them, "You better be worried about your God damned ass," and I walked away.

I got my sleeping gear, went to the edge of the perimeter and laid down. I figured I was going to die that night. I laid my gun conveniently beside me and went to sleep.

* * *

"Wake up Greene; get up, they want you on duty," Dakota said. I sat up immediately. It was full daylight, and I thought, I'm alive.

"What's going on?" I asked.

"They need you in the F.D.C. They killed several gooks inside our perimeter last night." That's all that was said, all that had to be. Everyone knew they were just probing for the future attack. I was lucky it wasn't last night. They would have slit my throat before I knew what happened.

I headed for operations. Out of the corner of my eye I noticed the gray, dusty bodies of the dead N.V.A. laid out at the edge of our perimeter.

When I got to F.D.C, I poured some water in my helmet and dabbled a little. I hadn't shaved or brushed my teeth in three days. I don't think anyone had. It didn't matter.

I'd slept like a baby, never woke, even with all the firing. As I remember, I felt alert when I stepped into the F.D.C. The captain and the men had been up all night. They were ready for some rest. But they weren't going to get any.

I had just set up and was firing when our colonel flew in – the colonel over artillery. He talked to the captain for some time. When he was gone the captain called us together. He said, "The colonel doesn't think we belong here. He'll have the birds here at 1700 hours (five o'clock) to pick us up if we can fire all our rounds and be policed up."

We fired so many volleys it burned the paint off the barrels and broke three guns.

During a break, I went out to watch. I noticed a major I'd never seen sitting on his gear. He was a man. Looked like a fullback to me. He said stoically, "They'll shoot back." He was talking about the South Vietnamese. I guess we had fired so many rounds, who knows where, that they might. Some of the men seemed not to understand. I did.

We got out of there at five o'clock, like the colonel said. They flew us back to Firebase Sarge. This part is fuzzy. I guess they replaced our downed guns, I can't remember. But I know no sooner than we had gotten settled in, it was reported that our last position had been overrun. There were heavy casualties. It was at seven o'clock, just two hours after we had left.

We weren't at Sarge long, but it was too long.

The major came over the radio, "POP YELLOW SMOKE," he requested "Our chopper's out of control."

They needed to know the wind.

I called it down to the guns. The captain and the men were waiting for him.

It wasn't but a few minutes later the captain came into the F.D.C. He was beside himself. "The major's been killed," he said. "The chopper went down in the wire. He got out, but went to get the pilot that was penned. The rotor turned and cut off the top of his head. Then the chopper flipped over on him. Get battalion on the private radio."

The captain left as quick as he had come. The men jumped up to follow but then realized. I told them to go on, I'd take care of it. I didn't want to see the major like that anyway. He was a good man, family and all.

We seldom used the secret radio. I got them up and said the captain needs to talk to you. They were insistent that I tell them, what for. I told them several times the captain needs to talk to you. Finally, I called down to the guns for the captain. He came immediately. Headquarters questioned his understanding of the situation. He was frank and disturbed in his detail. Him and the major were close.

We left Firebase Sarge at five in the afternoon the next day headed back to Mai Loc, The Montagnard village, where this adventure began. As before, Sarge underwent a massive ground attack, with heavy casualties, two hours later – at seven o'clock. We talked about it, but not much.

Once we got settled in to Mai Loc, someone turned on the radio. The NCAA basketball tournament was on, maybe the final eight. Anyway, Western Kentucky University beat the University of Kentucky by 30 points. Basketball is big in Kentucky and that was a historical game. That's how I remember the time, March of 1971.

We didn't stay long at My Loc. The choppers soon brought us back to our home base, Camp Evans. The whole battalion was out for us. It was a real home coming, steaks and cold beer.

* * *

It was Easter Sunday. We were moving. We'd partied several days with no duty and were now headed for Fire Base

Helen. Helen, like Rakkasan, was one of those mountain top outposts. They all looked pretty much the same.

We got settled in. We were on eight-hour shifts, as opposed to the twelve-hour stints. It seemed to keep us fresher. The captain had given us the okay.

We had just finished our shift. I got me a beer and walked the perimeter. There was no firing. It was strangely still. Everyone was asleep, except for the F.D.C. Even the infantry on watch slept. It kind of concerned me.

I got me another beer and sat down on a bunker. The night was light, but misty. You could see the mountainous jungle that surrounded us. I thought no one's on guard, but they probably wouldn't attack on a night like this.

I'd been in Nam nearly eight months. It wouldn't be long until I'd be a short-timer. I got to thinking about what I was going to do when I got home. Maybe law school. I'd graduated with a solid average with less than the proper effort. Well, my first two years, I was a little more attentive to the required classes. I had to be, but later, when in my field, I got real laxed.

The first two years, a good friend and me hitchhiked the 150 miles to school. We were real good at it. We were suit-casers. That's what they called those who went home every weekend. That was a real experience, but that's a story of its own. Our junior and senior year, we drove.

I had a child born to me during this time. She was beautiful. But it taxed my finances and I had to drop out of college. All the guys said you'll never be back, Greene. I let them know I'd be back.

I went back to construction, on a Firestone plant in Bowling Green. My stepfather and I shared a trailer. It was kind of depressing. I was off for the winter semester and through the summer. I made a small fortune and spent it at the Merry-Go-Around (a go-go bar), and any other places that had women and whiskey. I went back to college that fall with a 63 Falcon, a car payment and five hundred dollars They gave me a job as a dorm counselor and I worked at a neighborhood pizza joint on the weekends. I even worked construction during Christmas and spring breaks. It was enough.

I had trouble adjusting back to college. I wouldn't have kept my B average if it weren't for some early high grades. The last year and a half, I can't remember but buying only one book. But I took good notes. Before the test, I'd go through them a couple of times, then make a short outline. I wasn't that smart, I just had a system.

We had one professor with a serious ego problem. He taught the *New South*, and said his future book would revise it. There were about sixty students in the class. When the first test was passed out, there were two B's and a B minus. I had the B minus. There were a few C's and D's, but mostly F's. When the professor handed me my test, he gave me a look of disbelief.

Outside, after the next class meeting, a major in the army, the head of ROTC, wanted to know how I had done it. He said, "I read all the books several times, went to West Point and never failed anything in my life."

I said, "I don't even have a book."

"I don't believe it," he replied.

The other guys backed me up quick.

I told the major that his guy was an egotistical son of a bitch. I just take down everything he says and give it back to him.

The one book I had to buy was in Sociological Theory. The Professor was the head of the department. You had to take his class and have his blessing before you got your major. The first thing he told the class was that half of us would fail, and he meant it. There were some students taking the class for the third time. They had to have it to graduate.

I bought a used book, and borrowed when I needed them, a pair of eyeglasses. My eyes had gotten bad.

One day, the professor asked the class what indigenous meant? I popped out, "Native to, sir."

He said, "I'm impressed."

Hell! What luck! I had run into that word just a couple of days before. I aced the class.

I got drafted right before my last semester. I had to take the physical and when they got to the eye exam, the sergeant said, "Where's your glasses?"

"I don't have any glasses," I answered.

He came back, "Lie to me again, and we'll take you in today!"

I told him again, "I don't have any."

"We'll get you some," he said sarcastically.

The reason I got drafted was I fell behind a semester when I had to go to work. They drafted you if you didn't keep up.

I had one semester left and was determined not to go until I finished school. I got an appointment with the draft board to appeal. I told the lady that I had a solid B average and had never failed any course. I explained how I had to work my way through college and had to drop out a semester.

I said, "I'm not trying to get out of Vietnam, I'm just trying to get an education." I continued, "I'm not coming. You'll have to send the M.P.'s after me. But if you let me finish my student teaching, I'm yours."

I got my appeal.

That summer, when I was working good, I got some glasses. I thought I'd beat the army to it.

I was out in Fairdale in the late summer, and saw Mr. Hardin, my old principal.

Mr. Hardin said, "Greene, I see you are on the student teaching list. You're going to do it at Fairdale," he added.

"Oh, no sir, Mr. Hardin, that's taboo. They said no one in the history of the school had ever done their student teaching at the school they graduated from. They said, 'Don't even ask.'"

Well, a week later, I was assigned to Fairdale. What I didn't know was Mr. Hardin was a good friend with my college president. This was good news. I didn't know how I could afford living expenses somewhere else. I had a 3.9 my last semester. I think the glasses helped in my class work. I graduated in January, but never made it to graduation. Uncle Sam got me.

* * *

"Wake up Greene! Contact fire mission!" I was asleep on the ground right outside of the F.D.C. bunker. I allowed one man on duty, when quiet, to sleep at night, and it was my turn when Pockets woke me.

It was one of those defensive targets with data already computed. We had rounds out in eleven seconds with fourteen confirmed kills – that's as I remember it. The next day, the captain told us he had gotten word that the infantry owed us a steak dinner.

It was the dry season in the highlands. It was really quite pleasant. We were above the heat and mosquitoes. One day it came up a big rain. I can't remember who started it, but the whole bunch of us ended up naked in the rain. It was the best shower we'd had in over a month. We had our bar of soap and were enjoying it like children.

I believe I've seen some people have less fun at an amusement park.

The cooks would come out on some Sundays and cook us up steaks. It helped morale. The mess sergeant, the one the lieutenant hit in the stomach during the fights that Sunday on Camp Evans, was an old lifer. One of those Sundays, he came to me and really surprised me. He said, "Greene, when you first came here we all thought you was a real fuck-up. But the major always said you were the man."

"What the hell you talking about?" I asked.

"You know, I'm talking about you smoking dope when you first got here," he answered. He had to be talking about when I smoked with those two guys the first time I came back to Camp Evans from the field.

I said, "That was the first time I ever smoked dope in my life."

"Don't lie to me, Greene," he demanded.

"Now, why in the hell would I lie to you? Besides, I didn't even get anything out of it. I'd rather have a beer." We didn't say any more about it. But, later, when I had time to think about it all, it became clear. They set me up. I was already running the guns on my shift, and they were checking me out. That also explains the pothead-acting guy that showed up on Rakkassan right after the incident. He was assigned to my bunker and acted like a doper, burning incense and all. At the time I couldn't figure out why he didn't seem to have any duties. I couldn't smoke dope and run the guns.

* * *

I was crossing the hill when the captain caught me, "Greene, there's a special allocation to E-6 for you if you'll extend for another six months."

I didn't ask, just assumed, he meant duty in Nam. "Captain," I said, "I'm going home."

He seemed disappointed and a few days later he came to me again, "I think I can get you a battlefield commission. If you were here my first tour, you'd already have one. But with the war winding down they're already starting to rift officers. However, if you'd sign up for another year, I think I could swing it."

I let him know I was honored, but not interested. I just wanted to go home.

Pockets was sitting on a bunker coloring in his naked woman. He was a short-timer now. I asked, "Pockets, what are you going to do when you get home?"

"I don't even want to talk about it. You know how nervous you get in the end. When I get home, then I'll think about it."

He was right. Our worst fear was to take a hit at the end of our tour.

It was June, I'd been in Nam for some ten months. The lieutenant, Pockets, Savoy, and even Benji would beat me home, or so I thought.

We'd fired all night. There was a lot of enemy movement. I was tired. When our duty was over, I went straight to my bunker and laid down. Benji's shift continued the heavy fire, and Shinooks were bringing in sorties of ammunition, stirring up a dust storm. I thought, I'm going home today. Maybe I thought it other days. Whatever, before I'd fallen to sleep, Dakota came to my bunker. He said, "Get everything together. They're sending a chopper for you."

I knew what that meant. I was going home. What I didn't know, was why? By the time I got my gear together, my chopper was on the pad. The captain and some of the other men had gathered, I guessed, to send me off.

The captain said, "Your grandfather has died. Your sister contacted the Red Cross. Don't go Greene. Don't go."

"I've got to captain. My grandfather raised me. He was my legal guardian."

The captain made some reference to a close relative who had recently died and that he had stayed.

I told him, "Sir, if I don't go home for his funeral, I'd never be able to face my family again. I'll be back captain."

"No you won't Greene," he informed me. You see, I didn't know it at the time, but if you had less than sixty days left of your tour, they didn't send you back.

It was the last time I ever saw any of them.

I got back to Camp Evans and processed out. They had a Huey warming up on the pad to take me to Phu Bai. From there I would fly by prop to Cam Ran Bay, and then an R&R flight to Hawaii. I could catch a military flight from there, home.

I was headed for the chopper when the new C.O. stopped me. He had replaced the major recently and I really didn't know him. He said with an attitude, "You're not going anywhere looking like that! You're an embarrassment to the 101st. The chopper will wait. Go get that haircut, they're waiting on you."

He enraged me, but I didn't say anything. I knew one thing though, he wasn't like the major. I thought that he was a good candidate for fragging, but went on.

When I reached Hawaii, I couldn't get a military flight soon enough to make the funeral. I bought a ticket on a commercial flight and was on my way. I was still in jungle fatigues. I cleaned up the best I could and put on a clean set. But I think it was a couple of weeks since I'd even had a field shower. I must have been offensive.

I arrived at O'Hara with the sweats, a hangover and some strange feelings. I was home, Pap was dead, but I was alive.

My battalion, if tragedy a criterion, was legendary. Yet the men of Bravo Battery except for the major, had walked through the eye of war untouched.

Some thirty years later, I sometimes wonder ... why us ... why me?

Maybe there is purpose, or maybe, nothing at all.

For me, the war was like that Psalm I once learned in Sunday school. You know, the one with the verse, "Yea though I walk."

Big Dude Plays A Round Of Golf

* * *

Gary H. Baker

IT WAS LATE in the season and the chances of running into someone else to play eighteen holes with were slim to none. Pine Ridge Golf Course on a weekday, this time of year, drew a very low turnout. Maybe three or four groups all day long – a couple of threesomes and a couple of four-somes; also, there would be a small handful of hard core old men who preferred playing by themselves. Each of them had their own reason. Many times, the reason was that they knew their slower pace irritated the young players.

Seventy-year-old Carney McCubbin's reason was partly that, but also Carney knew that his penchant for building any casual, recreational golf outing into (in his mind) a dramatic, world class, competitive battle to the end ... well, his constant attempts to do just that, not only irritated those he might play with, it drove some of them to avoid playing a round of golf with him all together.

None of that ever registered in Carney's brain: When he'd say, "I got twenty bucks that says you can't reach that green with a six iron," because everybody knew a four or a five iron would be the correct club. When he'd say on the tee of a short par three, "Who's in on closest to the pin? Everybody but the closest does fifty push-ups." On and on it went. One day he found himself behind a tall tree on the second shot to a green that was one hundred and thirty-five yards away. A young stud he was playing with whose ball ended up three feet away from his own ball wasn't surprised when Carney challenged him with, "I got ten bucks says you can't put your wedge over this tree anywhere close to the green." The young golfer had no choice. Who would let an old gray- beard who never broke a hundred taunt him, dare him, design such a foolish challenge … who would let the old fart get away with it? Certainly not him. He lined the shot up, stepped up to the ball, and with a powerful, athletic sweep of his shoulders, he rammed the clubhead of his wedge down hard on the ball. It was a great shot, a beautiful shot; it couldn't have been any better, but it didn't even clear the top of the tree.

Today, though, Carney wasn't thinking about who might be over at Pine Ridge, who might be willing to play eighteen holes with him. It was one of those days that just being there, being on the golf course, playing the game he loved, was enough. He threw his clubs in the back of his truck and headed out over the back-country roads to Pine Ridge. As he drove he thought about why today was going to be a special day. He just knew it. How could it not be? It was Early November in south-central Missouri. There was still dazzling color in the trees. Life was abundant all around. The cool mountain streams in the Ozarks trickled and flowed with a beauty even a heathen would appreciate.

But mostly it was his ongoing dreams of recent months. The dreams had been providing him with a promise of something big about to happen. Strange and ghostly images of golfers had been invading his slumber. There was a warm glow to it all. Two, three, four golfers sometimes, sometimes many more, all in a spiritual golf nirvana, walking the fairways, taking their shots, smiling, effortlessly playing the game. They were all hitting great shots with an ease, a grace which was other-worldly. Carney knew he himself was a part of the dreams. He couldn't identify which of the many golfers he was, but there was no mistaking it – he was in the mix. Somehow he was a part of the nightly golfing nirvana. He wasn't just viewing it on a cold screen.

He pulled into the Pine Ridge gravel parking lot and judging by the seven or eight cars and trucks, he knew there was probably not going to be anyone to match up with. Today he would be playing as a single, not a twosome, threesome, or foursome. Because of that, he chose not to rent a motorized golf cart, but instead, he chose to pull his bag around on the two -wheeled hand cart his bag was already mounted on. Just another reason why he really didn't mind playing by himself. All of the young golfers preferred the motor carts because it sped up play. Carney couldn't help but thinking they were really missing the essence of the game – walking the course's five miles. Well, not him, not today! He was ready to enjoy eighteen holes of golf the traditional way – the way it was supposed to be played – walking it.

Carney went inside the clubhouse and paid his green fee, picked up a score card and a pencil and headed out the door towards the number 1 tee.

After recording a bogey on both numbers 1 and 2, he hesitated on the third tee. Before bending down to tee-up his golf ball, he removed the scorecard from his hip pocket and looked it over closely. *Hah! Starting out with two bogies. Not bad. Today just might be the day I break a hundred, for, let's see, what would it be? Uh … for only the second time this year! I knew something was in the cards today! I just knew it!*

He stood there on the tee, not quite prepared to tee his ball up and then address it, and then make the tee shot. No, he couldn't do it yet. He was still looking at the score card. He had his name printed under the player's name column, but after that there were no other names, none. He was playing alone. Well, of course he was, but he didn't like it, especially on this day of all days. Today was going to be something special. He knew it! Yet there was no other name on his score card, just his. Slowly he brought the pencil up to the card and before he even knew it he had penciled in another name – GOD.

Hmmmmmmmm, he thought. *Not a bad golf partner.* But how do you play a round of golf with GOD? Quickly he devised a scoring system that would accommodate his playing partner's particular needs. First, he would have to make the assumption that GOD would easily ace every hole if HE was playing at HIS best, and so, what was the point? Where was the competition? The final score would be GOD 16 (there were only 16 holes remaining), Carney 100 (or hopefully a little lower). Would GOD enjoy such a match? Carney was sure HE wouldn't, so, he made a proposal to GOD: "HEAVENLY FATHER, thank YOU for playing a round with me today. I know YOU are very busy and I just want to let YOU know how much I appreciate YOU taking the time to join me today here at Pine Ridge. DEAR FATHER, it has occurred to me that there won't be much of a challenge in the match for YOU. We all know YOU could easily defeat me, even playing left handed with both eyes closed. So … in order to, uh, let's say, uh … in order to even things up a bit, I think YOU'LL need to give me, uh, let's say … a four stroke a hole handicap. Let's see … four times sixteen remaining holes, plus … let's say YOU bogied the first

two holes, and, uh … assuming YOU ace the next sixteen holes, uh … if my math is correct … uh, that would
give YOU a final score of 89. Whaddaya' say FATHER?
Let me tell YA, I think that's very generous of me. Why,
I'd have to play the best round of my life to beat an 89.
Whaddaya' say, BIG DUDE, oops … I mean, whaddaya
say HOLY FATHER?"

"YOU will? Great! Let's get this thing moving along.
YOU'RE up."

Carney stepped aside to afford GOD the honor to
take the first tee-shot from the number 3 tee. When
Carney noticed a healthy gust of wind rattle a few blades
of grass somewhere just inside the tee marker, he said,
"Nice shot, YOUR EMMINENCE," but realizing he
(Carney) wasn't catholic, he wanted to retract it and sput-
tered, "Uh, look FATHER … uh, GOD …". He stopped
blabbering and finally, after a lengthy silence, he said,
"I just don't know what to call YOU. Most of the guys I
play with, I usually call them "Big Dude", you know, or
something stupid like that." He realized his mistake immediately. "Uh, I don't mean to say YOU are stupid or
anything." *Oh great. I've done it now.* The more he talked,
the more trouble he seemed to get in. But Carney knew
that was his nature. In fact, it was probably why he liked
to challenge everyone, about everything, all the time. He
loved to compete. Yes, that was the obvious truth. But it
was more than that. He always liked to push situations

to the limit – see how far he could go before something exploded. That was who he was.

"Well, here's the thing GOD. I think, if it's all right with YOU, I'll call YOU "BIG DUDE" today. Would YOU be cool with it? Look, the way I see it is … well, it would be a sign of respect. Really. You know, because that's what I call just about everybody on the golf course, and, you see, if I called YOU something pretentious or haughty, you know, like HOLY FATHER, or YOUR LORDSHIP, or, I don't know, … well I think that YOU would think I'd be treating YOU special, you know, different from all the other golfers, and who'd want to be treated like that? You know, after that first shot off the number 1 tee, we (us golfers) lose our protective wrap. Once a round gets started, we are all the same. We're balanced out – equals. Something happens out here that strips away any phony façade, any disguise we might be wearing. And now that YOU and me are playing together, it would just seem lame that I would treat YOU any different from any other golfer. It's not that I don't respect YOU and don't love YOU, no, it's just the opposite."

Carney realized he was jabbering on and on, *again*, blabbering on and on, so he did something he rarely did. He clamped his mouth shut and tee'd his ball up. He actually cut off the prattle. He hit a weak, leaking slice, barely a hundred and forty yards.

Carney and BIG DUDE walked off the tee in pursuit of their golf balls – BIG DUDE'S in the bottom of the cup, and Carney's in the deep rough with a down-hill lie, way over there on the right. Carney had been quiet for at least a couple of minutes by now, but he couldn't stand it any longer, "BIG DUDE, look at that lie. Tell YA what. That's gonna' cost YOU another stroke on my handicap."

BIG DUDE didn't say anything.

Scoreless Tie

* * *

Jim Harstad

ARGUABLY THE MOST beautiful beachfront acreage on Oahu is Kahuku's emerald nine-hole on an August Sunday morning. Here I am under a clear blue sky, one-fifth of a hastily cobbled-together fivesome: me, a New York Jew, a tourist from Atlanta, a local Filipino, and a French expatriate. "Five complete strangers?" I ask myself. "What've I got to lose?"

The local guy and the expat take left-handed practice swings. The Georgian torches a fat black cigar with a wooden match. The New Yorker finishes off a peanut butter and banana sandwich. "Energy," he says and drops his tee shot dead in front of the green. Inches in front.

They play the first two holes close to even. I'm only a little behind. When I shank my third-hole tee shot, the expat offers, "You looked op."

"I do that sometimes," I say.

The Georgian aims his iPhone at the rocky peninsula you can see from the fourth hole tee and clicks.

"Nice place for a house," the New Yorker says.

"You get one helicopter?" the local guy asks.

The expat sinks a forty-foot putt on the par four fifth hole for eagle, fist bumps all around.

Anyone notice I birdied that hole?" the Georgian asks.

"Did you?"

"Yay-ya"

More fist bumps.

I double-bogey that same fifth hole, flub the sixth so bad I don't even putt out, then triple-bogey the seventh. But somehow on the par four eighth I loft a monster drive, and a monster second shot, landing twenty yards past the green.

"Steroids," the Georgian says.

"Strong tail winds," I say and proceed to carve out my second triple-bogey in a row.

On the ninth hole the local guy drives straight up the middle of the fairway. Again. "Straight up the middle," I say. "Again."

"Lucky," the local guy says.

"Not luck w'en it 'appen ever' time," the expat says.

"More lucky yet," the local guy says.

I crush by far the longest tee shot of any of us on the par-five ninth, then finesse my way to an astounding quadruple bogey. It's over. The Georgian fires up another black stogie and we all shake hands.

"Anybody keep score?" The New Yorker asks.

"Hah!" I reply. "Didn't wanna embarrass you guys."

"Broke my pencil," the Georgian says.

"Los' mines," the local guy says.

"I am Franch." The expat smiles at me. "Mebbe you 'ear we do not gofe?"

A Drive One Sunday

* * *

Jim Harstad

IT EMBARRASSES HIM to hear the words crooning under his breath, oozing unwilled from his own mouth: "I'll ho-old you in my heart, 'til I can ho-old you in my arms." Who sang them? Ernest Tubb? Cowboy Copas? He can't remember now, but he could once have told you on the spot, via his own spirited approximation of the whole song as done by whoever'd done it, complete with nasal riffs and twangs. "T" Texas Tyler? Eddie Arnold? Corny cowboy stuff he loved as a little kid. Doesn't even know what made him think of it.

Sure he does.

He realizes his unspoken apology for outgrown musical tastes is aimed at the framed, softly tinted photograph that dominates the top of his dresser, indeed, his whole room. Those playfully impertinent brown eyes, that over-careful smile over over-perfect teeth. Lips. Heart. Arms. It makes sense, really, but would she understand? Could she? Why risk it? Why not

It's bright outside, the sun already too strong for unshaded comfort. Whitey's in his chair near the window, reading the Sunday Post-Intelligencer. Absorbing it, really, as he does every weekend, as he does the Sun every weekday, top to bottom, front to back.

"Any news?"

"The usual," Whitey replies.

"And the unusual?"

"Now and then. Keeps me coming back for more." He sports a fresh haircut, full blond flattop, white sidewall. Crisp.

"Uh, were you and, uh, Mom going anywhere?"

"Today?"

"Yee-ah."

"The car?"

"Ee-up," nervously, hardly perceptibly, rocking his feet on the woven grass living room rug.

"How long?" Whitey holds his safety-shielded shipyard reading glasses in his right hand.

"Mm-couple hours. Maybe."

"Three o'clock?"

"Sure! No later than. Sooner, probly."

"No smooching while driving?" Whitey asks, stretching his legs on the hassock so he can reach his pocket with his left hand.

"Probly none at all."

"Why go then?" Whitey smiles, tosses the keys a tad short but catchable.

"To find out."

"Keeps you going back?"

"Has so far."
"Don't speed."
"That's what she said."
They laugh.

* * *

The family Ford does not exactly match up to the strict requirements of most 16-year-old's dream car, but it has certain things going for it, important things. It's a 1955 Fairlane, almost-new and top-of-the-line. No well-maintained "family classic", like a 1949 Custom Six, for example. Also, it runs a 160-horsepower overhead valve V-8 through a three-speed stick, and here's the kick. Overdrive! Which means that when you're in third (or high) at say 60 mph, you've still got another gear to go.

Touted by Ford as a fuel-saver, it has not taken teenage cognoscenti long to see that high-over is really about speed. And even Whitey knows it, though he pretends otherwise, and occasionally, in spite of Mom's shrill protest, gives the family little tastes of it. Mighty powerful. A bit scary. Fun as hell.

There's no such thing as automotive sound systems in Whitey's motoring life, but his Ford's got a serviceable AM radio, a dangerous distraction he never indulges while driving. But Whitey's not here. So here we are on

KJR; we did arrive on Channel 95! Bebop a Lula, she-ee-ee's my baby doll, my baby doll, my baby doll. Yeah!

Heading north on the Old Belfair Highway, the Ford rolls lazily through alder-shaded curves in Bremerton's lush watershed forest preserve, its deep-treaded tires making reassuring gripping sounds. It's a gorgeous late-spring day, maybe the freshest, greenest day of the year. Almost the longest. Let's make it the best.

Channel 95 plays Elvis then Buddy Holley, Elvis then Little Richard, Elvis then The Big Bopper. El ... what? What's this he hears? Chuck Berry? "Maybellene'? Throbbing guitar a strong enticement to put your au-to-MO-bile through its paces ... started back doin' the things you used to do – or want to do sometime in the still-unexplored future. Clever fellow, this Charles Berry. How could he have known it would become their song, the one that when it comes on he points his finger in mock-accusation – why can't you be true? – as her head shakes no, no, no in mock-denial? It's as close as they've come to smooching while driving. Her name is not Maybellene, of course. That's part of the fun, of course.

And of course fast driving to rock'n roll rhythms could be a lot of fun, but this is Whitey's car, their four-door family sedan, and he wouldn't think of putting it at risk. As Nat "King" Cole's famous lady says, that's all there is to that. No smooching while driving and defi-nitely no speeding. He turns the radio down low, then off, and maintains his modest speed and actually catches himself once again crooning "I'll hold you in my heart," – Eddie Arnold, he thinks now and wonders again whether she would understand? Concur? Embrace? What must it feel like to be in love? Will he know when it happens? If it happens?

Coming out of the watershed and following the east side of Sinclair Inlet, he looks across the sparkling water at the mothball-gray shipyard on the other side and wonders what his life might be like right now if Whitey had left that employment and transferred to Pearl Harbor a few years back as he wanted to do? He'd been serious, and it looked feasible, but Mom wouldn't go. Too much water, an ocean of uncertainty.

Port Orchard looms ahead. Should he call from a pay phone and let her know he's on his way? Or just show up and surprise her? She'll like to be surprised. She'll think he's mysterious and romantic. Unpredictable. Real women like their men to surprise them off their feet, into waiting arms. No phone call.

He stops mid-town for a red light across from Hannah & Powell's Drugs, where he sees and rejects the stainless-steel phone booth at its entrance. Last chance, but the decision has been made. She'll love his unpredictability. No phone call.

Rumbling to a slow stop from the opposite direction sits Midnight Blue domed and decked, chopped and channeled 1946 Merc convert, deep-tan Carson top, recessed Olds headlights, an Olds grill, and classic – and illegal – blue-dot taillights. Under the hood a Buick V-8, racing cam, dual quads, headers, glass-packs. Full black leather tucked and pleated interior. Etc.

Widely acknowledged to be Kitsap County's koolest kustom, he knows it to be owned by one of the county's baddest bad boys. In his early twenties, Boyd Blake still hangs out near, and sometimes in, the high school parking lot before and after school. The Handlers are a kusktom kar klub specializing in general mayhem: fist fighting with wrist pins and brass knuckles, a bit of casual bullying, a lot of catch-me-if-you-can cop baiting.

Certain impressionable girls find them unpredictable, mysterious, and romantic. Heroic, even. Always fun. High school girls, junior and senior sexual sophisticates. Also, some freshmen and sophomores. Everybody's gotta have a party doll. But when one-fine lady rides even one time inside a Handlers' kustom, there' no going back to a normal life. But, really, who wants normal?

Boyd Blake, acknowledged Handler-in-chief, recently returned from the Navy, fit and tanned, a dark cloud of mystery hanging over him. He was only in uniform for, wasn't it less than a year? Ten months? Eleven, max. Who enlists in the Navy for eleven months? Were there medical reasons? An injury? Some mysterious disease? Gross dereliction of duty? Court martial? Dishonorable discharge? All of the above? And more? Nobody seems to know.

He sure doesn't seem physically incapacitated. Always a certified Bad Boy, he seems much worse now. Or much better? Older. Bolder. And even better looking, some girls say. Careless honey-yellow mop of hair, leering, sneering, totally open ear-to-ear grin. "What's happening, man? What's the skinny?" An invitation as much as a question. And always a challenge, of course.

The light still red, he reads the grin, the sneer, the leer across the intersection and through the cut-down two-piece windshield. He knows Boyd sees him too and recognizes, now that the light is green and he must concentrate on letting the clutch out smoothly, the connection between them: Her.

She sits next to Boyd, almost on his lap, almost straddling Boyd's kustom floor-mounted gear shift. She stares expressionlessly straight ahead at the center of Boyd's dashboard, those impertinent brown eyes most carefully avoiding his.

Whitey's Ford lurches and dies in the middle of the intersection as Boyd's Merc rumbles deliberately past in the opposite lane. Through his open window, he hears laughter, an indecipherable comment, then louder laughter followed by the velvet sound of twin exhaust pipes connected to a powerful engine holding second gear like a ballet fist of calibrated force.

The buzzing whirr of his balky starter embarrasses him into laying twin stripes of first-gear rubber across the heated concrete. No cops, he hopes. It's not like he's been silent or subtle.

Get the hell out of Dodge, he thinks, and never come back. Maybe Whitey can still get that job at Pearl Harbor, and he can go live in a place where nobody's ever seen or heard of him, a place where cars aren't important? Do they even have cars in Hawaii? Yeah, well, of course, idiot. But could it be a place where girls are nicer and more beautiful? "Proudly sweeps the raincloud o'er the cliff," he remembers from grade school choir. Is there such a place? Paradise? Really?

Past the cemetery and the bowling alley, he swings left toward Mile Hill, picking up speed and heading toward her house. But now there's no reason to go there. There's no her there. There's no her anywhere.

"Got it made in the shade on the downhill grade," his mouth croons to the sound of rubber tires rolling fast over hot asphalt. "Man, I've really got it made." Wayne Ormiston and the Hydra-Matics, local one-hit wonders sometimes called the High Dramatics by the irreverent.

* * *

He finds himself heading toward Price's Dairy on Long Lake Road, a quiet, well-maintained two-lane blacktop perfect for what he's got in mind. Whitey's speedometer reads up to 120 mph, and he thinks 160 V-8 ponies with an overdrive tranny should do ... at least that. There's a little open space after 120. Let's fill it with red needle.

The early part of the highway is hills and curves, houses and trees, but it opens into flat, straight meadow-land where Golden Guernsey milking herds graze incuri-ously behind taut wire strands. He visited this dairy on a field trip with fellow second-graders many years ago. He remembers that Guernsey cows are famous for the high butterfat content of their milk.

He pushes his speed up to 75 to see how it feels. It feels fast. Then he slows down and looks for a place to turn around. He hasn't passed a single car since turning onto this road. Perfect. Clear sailing. Made in the shade.

Now, turned to head back toward town, he sits for a few minutes with the engine at quiet idle. The speedom-eter sits in a kind of bubble, higher than the rest of the dashboard, directly behind the steering wheel. A visual safety feature. Even at high speeds, you'll never take your eye off the road to see how fast you're going. Even very high speeds.

But the dash it sits on is not padded, the steering wheel will not collapse on impact, and there are no seat belts. Not even lap belts. Is he sure he wants to do this? Yes, he is. Is he sure he can do this? No, he's not. Then why ...? To find out. Of course. And to have a story to tell. Of course.

He has taken the transmission out of overdrive because he wants to compare. He'll do the first run just using the standard three-speed, and the second run, the big one, he'll do in overdrive. Then compare. Would top speed go from, say, 105 in straight stick to 115 in overdrive? But couldn't he gain more than a paltry 10 mph?

That's what he plans to find out and what he plans to tell Whitey as soon as he gets back home. Ha ha. Sure he does. Maybe sometime in the far distant future over casual backyard beers? Maybe some Father's Day? "Hey Dad. You know that blue Ford I learned to drive on? What's the fastest you ever took her?" And when Whitey admits to a modest 87 or 93, he'll tell him this story. "You know that straight stretch next to Price's Dairy on Long Lake Road?"

The radio's off, the windows all rolled up, the road clear coming and going. The Ford does not buck to a shuddering halt this time as he lets out the clutch and takes her smoothly to a strong 20 in first, 35 in second. In third he puts the pedal to the metal, as they say, and watches the needle climb swiftly through the 80's and 90's before hanging fire around 107 or 108, when he decides to rein her in.

Just in time too, it seems. He realizes almost too late how little time has passed and how much road he's covered. Thank God he backed off when he did. If it hadn't been for the engine's braking ability, he could've been in real trouble. A hundred and eight is a lot faster than 50 or 60. Change in plans. Can he clock 110 on the way back, still out of overdrive?

He is surprised by the engine's metallic popping and snapping as he turns around in a driveway beyond the pastureland. Cooling itself, relieving the strain of overexertion. His knees feel a little weak, his hands a bit trembly as this time he takes her to 25 in first, 40 in second.

After an almost-111 mph return run, the engine is really popping and splanging. It's hot, of course, hot and ready to beat 111 by more than 10 in overdrive. Hell, he'll bury the needle in overdrive, 125 and still gaining. Let her cool down a bit before the final run, the big one. Really, though, who knew 111 mph could feel so fast?

Before letting the clutch out, he left-hands the sturdy chrome tee-handle of the overdrive bar as far forward as it will go. It is located just beneath the dash, halfway between the steering column and the larger tee-handle of the hand brake. Both handles are clearly marked. BRAKE. OVERDRIVE. More safety features.

Time to go. He lets out the clutch with practiced smoothness now and shifts gears at 25 and 40. As he reaches 80 in third, or high, he quickly releases the gas pedal, feels the overdrive gear kick in, then really puts his foot in it. There's a strong floating, gliding, soaring sensation, enhanced by the freewheeling nature of the specialized drive train. Sometimes the engine can't keep up with the wheels it's supposed to drive. At no time does it provide braking capacity.

That complication is not foremost in his thoughts as he desperately urges the red needle past the 112 mph mark it seems glued to. Why 112? Why not 120? Or more?

Oops, too far, too fast, and letting off the gas doesn't help and standing on the brake doesn't help, and, Good God Almighty there's a 1951 Plymouth Cambridge pulling slowly into his lane a quarter mile away. He barely manages to get into the oncoming lane and somehow past the Plymouth when the fishtailing begins.

Actually, it began as he slid almost sideways past the Plymouth, then across the road in front of it, then across the road the other direction, then across one more time before he feels the speed decreasing and something like control returning. No seatbelt means he's sliding back and forth on the smooth bench seat with nothing to hold onto but the steering wheel he whips back and forth, but hold on he does until Whitey's pride and joy - the Ford, not him – is once again headed straight down the road trailing billowing clouds of dust from both shoulders and approaching a series of hills and curves at a now stodgy-feeling but still formidable 70 mph.

There's still no engine braking, of course, but the brakes themselves seem marginally functional once again as he works his speed down to a sedate 35. He wants to stop and crank down the windows, but he's afraid he's been reported to the cops and wants to keep moving. The only choice is back through Dodge.

A quarter-hour later he's crawling through Port Orchard at 25 mph, doing his best to be invisible. He's got his front windows cranked down, so it's impossible to completely ignore the loud popping and crackling of overheated metal, the smell of hot motor oil and engine coolant, the skunk like stench of burnt rubber. Luckily, the traffic light is green and he doesn't have to stop downtown in front of people who might recognize him, might even hail him.

Would they recognize him? Hasn't he changed? Hasn't he, like, returned from the dead? He sincerely believes he has. Or could have. It makes as much sense as … Did he really do what he just did? Or dream it? How could he not have rolled over and be, well, let's say transformed. Out of? Into?

At the start of the watershed, he pulls over to crank down the rear windows, and turn the heater on full blast for a slow, engine-cooling drive through shade-giving maples and alders. He feels weak and trembles uncontrollably. His clothes are wet through with sweat that permeates the seat cushion. He doesn't think he pissed his pants. He most sincerely hopes not.

That Plymouth Cambridge, that momentary exchange of fear and danger lasting an eternity of micro-seconds, is imprinted permanently oh his mind. He knows that as surely as he knows the 30 mph he now travels will take him home much faster then he wants to be there. It was a family of four well-dressed Latinos out for a Sunday drive, and he still sees the terror in their gestures, their horrified eyes, as he bore down upon them from behind. But surely he didn't have time in those few seconds to actually see those near-victims apprehending their final forever? Surely he is making it up.

Surely he is not making it up. He knows they heard him exploding toward them and turned to stare hopelessly out, even Mama, clutching her purse. Even Pappa, clutching the steering wheel, And the two children in the back seat, their eyes staring wide, their mouths gaping in absolute terror. He saw them like that in that brief moment, and he sees them like that now. He knows he will be seeing them like that for a very long time to come.

Instead of driving past the house and taking a slow trip to Hood Canal to let everything cool down, he turns into the driveway and parks the Ford in the garage. It's still popping and snapping like the Fourth of July. It still smells like a junkyard fire. He can't help it. His arms turn the wheel, his feet work the pedals. Not him. He works nothing at all.

His hand lays the keys on the kitchen table. His eyes see Whitey, still in his chair. Still reading the paper and looking up in acknowledgement. "Didn't expect you back so soon," Whitey says.

"Nobody home," his mouth replies. The words sound strange to him. Whispered, almost. Does Whitey notice?

"Should've phoned," Whitey says.

"Yep," his mouth replies in that strange voice. "Should've."

His feet carry him up the stairs to his room, and his hands lay the framed, tinted photograph gently on its face. His feet carry him past the open ventilation door to his bed, where his ears and his nose tell him that the Ford is still cooling. Now recumbent, his mind wonders whether it will cool completely before Whitey notices and whether his strange new body will stop sweating and trembling before Mom serves Sunday dinner. Or ever.

We Called Her Oink

*** * * ***

Jim Harstad

OUR PIG OINK Johnson wasn't even really our pig. It or, rather, she was the neighborhood pet, a long-snouted feral throwback with a soft black and white pelt and an expression that seemed to beg for tolerance and understanding. From the beginning she seemed to know she wasn't with her own kind in her own neighborhood, but it wasn't her fault and there wasn't anything she could do about it.

Our young son was the first one to run into her down the street on his skateboard. He bumped and rattled proudly over the lumpy asphalt on his new fiberglass wheels. "Dad! Dad! I just saw a pig!"

"What kind of pig? Where?"

"Just down the street. A baby."

"A baby pig? A piglet? Not a dog?"

"No. It's not a dog. Come on."

I followed to where he said he saw it, but it wasn't there, and that was that. "So, was it pink and fat?"

"No. It had black fur and a long snout and looked like it could run."

"Couldn't you tell? Was it running? Sure it wasn't a dog?"

"I said it wasn't a dog."

It wasn't a dog, as I found out a week later when it showed up in our back yard, peering over our low rock wall, snuffling around in the dead leaves for something to eat. Sometimes it would stop and hold its nose in the air, catching a waft of something we couldn't smell and looking at us sideways like we'd do her harm if she wasn't alert. Suddenly she wheeled around on her back legs and crashed into the brush and was gone.

She came back several times after that, and once I managed to get a very good photo of an almost-intimate moment between her and my son. I'd love to know what happened to it. I'd love to have it. Two buddies looking directly into the camera, posing, smiling. I swear, smiling! I called the picture "Oink and Doink".

Then one day I found a pair of ravaged amaryllis pots that I'd been growing on top of the wall. She'd never shown any interest in them before, so I thought they were safe. She must have known she'd crossed a line because she didn't come back for maybe months. Enough time for me to forget the amaryllis.

Th next time we saw her she was still not full-grown, but she was getting there. I think that's when Oink

Johnson became her "official" name. We never called her the pig again. And the next time we saw Oink she had grown tusks and was there. Really big and really there. Oink in full.

By then she'd carved a skinny trail diagonally across the steepest part of our steep back yard. The delicacy of her trail told us she was nimble as a goat. Gradually we realized that she'd cross every afternoon at about five and head for one of our neighbors' back yard for dinner. They too had given her a name, Petunia or Alice, I think.

To us she was always Oink, and even though we never fed her we felt that she was at least as much our pig as theirs. We'd seen her first, and we allowed her to cross our property. Sometimes when we had guests we'd move the party to the back yard just before five so everybody could watch. At first she didn't quite trust it. She'd sit on a small knot of ground at the side of the yard, nose up, snuffing the air. Then she'd gather herself and race quickly across.

"Oh, isn't she cute!"

"She's so handsome!"

"I knew pigs were supposed to be smart, but I didn't know they could be graceful."

After a while she seemed to understand that she was being admired, not threatened, and she liked it. Now there'd be only a momentary pause until she knew she had everyone's attention, then trot nimbly down her path to dinner.

"She's almost like she knows we like to watch her. Is she that smart?"

"She could be a lot smarter than that."

"Really?"

"Really."

"How do you know?"

"I just feel it. The way she looks sometimes. Her expression. Trust me, she's very smart."

"Yeah, I guess maybe so." But they didn't really think so. Smart, maybe, but not *that* smart.

But I thought so and should have known better than to do what I did next. At some point I decided to make my hillside fruitful and productive, so I bought two citrus trees and an avocado tree and planted them spaced evenly in well-mulched holes. They were all near Oink's path but did not interfere with it and would never encroach.

They'd been in place for about two weeks and doing well. I watered them with a hose every afternoon and checked up on them several times a day, beginning first thing in the morning. I think it was a Saturday afternoon that I stood there giving my new babies a good soaking when I heard the unmistakable sound of Oink breaking through underbrush before suddenly appearing at the edge of our yard. Seeing me, she ambled confidently past, showing me her now bristly, mud-covered coat. It was probably good protection against flies and mosquitoes, but it was no longer beautiful.

Was I offended by her inelegant appearance? Just because she was a pig didn't mean she had to look like one? Maybe? Whatever I was thinking, I aimed the hose full-force at her receding back and hindquarters. She grunted, lurched forward, and was quickly gone. I'll admit to some feeling of accomplishment, having aimed at and hit a moving target, a wild beast, a prey.

I stayed there stupidly watering my precious young trees when I noticed an unfamiliar thudding sound that seemed to come from the flattened area of abandoned quarry roadbed directly above and behind us. Heavily grown over by shady haole koa, it was where she apparently spent most of her time. In one place she'd dug herself a swale that collected and held cooling moisture. Thus her muddy hide.

But I'd never heard the galloping sounds I was hearing up there now, and I'd never heard galloping sounds that seemed to turn and come from the direction Oink Johnson traveled daily, and I'd never seen Oink Johnson bearing down on me from that direction, nose and tusks like the cowcatcher on a steam locomotive aiming right at me then past before I could make a move in any direction.

What I felt then captured the most literal meaning of the word "thrilling". I was shocked and stunned and numb and scared. And I was thrilled, thrilled to still be in one piece, thrilled to still be alive. She'd actually brushed my knees as she blasted by, just a delicate little brushing, a very small taste of the dinner she could have served me, my tusk-skewered butt on a platter. Thrilling.

If anyone doubts that a pig can have not only intelligence but a sense of injured pride, a deep sense of moral injustice, please read on.

As I turned off the water and coiled the hose, I pondered the lesson this pig had taught me. She could have done serious harm, and there was no doubt that she knew it. As I gave each of my healthy new trees a last solicitous look, I marveled at her restraint. She'd held all the cards. Why didn't she just take me out? "Because she's a gentleman," I faint-heartedly chuckled to myself. Indeed, my faint heart was still working overtime, and I was suddenly sweating like a … well, like a pig. That evening I showered before dinner.

The next morning, I took my customary saunter into the back yard. And stopped short. My beautiful trees, my beautiful trees, beautiful young saplings, were each snapped off at the trunk, from which they still dangled by threads of mutilated bark. Ravaged. Savaged.

I liked to play games did I? How's this for a game, Mr. Big Hose Man? Your move next, Boss, if you want to keep playing. Maybe you'd like to find replacements for your babies and start all over again? Not? I thought not. See you later, Bigshot.

And talk about smart. Consider this: Not only did she snap the trunks, she made sure she snapped them in the right place, below the graft, almost at ground level. Even if they somehow managed to survive, they'd never bear edible fruit. I call that no accident. I call that on purpose, and I call it really smart.

After that we rarely glimpsed her. She'd stopped going through our yard and went the back way to be fed as Petunia or whatever. We were no longer worthy. She'd probably always wondered about the Oink Johnson bit. Wasn't that a bit too cute, don't you think?

Another neighbor, near the one who fed her, was clearing heavy brush from a good-sized lot, preparing to build a house. He'd hired some strong young men with machetes for the job, men who'd spent their boyhood in the jungles of Southeast Asia. They noticed pig signs, they said. Were there pigs here?

Only one pig, they were told, and it was the neighborhood pet. Pet? It didn't seem like much of a pet to the young men. Who keeps a feral pig for a pet?

One very hot weekday afternoon in July when the brush clearing was over, our sleepy neighborhood was brought alert by a heavy thrashing of brush, and indignant then terrified squealing, then a loud, prolonged scream followed by summer silence. People came out of their tidy white houses tentatively, dazed, half-sickened. We were all looking toward the thick brush behind our houses, the spot where the atrocity had taken place. The men carrying the heavy carcass on a pole were so deft and quiet that they appeared unexpectedly far down the street from where everyone was watching and where quickly the waiting pickup was gone.

Somebody called the police, but they said they couldn't do anything unless somebody wanted to file a lawsuit. Did anybody? No. Nobody. And that was pretty much that.

The nice family who fed her gathered personal anecdotes from neighbors, including mine, and took up Oink's cause with the SPCA, but of course nothing happened. What could anyone do? Nothing. Best just forget about it.

I'd just about forgotten about it a couple years later when the nice family moved out of the neighborhood and returned my photo of Oink and Doink. There they were, smiling buddies, Oink the pig I befriended and betrayed, and Doink, a name we never really used to describe a son who has grown well beyond skateboards and piglets. I'd really like to see that photo. I'm sure it's around here somewhere.

An Introduction

* * *

 The confused housefly,
or as the wife exclaimed,
The Frustrated Artist

AND SO THE writer picked up his pen and began to write. Where he was going he wasn't really one hundred percent certain. But that fact didn't concern him too much. After all, he'd started four decent novels in pretty much the same manner. He knew he had something to say; he wasn't exactly sure how he was going to say it, but most of all, he knew he had to have faith in and confidence in the fact that if (as writers and editors are prone to point out) he let the story tell itself, let it go where it took itself, he would end up with a work he'd be anxious to share with the world. And, in this writer's case, he knew that wherever the story ended up would be a good place – a better place than if he'd not written anything.

The writer knew this to be true because, as always, he knelt in prayer before writing one word, and he asked God to give him the words to write and how to write them.

For days the writer had been searching for a worthy short story idea – a concept, an image, a twist he could mold into pure literary nirvana. He had failed. He scanned and re-scanned his list of story ideas. Nothing ascended from the page that the ideas were written on. None of his varied and (he thought) colorful list of personal history and exploits seemed to demand he act on them. And pure fantasy? No, he wasn't very good at that. Deep down he questioned the philosophical credibility that fantasy writers operated with. Then of course, he'd have to remind himself of the many serious writers he could name. Why ... he'd read them himself; writers who employed the most brazenly outlandish and preposterous fantasy to reveal some of creation's basic tenets and truths.

What a mess he was in, a road block to his pen, a virtual quagmire of nothing to write about, a wall facing him that said, "That's right, there is nothing to write about, move on, get a life, get a "real job", go do something important, and then write about *that*."

At this point, our writer, or should we say "our frustrated artist" felt even more helpless. He'd *had* real jobs and he'd written about them. He'd done *important things* and he'd written about them as well. What was left to write about?

And then the answer came to the frustrated writer. He aimed his pen at the paper and he slowly wrote the new short story that God had just now suggested he write. He called it:

YOU BE THE JUDGE

You Be the Judge

* * *

Gary H. Baker

THE COUNTY JAIL was not a happy place. The normal prisoner population was around three hundred, and a high percentage of them represented a good deal of the county's poverty, addicts, drug dealers, mentally ill, criminals, and trouble makers. Under the heading of trouble makers, one could further sub-divide the incarcerated into three camps: drunks, the lazy, and minor offenders of laws and ordinances dealing with auto registration, traffic laws, property taxes, and the like.

Billy Overton just could not understand how or why he'd been locked up. The 2002 Chevrolet he'd put three hundred down on and had "lot financing" for the remaining thirty-eight hundred, well, it was that Chevrolet that was the reason he was in jail. But Billy just could not understand it. He remembered at the hearing, the DA had said something about it being illegal to re-sell an automobile prior to possessing a clean title on it. And what the DA didn't have to say was that when someone drives such an automobile across state lines for that very purpose, you've then broken additional laws. Not only that, when an individual attempted to disappear with the cash from the out of state sale, well ... another law had been broken.

Billy just could not understand it. Some folks said he was "slow", his elevator didn't go all the way up to the top floor. Some thought Billy was a good actor, that he feigned his IQ in order to play the poor, abused, country bumpkin, always snookered by slick operators.

But Billy wasn't faking the current problems he was dealing with. He was fifty years old, grossly overweight at three- fifty, his heart was failing, and diabetes had set in. And then there was the high blood pressure, the gout, a whole list of other medical issues, and the worst problem of all – he was getting out of jail.

One day, a couple of months before Billy's release date, Billy was listening to a couple of inmates who shared his fifteen-man communal living area – Charley pod in Alpha block.

"Church call will be in about fifteen minutes. You going?" Ray Trindle asked.

"I guess I will. What's today, Wednesday? It'll probably be the new guy. I think he comes every Wednesday." Jarvis Rexrode answered.

"You heard him before?"

"Yeah, he ain't bad. He's not an ordained preacher, just a volunteer. But, you can tell, he's been around, you know what I mean?"

"I ain't never heard him."

"Well, don't get me wrong, I'm just saying, he gets right to the point. It's Jesus this, and Jesus that."

"Well, that's the way it's supposed to be, ain't it?"

"Sure, if that's what you want to hear, you won't be disappointed."

Twenty minutes later Billy joined Ray and Jarvis and three others from other pods in Alpha block. Two guards fetched the six of them and were walking them to central booking where the "church service" would be held in a nearby drunk tank, a holding cell roughly sixteen feet by twelve feet. There was a stainless-steel commode/urinal and a long concrete bench attached to one wall. The wall facing the elevated command post of central booking was unbreakable, reinforced, two-inch thick glass. This allowed the guards to observe the activities of the prisoners at all times.

The six were sitting on the concrete bench not talking much about anything. Jarvis Rexrode could see through the glass that the volunteer jail minister was coming their way. "Here he comes."

A guard unlocked the door with one of the twenty keys on his belt, and all six men immediately realized that the volunteer preacher was already different in at least one way from the many preachers and jail chaplains that usually led services. He was bringing a chair into the holding cell to sit in, not a pulpit that the guards would always set up for the others.

Jarvis had seen the new guy do this before, but the other five, if you could have read their minds, were probably thinking, "Well, I'll be … He's going to sit down and talk with us."

When the guard had locked the door and as the loud metallic CLANK reverberated around the holding cell, the new volunteer preacher positioned his chair in front of the six men on the bench and at about five feet away, facing them, he sat down and started talking.

"Thank you for coming. You know, Jesus said, 'Where two or more are gathered in my name, that's where the church is'. Today we have a church of seven. Let's see if we can do something good today, something to please our Father in heaven. Let's study God's word and see where it takes us today, what He wants to reveal to us. Let us pray.

"Our Heavenly Father, we come to you today asking that your love, your guidance, your strength, your mercy be on every man in this place. May the Holy Spirit roam freely in this place today Father. May every prisoner, every guard, every volunteer worker, may we all sense Your holy presence. And Father, we ask You be with the families of these men who are behind bars. Brothers, sisters, moms, dads, wives, children, friends, all those on the outside that need your protection. Be with them all. And Father, we pray today, that if there is a man in our midst who's never asked Jesus to take control of his life, we ask that that man's heart would be opened today and that he'd ask Jesus to take him today so he would experience that peace that passeth all understanding, so that he will dwell with You eternally in heaven above. We ask all this in the name of Jesus Christ Our Savior. Amen."

The next thing that happened was the new volunteer jail preacher had asked all the men to stand, and then he said. "Take the hand of the man next to you." They all did, and then the new volunteer jail preacher stood and stretched out his hands and grabbed the men on the end. One of them was Billy Overton.

They now had a tight circle of seven men holding hands, and the new volunteer jail minister started praying again. He repeated much of what he'd prayed on before, but he also started off in a direction that not so much questioned each individual prisoner about his belief and/or commitment in and to Jesus Christ, but challenged them as to whether or not they had *made* a commitment, and if so, what kind of a commitment was it? How strong was it?

Billy Overton was somewhat ruffled, maybe flustered was a better description of how he felt, and he didn't know why. He just did.

When the prayer ended, everyone sat back down, and the new volunteer jail preacher started talking again, "How many of you have been with me before?"

Only Jarvis Rexrode rose his hand.

"Okay, then we need to do two things: put your names on this paper for me. I have to turn in a list of everyone that attends a service. And while you're doing that, I'll tell you who I am and why I'm here.

"My name is Cliff Garrett. I'm from Spring Valley United Methodist Church. I'm not an ordained minister. I'm what they call a lay-speaker. I fill in for the real preacher when he or she is out of town. I'll be honest with you. There are only two things I have that qualify me to come to jail and talk to you. The first thing is, I love Jesus and I like to tell people what my experience has been following Him. The second thing is …"

Cliff always caught himself when he reached this part of his self-introduction. It wasn't a conscious pause, it was just something that always happened, as if what he was about to say, he couldn't believe himself. He didn't choke-up when he said it, but always, down deep inside, the words had a cold and empty ring to them, that left him feeling as if he were in a free-fall from a cliff with no bottom.

"Six months ago I lost my son to suicide. From that entire experience, I think I learned something very important. Not too long after we lost him, I was watching one of the big TV evangelist early on a Sunday morning before church. You may be familiar with him – Dr. Charles Stanley out of Atlanta, Georgia. That morning Dr. Stanley was preaching on the subject of suicide. I

287

remember telling my wife I didn't think I needed to sit there and listen. But that's what I did; I listened to the entire sermon.

"As Dr. Stanley was speaking, needless to say, I was expecting the worst. He talked about the general nature of sin, about all sin being equal. That not feeding a hungry person is as bad as murder, is as bad as suicide. Yes! Suicide is a horrible sin. My son had committed a horrible sin. But that's when Dr. Stanley taught me the important lesson, why I'm here today. As bad as suicide is, it's not an unforgiveable sin. There is only one unforgiveable sin, and it is not suicide. My heart was beginning to breathe again. For a moment I wasn't sure it would. But when he said that, some kind of a burden began to float away. You see, I always felt like my son had been searching for Jesus. You know, Jesus said, 'I stand waiting at the door, knocking. If you open the door, I will enter.' Well, I always felt my son was trying to open the door, but then of course, he somehow got lost, and he did what he did. But I know in my heart, now, he is with Jesus.

"And then Dr. Stanley quoted a scripture that said the only one unforgiveable sin isn't suicide, it's blasphemy of the Holy Spirit. I let out such a sigh of relief, for you see, I knew my son couldn't blasphemy the Holy Spirit. I knew as well as I know I'm breathing air; he couldn't do that. And I knew, stronger than I knew before, my son was in heaven with Jesus.

"That's why I'm here with you today. You see, until I learned that the one and only unforgiveable sin is blasphemy of the Holy Spirit, I didn't know if I had a good message for men in jail. One of the chaplains had asked me if I'd be interested in volunteering for jail ministry, and I told him I'd think about it. Then I lost my son, and then I learned from Dr. Stanley what the scripture says, and then, I *knew*, I *did* have a message for men in jail. No matter what it is you've done to get here, you have the opportunity to spend eternity in paradise with a merciful, forgiving, and loving God. The only thing that would stop you is if you commit blasphemy of the Holy Spirit. And there is one other requirement. You must ask Jesus to take you. And you must mean it."

Billy Overton and others in the group felt a jolt of something run through them. An old memory perhaps, of better places, better times? Or was it new and fresh? Could it be hope, maybe a vision of a positive future, maybe a dream, maybe a dream worth chasing?

As they relished the idea of something to grab ahold of, they, at the same time, dropped right back into the reality of their current situation, they were locked up; one on assault and battery charges; one on domestic abuse; one on his fourth DUI; one on possession with intent; one on trafficking; and Billy Overton was in jail on out of state re-sale of stolen property.

But still, for most of them, the last few words from Cliff Garrett were ringing in their ears, "No matter what it is you've done to get here, you have the opportunity to spend eternity in paradise with a merciful, forgiving, and loving God."

For the next half hour Cliff Garrett shared scripture with the men, he listened to them, he talked with them, and he told them the four words he had voiced forty-two years ago when he was at his bottom – "Jesus please take me." He told them that when he said the words, he did not hear the voice of God, so much as he *felt* God lift him up and take control of his life.

After final prayers and good-byes to the six men, Cliff Garrett walked out of the jail and drove home.

It was two months later, Cliff was at home one evening at around 9:30 pm, and a call was coming in on the phone.

"Hello."

"Mr. Garrett, this is Billy Overton."

"Uh, okay. I'm sorry, I can't place your name."

"You know, over at the jail. You preached to us one day."

"Oh, okay, I see. How long ago was it? I see a lot of men over there, and I almost never see the same group twice."

"Probably about two months ago. I come out of Alpha block."

"You said Billy Overton?"

"Yes sir."

"Yeah, yeah, I remember you now. How are you doing?"

"Well Mr. Garrett, that's why I called you. I ain't doing very good. I got out of jail this morning and had to go straight to the hospital. You see, they didn't give me no treatment for my heart when I was in jail, and when I got out this morning, I was in pretty bad shape. I took the only money I had and got a taxi to the emergency room. I been here all day. They said I should be pretty stabilized by tomorrow, and they're going to turn me out at noon."

"Well, that sounds good. I guess you'll be going home then."

"No sir. I wish I could …"

"What do you mean. I don't understand." Well, no, that wasn't exactly true. Cliff didn't understand everything, but he did understand a little.

"I ain't got no place to go to."

"Do you have any money?"

"No sir."

Cliff didn't say anything. He was just letting it sink in – the part he was beginning to understand more and more each second. He still didn't say anything, but he was thinking about the options he had: simply tell Billy he was sorry, but he wasn't in a position where he could help with any money. He dismissed that option quickly because it would have been a lie. He and his wife were retired and had a very small nest egg they could tap into in the event of an emergency. Then Cliff thought about his small church. They had been able to help people in a financial pinch in the past. Maybe they could do it again. He also thought about that huge Baptist church on the other side of the county. He'd helped stranded travelers get help from them in the past.

"Billy, I can't promise anything. Let me make a few phone calls to some churches and see what they might be able to do. What about your family, Billy? Can you get any help there?"

"No sir, none of them wants me around. And my girl-friend, she, uh … well Mr. Garrett, I ain't never said I was a good man or nothin', and my old girlfriend, she, ah … she never lived no kind of Christian life, you might say. She probably ain't got nothin', but even if she did, I don't think I need to go back there."

Billy was quiet for a moment, and Cliff Garrett didn't say anything either.

"But you know what, Mr. Garrett … that day you talked to us in jail, you got me thinkin'. I thought about what you said, and now I want to be baptized. Maybe I could come to yals' church."

"Billy that would be a good thing. You come and worship with us. I'm sure our pastor would love to baptize you."

"Yes sir, I'll be doing that. It's just I don't know what to do tomorrow."

"Call me back in the morning Billy. Maybe I can find a place for you to stay for a few days, until you can get back on your feet."

"Yes sir, Mr. Garrett. I thank you."

Around ten the next morning Billy called Cliff Garrett from the hospital, and Cliff informed Billy that his little Methodist church would put Billy up in a local motel for a few days.

At noon Cliff drove over to the hospital and as a nurse wheeled Billy out, Cliff recognized the face of the prisoner from Alpha block from a couple of months ago. He got out of his car and went around to open the door for Billy. Billy had with him everything he owned in a small bag.

As they were driving out to the motel about five miles from the hospital, Billy said. "If I could just get me a cell phone and a month's service plan, I think I could get me a job. I've got a few contacts you know. One man over in Tolson Gap was about to put me to work for him, but that's when they put me in jail."

Cliff realized there was no one else that was going to help. It was him that would have to step up to the plate. This was his opportunity to put his faith, his discipleship, his commitment to follow Jesus on the line. He knew all of this, and he knew he should do it willingly and be a "cheerful giver", yet he had some black hole in him restricting him from coming forth willingly and living out his Christian beliefs that he went around proclaiming everybody ought to be happy to perform – or should he have said, *everybody else* ought to be happy to perform, everybody but him!

The rubber was about to meet the road. If Cliff was going to help Billy, then Cliff was going to have to get his hands dirty. He was going to have to get down into the thick of it. The man has nothing: no money, no home, no food, he doesn't have any clothes other than what is on his back.

Cliff thought about the phone for a minute and he realized Billy was right. How was he going to find work without a phone? Cliff stopped at Walmart and paid for a new phone and a thirty-day service plan for Billy. He also purchased food to last a few days and before dropping Billy off at the motel, he told him he'd be bringing over some clothes for Billy tomorrow, and he laid fifty bucks on him.

Billy was very thankful for all of these things, and he promised Cliff he wouldn't be sorry. Billy was upbeat about finding a job and then repaying Cliff for everything.

After the first four days Billy had spent in the motel room, Cliff drove back over there, parked in front of the office, and walked in to have a talk with the manager. The proprietor, Mr. Antif Khurana, slipped through the curtain that was the portal back to his families' living quarters, and looked absently in the approximate direction of Cliff Garrett. No "yes sir", or "can I help you?" was given.

"I'm from the church that is helping out with Mr. Overton in room 231," Cliff offered.

Mr. Khurana's eyes registered nothing, and he looked as if he might turn around and go back through the curtain.

"It looks like we will need to pay for another week," Cliff said.

"Oh no, we cannot do that. Tomorrow morning check out time is 10:30." No expression came from Mr. Khurana's face. He might have been talking to a tree in the forest. "If he is not gone, we put his things out on the street and we call police."

"What's happened? We need a room for him. I'll pay right now." Cliff wasn't in the habit of being snubbed, and this … this treatment from the cheapest motel in town; what could have happened?

"I told you. Tonight his last night. He must go tomorrow morning." Again, there was no explanation, only the hammer dropping.

"Look Mr. …" Cliff noticed a tray of business cards on the counter and picked one up, "Mr. Khurana, I don't understand why you are doing this. The man needs a room. It's cold out here at night. Surely you won't put him out. We can pay. We've already paid for four nights. Can you please tell me what the problem is?"

"We in busy season now. Room 231 we need for other customers. Sorry, he cannot stay there."

"Well, don't you have any other rooms?"

"Maybe we have one room left. I look." Khurana pushed a couple of keys on the computer, and the look on his face was icy and indifferent, and then he grudgingly said, "Look like maybe I got one room left."

"Okay, good. How much do I owe you for a week?" Cliff was reaching for his credit card.

"Four hundred fifty-five dollah'." Khurana's face was as blank as a sidewalk.

Cliff was wishing he were in the woods with his chainsaw gathering firewood for his woodstove, or maybe over at the golf course, teeing off on number three – his favorite hole. What was he doing in this dive bickering with a rag-head for the benefit of a jail-bird he barely knew?

"Four fifty-five? That's way over twice the rate you charged us for four days!" *What in the world has Billy done to stir this up?* Cliff was thinking.

"It busy season. You want him to stay here, he must move to new room. Four fifty-five for one more week."

Khurana turned to walk back through the curtain. He was through negotiating.

"Wait! Okay." Cliff handed over his credit card and knew that the church finance committee would reimburse him again. He also knew that a good percentage of the balance on hand for benevolence could be traced to his wife's and his own tithing. He hated even thinking about his own cheapness. Scripture came to mind about it being nearly impossible for a rich man to enter the kingdom. *I'm not rich*, he fumed. Then what really burned him – the woman that gave out of her poverty! What was the story? She only gave two talents, but it was all she had.

He wanted to slither away into the grass – snake that he was. By the time he got up to room 231, he was ready to rip the door off and find out what he could about this motel situation.

He knocked and in a moment or two Billy opened the door. The noise from the stupid game show on the TV assaulted him like a freight train was blasting through the room.

"Hey, Mr. Garrett! Come on in!" Billy was clad in baggy shorts Cliff brought him a few days ago and a scraggly t-shirt he had from the jail-house. His ankles and feet were swollen up badly, an ugly dark purple. Still, the room looked in good order. Billy had the few possessions he owned organized in one or two clusters, the most obvious, his billfold, a few papers, his phone, and what looked like some medicine from the hospital; all these grouped together on the small table. What was left of the food from Walmart was likewise organized up on the top of the low-cut dresser, sitting next to the TV. The clothes he owned were on two hangers on the clothes rack, not scattered haphazardly around the room.

The TV was still pounding away and Cliff sensed Billy wasn't going to do anything about it. He picked up the remote and switched off the power. "Billy, what's going on?"

"What do you mean Mr. Garrett? Hey I really want to thank you for the room and everything. And I been looking for work. I called a man over in Trasperville, and he wants me to start work next week. But he said I need to come over there tomorrow so we can talk about the job. He's even got a place there for me to live in."

Cliff didn't say anything, and so Billy continued on, reporting all of his job hunting activities. Finally, Cliff broke in, "Billy, what happened here at the motel?"

"What do you mean, Mr. Garrett?"

"Come on, just tell me what happened?"

"Oh, I guess you mean Mr. Khurana. He don't like me, that's all."

"What happened?"

"I don't know. He come up here complaining about something I guess. I don't know. He called me some names, and I guess … well, I probably called him some names too. He just don't like me. Plus, he said I've got to leave tomorrow."

"No, you don't have to leave. We got you another week here."

"Aw Mr. Garrett, I'm sorry about all of this. I really thank you for all you've done. I know if I could get over to Trasperville tomorrow, I could get that job, and I'll start paying you back."

"That's not important Billy. What's important is you start taking care of yourself. You gotta' learn how to do that, you know. Let's pray on it."

As Cliff was driving home from the motel, he was actually feeling a little better than he was right before he knocked on room 231's door. He hadn't torn into Billy as he thought he might, and now, thinking back on it, he knew it was also a good thing when he told Billy he'd drive him the forty miles over to Trasperville tomorrow. The sooner Billy found work, the sooner Cliff could wash his hands of him.

The job interview the next day didn't work out. The man needed an auto mechanic for a used car lot he was opening. Cliff waited nearly an hour while Billy and the man were talking and looking around the prospective car lot. On the drive back to the motel Cliff was able to piece together a good bit of Billy's work background. It had been mostly mechanic work and truck driving. Having been a truck driver himself, and knowing there was always work for people willing to jump into that sort of grind, he asked Billy, "Have you thought about driving a truck again?"

"Well, I was hoping I could find something else. I don't like being gone all the time, you know."

"Do you still have your commercial driver's license?"

"Yes sir."

"Well Billy, I know there's plenty of truck companies out there that would put you on. Think about it – you'd have a place to live, no rent. And making money at the same time. Not only that, after ninety days, they put you on their health insurance plan."

"Mr. Garrett, I'd sure like to find work here local. I been out on the road. I know what it's like out there."

"It's your choice. I'll help you anyway I can. I just didn't know if you'd thought about trucking or not."

Four months later Cliff got a call from Billy. A lot of things had transpired since the last time he'd heard from him. Eventually Cliff had taken the stance that "tough love" was the best way to handle the situation. He refused to put money out for Billy, but he would always answer the call when starvation itself was an issue. Also, he helped Billy locate a large men's mission in a neighboring town. This afforded Billy a roof over his head on many nights. And of course Cliff was available most of the time to drive Billy to job interviews.

All during that four months, Cliff had no clue what calamity, misfortune, or turn of luck might have befallen Billy. He'd tried to distance himself from the experience.

In some ways he felt he'd done all he could have done for Billy, but deep down, at the level some folks might describe as that room where the "real self" is introduced to the "real self" and they say to each other, "Why, I know you, I know you completely, I know you hugely, I know all about you." In that place, Cliff was not proud of what he saw – a selfish hypocrite. Always talking about the Bible, about Jesus, about doing the right thing. Well, the right thing would have been to bring Billy into his home, wouldn't it? Give him work right there on his four-acre mini-farm, feed him, build up his confidence, love him. That would have been the right thing, wouldn't it?

But Cliff hadn't done any of that, and in fact, even when he prayed for Billy during that four-month span, he felt as if he were committing some sort of lie.

Then Billy called that night, and Cliff tried to prepare himself for whatever was to come next.

"Hello."

"Mr. Garrett, it's me, Billy Overton."

"Hey Billy, how in the world are you?"

"Well, I ain't too good right now, Mr. Garrett."

"It's been quite a while Billy. Fill me in on everything."

"Yes sir, it's been rough, but I been making it best I can. You know I ain't no quitter, Mr. Garrett. Back when you was talking about going back to truck driving, … well, that's what I done. A man with a small fleet of regional trucks put me on, and I was driving back and forth on a dedicated route about four hundred miles a day. "Course I was living in the truck, you know, and I was saving up a little money too. Then I got sick. My heart gave in. I blacked out and on the way to the hospital it quit beating. They say I was dead for a while but I came back. I don't remember a thing about it. But I guess it was God that said it just ain't my time to go." Billy stopped to catch his breath. To Cliff, it sounded like he was quite winded.

"That's amazing Billy. So, you don't remember anything after you went out?"

He wanted so much for Billy to be able to confirm a heaven experience, a Jesus experience. Cliff had been a big NDE (near death experience) fan for years.

"No sir, I don't remember nothin' about it."

"Where were you Billy?"

"Just outside St. Louis. They kept me, aw, probably five or six days and they turned me out."

"Did your insurance pay for most of it?"

"No sir. I was on the eighty-seventh day of the ninety-day waiting period. They say I owe them three hundred and fifteen thousand dollars."

Cliff's heart shrunk. Three hundred and fifteen grand? He realized that if the shoe had been on the other foot, and it was himself with such a bill, and if he'd had no health insurance, why he'd be homeless in a matter of months.

"Look Billy, that's the least of your concerns. They write off similar cases every day." It was then Cliff realized that Billy was probably homeless right now, again.

"Where are you now, Billy."

"I'm in the same hospital you picked me up from. I've had two more heart attacks since that day in St. Louis. I was able to get back here, and then these two hit me."

"What can be done, Billy."

"I reckon I'll just die if it happens again. I don't want to. I ain't no quitter. I still want to come to yals' church, but they going to put me out again, tomorrow morning."

"Where you gonna' go?"

"I got just enough of my savings left; I got me a room for two weeks, and the social worker here helped me apply for disability."

Cliff didn't have the heart to break the bad news to him – social security disability claims take a minimum of six months to process. Usually they take a year or two or even longer.

"Mr. Garrett, I was wondering if you might be able to pick me up tomorrow and drive me to the room. Instead of cab fare, I figure I'll need that money to eat on."

"Okay Billy, that won't be a problem."

The next morning Cliff was waiting outside the hospital for Billy. A nurse helped Billy out of the wheel chair and helped him into Cliff's car. Cliff was surprised. Billy was even larger than the last time he'd seen him, and his color was awful – a sandy gray with bad, red-flaked eyes.

After Cliff had driven Billy to the dump called The Circle Three Boarding House, and got him into his room, he drove away wondering when he'd get the next call from Billy. It didn't take long; it was three weeks later when the call came.

"Mr. Garrett, I'm over here at a big hospital, not the same one as last time."

"What are they doing for you?"

"Well, something about some stints and another by-pass, whatever that is."

"You're getting good care it sounds like."

"Yes sir, they treating me pretty good. Mr. Garrett, I was wondering if maybe you could bring me a few things?"

"What do you need, Billy? I'll try."

"I need some underwear and a pair of pants to wear for when I get out. My old stuff don't fit me."

"Okay, I can do that."

The next day Cliff walked into the hospital with a bag of some things for Billy. He got to the floor he thought Billy was on and found the correct room number, but the patient in there was not Billy, it was a young woman, who like many on this floor, was hooked up to all kinds of tubes and electronic monitors.

Cliff's thoughts froze in anguish, *My God, Billy's passed away, and I sat idly by doing nothing for him.* He turned and walked back to the nurses' station.

"When did Billy Overton pass away?"

"Uh, … Sir, he didn't pass away. He was transferred to another facility."

"Oh, oh. I brought some things for him. Can you tell me where he is?"

"No sir, uh, you'll have to go down to admin. There will be a business counsellor you can talk to."

"Okay, thank you."

A few minutes later Cliff was sitting in a small cubicle with a heavy-set middle aged woman who had a cheery smile bulging from her fat lips. She hit a few keys on her computer and said, "Let me see … Yes, we moved Mr. Overton to Saint Teresa's early this morning." She looked up and had nothing else to say.

"I see. Look, I'm wondering if you could give me a little insight into his overall situation. Not so much his medical status, but you know, the money picture. How will a man like Billy be able to absorb these huge medical bills?" There was another way he'd wanted to ask the question, and there was a lot more he wished they could tell him about the entire situation.

What he got from the administration specialist who dealt with indigent patients was, "We can't share any

private information with you. But what I can tell you is
that generally speaking when a patient has absolutely no
resources of any kind, they are moved from one facility to
another quite quickly. It's unfortunate, but I'm sure you
understand. The financial exposure is just too great. I'm
sure Saint Teresa's will do all they can do."

The next day Cliff found Billy in a nice room at Saint
Teresa's. "You are a hard man to keep up with. Here's the
things you asked for."

"Thank you Mr. Garrett." Billy looked defeated. As
they talked there was no "I ain't a quitter" from Billy, but
he did share some of his last ditch plans with Cliff. "You
know I ain't got no money Mr. Garrett, but I do have a
good pick-up truck and a Harley Davidson motorcycle."

"I didn't know that."

"Yes sir. They're both in good shape. I guess I'll have
to sell them to live off of 'til my disability comes in."

"Sounds like a plan."

"You want to buy a good truck Mr. Garrett?"

"Oh, no. I don't need a truck." The truth was, the old
beat up farm truck he had was on its last round-up, and he
needed to find another truck as soon as he could. But when
he remembered Billy's affinity for selling vehicles without a
clear title, well … he wasn't about to do business with him.
And this made Cliff, once again, feel like a low-down snake.

It was four days later before Cliff heard from Billy
again.

"Mr. Garrett, it's me, Billy Overton."

"Hey Billy. I bet you've got good news. You're going to tell me they've fixed up your heart so good that you're going back to work tomorrow."

"No sir. They're putting me out on the street this afternoon. They're not sending me to another hospital. And I can't hardly walk no more."

Cliff couldn't say anything even if he'd wanted to.

After more silence Billy said, "I don't know what I'm going to do."

"Billy there's no way I can get over there this afternoon. That hospital is seventy miles away. Let me make a couple of calls, see if we can't find a room for you tonight. Can you call me back in forty-five minutes?"

"Yes sir."

"Okay." *Oh brother! It's coming undone this time. I'll probably slide down in the pit with him by the time this is over.* Cliff haggled with a motel proprietor close to Saint Teresa's in the town seventy miles away. After a half hour of electronic confusion and internet connections, Cliff had a cheap motel room reserved for Billy, with a cash payout to the taxi driver that would haul Billy to the motel.

"Mr. Garrett, it's me."

"Okay Billy, I've got you a room set up and I ..." he was cut off by Billy.

"Mr. Garrett, thank you for doing that, but I won't need it now."

"You won't?"

"No sir. You know that man I drove the truck for, well he's going to buy my pick-up and my motorcycle and he's gonna' let me work over there on his lot, and there's a room I can stay in too." Billy's spirits seemed to have taken a decidedly upward trend.

"He's coming over here this afternoon to pick me up and take me back with him."

"Well, well. That's good news Billy. You know good things happen to those that wait upon the Lord. I better call the motel right now and cancel the room."

"Yes sir. Thank you again ... for everything."

"Billy, ah ... you're welcome."

Cliff cancelled the room reservation and was told they would make the credit entry back on his credit card. *Right! I'll bet.* What was the matter with him? Why couldn't he trust anyone. He didn't know why. He just knew that that *was* a very accurate description of his true psychology. He didn't want it to be that way, but it was.

Around 4:30 in the afternoon Cliff got a call on his cell phone. "Mr. Garrett, it's me, Billy Overton."

"All right."

"Mr. Garrett, the man can't come to get me today. He ain't changed his mind, but he can't come 'til tomorrow morning."

"Aw Billy, you're kidding."

"No sir, I ain't kidding."

"Okay, I'll tell you what I'm going to do. Instead of trying for the motel room again, I'm going to call the hospital administration and see if they can keep you one more night. Is that okay with you Billy?"

Billy wasn't sure if Mr. Garrett wasn't trying to be a smart-ass. Actually, Cliff wasn't sure of it either.

Billy said, "Mr. Garrett, it looks to me like there ain't nobody that's gonna' help me. I'm sorry I been a trouble to you. You don't got to worry about me."

"Billy, I told you I'd call administration. Let me see what I can do."

"All right."

After convincing the authorities downstairs in administration that Mr. Overton had a solid job starting tomorrow morning and that Mr. Overton wanted nothing more than to depart their hospital, and that unfortunately there was no prospect of finding other shelter for the night (a lie), could they possibly make an exception, just this one time, and allow Mr. Overton to remain in his room this evening.

He was totally amazed when they said, "Yes." They would do it, this one time.

It was another two months before Cliff heard from Billy again. He was almost convinced that maybe this time Billy really had found a permanent place, a solid footing he could live his life on. But still there was a nagging worry that the worst was yet to come.

"Mr. Garrett, how you doing?"

"Hey Billy, everything is fine here. How are you doing?"

"I'm in a nursing home. I broke my ankle, and my heart still ain't working very good."

"I'm terribly sorry you're having such a difficult time. Where is the nursing home? I'd like to come pay you a visit."

"It's over here in Cliptonville. It's my hometown where I grew up. You know where it is, don't you?"

"Yes I do. Only about forty miles from here. Look, I'll try to make it over there this week. Is there anything you need that I can bring you?"

"No sir. Thank you."

"I'll see you soon Billy."

A few days later Cliff found Billy being wheeled down a hallway, on the way to physical therapy. The nurse left them alone for a couple of minutes. Cliff learned that Billy still had a little money left from the sale of his truck and motorcycle. There was no reason to believe his heart would ever be any stronger, but still, Billy was optimistic about his social security claim coming in someday soon. The two men shook hands and as Cliff drove away he was beginning to finally feel a little better about the way he'd been handling the entire eight-month ordeal with Billy. Yes, he'd harbored some deep seated regret that he had ever got involved in the first place. Most of it probably having to do with his selfish and sordid nature as an unpolluted hypocrite. No, he was not perfect, but he *had* answered the call to some degree, every single time. And what about today. He actually *wanted* to pay a visit to Billy. He really *wanted* to know how he was doing. All in all, Cliff was a little more comfortable with himself this time.

Billy called Cliff three weeks later with good news and bad news. The bad news was that he had been transferred to another nursing home. They took good care of him, Billy said, but he just couldn't understand why all these hospitals, rehab centers, and nursing homes kept moving him around. Why wouldn't someone keep him under one roof until his medical issues were fixed?

The good news was that the cast on his leg was ready to come off, and that he knew that this time when he returned to work everything was going to be just fine. "I ain't no quitter, Mr. Garrett," he had said.

The next time Billy called it was late fall, night-time temperatures were flirting with freezing already, and Cliff always cringed as soon as he heard Billy's voice. "Mr. Garrett, it's me, Billy Overton."

"Hey Billy, what's up?"

"Aw, nothing much, just wanted to see how you and your wife is doing?"

"We're fine. How about you? Did that cast ever come off?"

"Yes sir. I can get around a little bit, but not much."

"Where are you staying these days?"

"At my daughter's house."

"Your daughter?"

"Yes sir, it's hard to believe, but I found a daughter I didn't know I had."

"You don't say?"

"Yes sir. Well … really, she found me I guess you would say. You know, I think I told you about my old girlfriend, didn't I? But I never told you about my ex-wife. Oh, she was bad to me, Mr. Garrett. When we split up, she took everything I had. She was just plain mean. And that husband of hers, he's the main reason nobody in my family will help me. He's been telling lies about me from day one.

"Well, anyway, one of the kitchen workers over at the nursing home was talking to me one day, and when she found out who I was, she told me she knew my ex-wife really good and that she'd been holding back a big secret from me for years. She asked me if I knew a twenty-year-old girl named Lewellyn, and I said, 'No, I sure don't'. 'She's your daughter', she told me, and she said, 'If you want me to, Billy, I'll tell her you're here. I know she'd like to see you.'

"She come to visit me and before I knowed it, she asked me to come live with her. She's got a good husband. He's a carpenter and he cuts wood on the side. And Mr. Garrett, I got two grand babies! We all live in a small trailer, and I'm helping them out with what's left of my money from the truck and the motorcycle."

"Billy that's wonderful, just wonderful! Look at the amazing things He hath done."

"Yes sir! God's been good to me, and Mr. Garrett, you ought'a see that little grandson of mine. He follows me around like a little puppy."

It was bitter cold on an early January day when Cliff hit the receive button on his cell phone, "Mr. Garrett, it's me, Billy."

"Hey Billy, how you been doing?"

"My daughter and her husband had to move and said I couldn't stay with them anymore."

"Oh no, Billy. I'm sorry to hear that. Where are you?"

"I got me a room for a few more days, and then I don't know what I'm going to do. I spent most of my money on Christmas for my grand babies and my daughter."

"Aw … Billy … All I know to do is keep praying for you."

Cliff knew there was a lot more he *could* do, but as he clicked off his cell phone in a couple more minutes, he knew he wouldn't.

Cliff went about his semi-retired routine the next couple of weeks in a low-down funk. He knew why that was, but he still just could not mount whatever it took to do the right thing – the one thing that needed doing, the one thing that would remove his name from that pitiable list of authentic, unpolluted hypocrites. He continued his once a week jail ministry, and his part-time medical transport driving job, and the endless yard and gardening work on his four-acre home site, but he was always wondering why he had a backbone of mush when it came to actually giving physical aid to people who needed it, giving himself to people who needed him.

He also continued his church activities at the tiny Methodist church he and his wife had been a member of for over thirty years. As a Methodist Lay Speaker, he was routinely called on to present the sermon on Sunday morning from time to time – as he always told the prisoners at jail, when the "real preacher" was out of town or ill. The very next Sunday he'd been called on, so Cliff sat down at his desk and began studying his Bible in order to prepare a lively sermon.

He came across scripture passages in John's Gospel that spoke to him in a special way, in an intimate way; they were the words of Jesus: "He who abides in me, and I in him, bears much fruit; for without Me you can do nothing." "If you abide in Me, and My words abide in you, you will ask what you desire, and it shall be done for you." "This is my commandment, that you love one another as I have loved you."

Yes, Cliff thought to himself, *these scriptures are talking to me.* He kept thinking about them and searching them for meaning. It didn't take him long. The light came on.

Okay, "Without me you can do nothing." Of course! And what have I been doing with Billy? I've bailed him out of two or three bad situations and then left him to wallow around in the pit. I've never tried to teach him to depend one hundred percent on Jesus! I have not done that! Of course! I'm such a simpleton! Not only have I not tried to teach Billy, I've demonstrated by my own actions that I must not believe it myself. "Without me you can do nothing." I've been acting like the most important thing was seeing that his physical well-being was being taken care of, and I haven't even done a very good job of that. But the real issue should have been ... does Billy know Jesus, does he want Him, can he depend on Him one hundred percent!? And the "If you abide in Me, and My words abide in you, You will ask what you desire, and it shall be done for you."

Of course it will! How come my prayers haven't been, Oh Lord please help Billy open his heart to you ... not, Oh Lord please let Billy find a job, a home, food!

And, "This is my commandment, that you love one another as I have loved you." Of course! If I had loved Billy first, helped him get swallowed up in prayer and dependence on the Lord, I know, no matter what, I know he would be safe from all harm – safe from all harm, now and forever.

Sunday's sermon went off without a hitch. As usual, Cliff could sense that some members of the congregation were tuned into what he was preaching, and some might as well have been sleeping. And of course, some *were* sleeping.

A few days later Cliff was driving home after having dropped a patient off at a hospital. The medical escort driving he did was just about perfect for his semi-retired lifestyle. It was only part-time, maybe one or two days a week and left him plenty of time for his other activities. It was cold and there were a few spits of snow flurries. He was out in an area that was run down more than the small town it was close to – trailers, junk yards, auto repair shops, and a few other small businesses scattered here and there. Where the two lane highway cut through a section of higher ground, there was a steel guard rail on Cliff's side blocking a pretty steep drop off to the creek bed below. As Cliff sped by, he saw a man sitting on the guard rail. *Was that Billy?* He wasn't sure at all that it was him. He'd barely caught a glimpse of him. But he couldn't say for certain it wasn't him. He thought about turning back and checking on the man, whoever it was, but he didn't.

On the way home he started beating up on himself again. *What is wrong with me? Why won't I help people?* But then he remembered what he'd promised himself last week when he'd stumbled on the scripture from John. He immediately began a lengthy prayer, that if he had not already done so, that Billy would go to his knees and pray that Jesus would take control of his life. Cliff prayed and prayed. He wanted to touch all the bases concerning the saving of Billy's soul.

It was maybe five days later that Cliff got the last phone call from Billy.

"Hey Mr. Garrett."

"Billy, how are you? I've been praying for you."

"Thank you sir."

"Are you all right."

"I'm pretty cold."

"Where are you Billy?"

"I'm in town."

"Do you still have your room?"

"No sir, my money ran out a few days ago."

"Where have you been staying?"

"On the streets. I slept here on this park bench last night."

"Do the cops threaten to haul you in? I mean … maybe that would be …" Cliff's voice faded away.

"They just ask for ID, that's all."

"Have you been to the mission?"

"Yes sir. They won't take me in."

"Well Billy … I, uh … I don't know what to do. Let me make a couple of calls. Can you call me back in half an hour?"

"Yes sir."

Cliff got the number to the City's Human Services Department and dialed them up. After two receptionists passed his call along he was finally talking to a social worker, Ms. Shequita Harrison.

"Yes mam, my name is Cliff Garrett. My church and I have been helping out a little with a single man who has finally went through his own resources and what little we could help him with. He's living on the streets now. Are there any programs or any help that Human Services might be able to offer this man? He's only a few blocks away from you right now. And I know it's going to be really cold tonight, and …"

Ms. Harrison cut him off, "He would have to come in to our office, and we'd do an assessment. Has he been to the mission?"

"Yes mam. He said they wouldn't take him."

"No, that's not right. They will take any homeless, that is unless he's got in trouble over there."

"Trouble?"

"Yes, you know, if he's a trouble maker – fighting, stealing, whatever."

"I see."

"Anyway, he would need to come in so we could do an assessment."

"Okay, I'll let him know that. Like I said, he's not far from you right now. What time do you close today?"

"Three thirty, and Mr. Garrett …"

"Yes mam."

"If he can't make it today, we open at eight tomorrow morning."

"Thanks for your help. I'll tell him."

Cliff scrolled down his contact list on his phone to Billy Overton and keyed the "dial" button. As Billy's cell phone rang on the other end, Cliff was wondering if he should ask Billy whether he'd been in any trouble at the mission. He remembered that Billy had spent some time there back in the summer before he got his truck-driving job. He finally decided he wouldn't mention it.

Billy's phone rang and rang. Finally, a recording came on that said, "We are sorry. You have reached a number that's not in service at this time."

Cliff figured that eventually Billy would call him back, but he never did.

The Deal

* * *

Gary H. Baker

Monday, June 19, 2017, Edgewood Tennessee

My alarm goes off at 4:10 A. M. By 4:30 A. M. I've had my first cup of coffee and I'm halfway dressed in my running outfit. I have my running shorts on, and my t-shirt, but not my running shoes and socks. They don't go on till' I'm ready to go out the door – just another pre-run ritual I've constructed over the years.

I won't need any sun screen lotion nor a large-brimmed hat as I'll be through running before the sun comes up. I do a few stretches, making sure I work on my lower back. The only problem I note is that nagging right hip joint that's been acting up lately.

I drink plenty of water and I'm out the door by 4:40 with my second cup of coffee in hand. Tomorrow is the first day of summer, so as I walk up the small hill to the back of my property, I'm not surprised to see the black night begin to die and a spidery cobweb of different shades of gray begin to assert themselves beyond the low hills to the east. The dew is thick on the grass and in five more minutes it will probably be light enough to detect some patchy fog that I'm sure I'll see in some of the fields and over the little branch running cool a quarter mile away at the base of the bluff.

The second cup of coffee is going down now. Boy! Do I love good coffee! And gee! What a swell morning it's shaping up to be! (Forgive the Sinclair Lewis sound-alike.) The thing about this morning is that I just *had* to get out early and see what two or three miles would feel like. I've been eating way too much lately, and running way too little. It was about three months ago, I remember, my most recent attempt at losing some serious weight by re-booting my one time, long ago, running lifestyle. That was just before my dermatologist removed a squamous-cell skin cancer from my left leg and replaced it with sixteen stitches. Yeah, I had a pretty good excuse that time. But, no excuses this time. My part-time gig of transporting medical patients around to various clinics in Middle Tennessee has dispatched me on just a very few trips lately, but I do have one later this morning at 10:00, so an early morning run is going to fit nicely.

It's close to 5:00 now, that second cup of coffee is in my belly and that fog I suspected would soon show itself is doing just that. But it's not heavy, not dense, just a sheer, see-through lace curtain, haunting the low spots and the slow, easy moving country stream, known all over rural Tennessee as a branch.

Time to quit puttering around Red Neck Clubhouse; it's time to start running. Red Neck Clubhouse is my outdoor man-cave where I mostly drink in late afternoons and early evenings by campfire, and it's the focal point of my Par Too Nine Hole Red Neck Golf Course. The golf course doesn't have any putting greens or decent fairways, just some stripped down saplings stuck in the ground with red rags hanging off them pretending to be pins. The large sign welcoming visitors to this corner of my modest three-and-a-half-acre slice of heaven says: Welcome To Red Neck Clubhouse and Par Too Golf Course, Delightfully Tacky, Yet Unrefined.

Okay, start very slowly. Do the one hundred yards downslope and act like you are a turtle (that won't be hard). Ouch! What's going on with that stupid hip? It feels like some sand found its way into the joint.

The same worry I've had for at least the last three or four months is sneaking up on me again – the worry that *this time* there is something really wrong with my right hip joint; that *this time* it's not just the ordinary pain and discomfort that seventy-one-year-old used-to-be runners put up with continually in and around most of their major joints. Yeah, the recent worry has been centered on this stupid right hip joint. And why shouldn't it be? My older sister, Donna, I mean, did she not just have her second hip-replacement done? Bad hip joints evidently run in my family!

Quit whining, start running. You know good and well that most minor joint pain and discomfort tends to disappear as soon as you do the first mile at a slow jog. That's true – it always has. Well, not always. There *was* that time in 1986 I did my Forest Gump impression and set sail to run all the way across the country, 2,700 miles … and did. Well, not exactly. I had to walk about a third of the mileage because, this time, the pain (in my knee) would not go away. And, just to make sure the record is straight, it really wasn't a Forest Gump impersonation, a copy-cat experience. No, it couldn't have been. It was eight years before the movie came out in 1994 that I ran and walked across the United States on behalf of The Just Say No movement of that era.

That was thirty-one years ago. Quit whining and start running, or you might as well go back in the house and waste away the morning watching all the lefty talking heads do their best to end Donald Trump's presidency.

"You're right, let's get moving," I said to myself. Okay, here we go, nice and easy, a hundred and thirty yards down the hill, over by that far fence line. Not too bad, a little pain in the hip; It'll go away.

Coming back up the gentle slope now, right along that same white board fence which is the out of bounds border for the number seven hole on the golf course. I am halfway up the slope when it hits me – Ouch! Ouch! Ouch! It's the hip! Feels like bone on bone! The initial stab of pain is quick, just a second, and it brings me to a halt. But I start jogging again, slowly, because that first jolt of pain left in its wake only the same mild discomfort and tightness I had earlier.

Going ever-so-slowly now, but still jogging. Shifting my attention away from the hip pain itself to the mental aspect of what this means. It doesn't take long to realize that when you have sharp, bone-on-bone pain in a hip socket, that your running days may be over. No! It can't be! I'd never dreamed it would all come to an end because of a bad hip.

It was time to turn to the one place I knew I could get some answers from, or at least get some wisdom as to how I should handle this new curve-ball life has thrown at me.

"God, is this it? Is this the end of my running?" I waited for an answer. What might the Heavenly Father have to say about my situation? Still I waited for an answer. And then He answered me. "That depends on you, Gary." Oh crap, why does He always throw it back on me – where it belongs! Sometimes I just hate the wisdom He so effortlessly tosses around.

"It depends on me?" Now, let it sink in. Think about it. What is He saying? After a moment or two I think I begin to understand. He is wanting me to do something. What? Do we have a "deal" in the making? But wait, I know that's not the way it works. I know you don't make deals with God. But, I also know, He is perfectly willing to make deals with us. There is a big difference.

I'm still jogging very slowly, hoping a white-hot zinger won't rip that hip joint again. What does he want me to do that might allow Him to see fit to extend my running aspirations? And I'm talking *right now;* I'm not contemplating years and years of future running. No, I'm talking today! Now! The next sixty seconds! That would be enough for me, I thought.

Then it came to me. He wants me to quit drinking. Well, of course He does. He always wants good things for His children. *I* want me to quit drinking too. I've done it lots of times before, one time for seventeen years. That was when the kids were still at home and I wanted to be a visible role model for them. And then … and well … and well… I drank off and on ever since – mostly on. Not crazy drinking – most of the time. There were a few nights of over indulgence, but not many.

"Okay Father, I'm in. If You are setting up for me what I think You are setting up for me, I'm all the way in. I will stop drinking if you will keep my hip joint together in order that I may continue running."

There! It's done! The deal was made, and guess what? That morning, before the sun ever came up, I finished a decent two-and-a-half-mile jog with no more white-hot-zingers ripping through my joint. It looked to me like The Big Man Upstairs had given me one more chance to extend my lifelong running obsession. He'd given me a sign and He'd offered me a deal that I accepted.

Now, the question was, could I live up to my end of the bargain?

Well, the first five days were swell. I didn't have a drink of any kind. Then one night I had a glass of red wine with a meal. Then a couple of nights later I had a couple of cold beers after a round of golf. And then a couple of nights after that, the bourbon, the campfire, and myself, and well ... let's just say, we all had a very pleasant evening.

Crap! I haven't lived up to my end of the deal. And so, I have every right to expect a white-hot-zinger to rip through my hip socket. Would you not agree? We'll find out later today as I plan on lacing up the running shoes and seeing what a three-mile jog might feel like. You see, I've not tried a three miler since that pre-dawn adventure previously mentioned which occurred a couple of weeks ago. I've been very busy. But today, we will see.

Okay, here we go. It's 7:30 A.M., the sun has been up almost two hours, and I've got plenty of coffee in me, and I've got the preliminary stretching out of the way. Will the three- miler I'm contemplating be mostly pain free or will that hip joint explode with blinding pain?

Here's the answer: just like two weeks ago, the first two hundred yards wasn't bad at all. Then, coming up that same hill – WHAMO! It felt like a dump truck had unloaded a ton of rocks and gravel into the hip joint. I nearly went to the ground but instead heard myself scream out a series of four letter expletives which started with the letters S and F. They might have been in reverse order, F and S. I don't remember. But I do remember thinking that God did not forget the deal He had made with me.

Will I ever run pain-free again? Will I ever *run* again? I had not lived up to the deal the Big Man Upstairs had so generously laid out for me. And it doesn't mean I'm condemned to hell. No, it does not. What it means is that once again I have failed to be the child He wants me to be. I'm still His child. I'm still saved. My sins are still forgiven, but alas, I have fallen short of the desires and expectations He has for me. It doesn't drag me down, it doesn't make me love Him any less, because I know He doesn't love me any less because of my failures and short-comings.

Last Sunday the members of our adult Sunday School class were in a deep discussion about the nature of God. Our pastor was with us and after many attempts by us all to describe His nature, our pastor finally stated, "Well, I just can't put it into words. I'm afraid I'm incapable of describing the awesome nature of God."

Without any hesitation, I spoke up assertively and said, "I think I can. How about this: God is pure love. His love is eternal. It always was. It always is, and it always will be, and it is unchanging."

Epilogue

It's been a month since my last white-hot-zinger exploded in my hip. One day I jogged a good four miles. A couple of other days I was able to do a mile or two. And there were several days I'd start out slowly and after a quarter-mile decided against continuing – there was pain, but no white-hot zingers.

What does the future hold for me as an aging runner? I don't know. But I do know that I will continue to make the effort a couple of times a week. I will get up early, stretch, drink my coffee and head out the door. I will start slowly and if I can go a mile or so, I will try to pick up the pace. If the pain stops me, it stops me. But it won't be God's fault one way or the other. It will all be on my shoulders. God showed me a way to get it done, and I have not chosen His way. His way, His wisdom is perfect. Ours is flawed. He only wants the best for us. And, He forgives us when we fail.

A Willing Vessel

* * *

Gary H. Baker

THERE WERE SIX or eight drivers milling about at the check-in window, each one wanting to get his or her dock assignment. Danny Nalley already knew what his load was – auto parts – and where it was going – Salt Lake City. The drivers all wanted to get loaded and skedaddle out of this distribution center near Little Rock. You're not making any money unless you're moving.

Danny had been driving a truck for a long time. He was fifty-one years old. Little did he know, that four years in the future, on the day he would turn fifty-five years old, it would be the same day exactly that he drove his six -millionth mile. Things always seemed to unfold in singular, uncanny ways in Danny's life.

Danny was born in Yakima, Washington in 1962, and just a week later, his family moved to a little town in northern Arkansas. Danny has a gift of excellent memory. He recalls with great detail most of his life. He told me that, "Times were hard and things were bad in north-ern Arkansas as me and my two brothers and my sister began growing up. My parents, each year, would go out to Washington state and pick fruit. That's what you would call "fruit tramps." They'd go out there and pick fruit through the harvest and make good money, then come back home and with the wages they made in North Arkansas to go with that, we'd survive through the year."

I asked Danny about his memories of growing up in Northern Arkansas. "The very first memory that I had was in the back floor-board of a 1953 Ford punching it out with my brothers. My two older brothers and me, we always fought, fist fights, and most of the time it was just for fun, I mean it was just how we were raised. The things that stand out in my mind on all of it, looking back, is once in a while going to church with my grand-mother, uh, just once in a while. I didn't have no idea what kind of an impact it would have on my life eventually, but, through all these years, the love of my mom and my dad, the togetherness of the family was complete. My mother would fight a circle-saw, just like she would stand flat footed and fist fight any man who drew a breath over one of her kids, and she done it before," Danny laughs a little.

"But, as for my dad, the same thing. With that being said, my grandpa, my mom's dad, he stayed out there after harvest one year and bought a log truck. He had a good job in the log woods, and he bought a log truck. When

I was four years old, I went with him to work in the log truck one day. From that day forth, I knew my life-long dream was to drive a truck, a semi-truck."

I asked him, "Four years old?"

"Yep."

"Okay, how old you reckon you were when you gave your life to Jesus?"

"About forty or forty-one."

"What happened then?"

"Um ..."

"How did you know you wanted to, uh ...?"

"Well, I made a deal with the Lord. Prior to this, other than driving a truck, after I became a teenager and started driving when I was sixteen years old, my biggest deal was to get drunk in every state in the United States, and have a bar-room fight in every state."

"Did you achieve that dream, in every state?"

"Every continental state, and then in every Canadian province, and Alaska, and in Old Mexico."

"Wow!" Is all I could say.

"But I got into a spot of trouble, a very bad spot of trouble with some bad fellers. We'll leave it at that. I made a deal when I got into that lion's den."

I said, "This is aside from the story I'm going to write about what happened at the Pilot truck stop in Tacoma. Uh, do you want it to stay private, or not?"

"Um, just put that I found myself in the lion's den, and I made a deal. I got on my knees and I prayed to the Lord. I said, 'Lord, if you'll deliver me out of this lion's den, like you did Daniel, I promise you, I'll never take another drink of alcohol and I'll do my best to serve you from this point forward.'"

"About how old were you then?"

"I think about thirty-seven or thirty-eight at the time. And it isn't just an instant change for somebody that's had my lifestyle prior to this."

I understood exactly what he meant by that. I asked, "This encounter with these bad guys, did they succeed in what they were trying to do?"

"Un ugh, no, no. The Lord delivered me just like He said. You don't really make a deal with the Lord, but if you do, you better stick to it."

I laughed a little bit, "You ain't going to believe this. I wrote a story two weeks ago called <u>The Deal.</u>"

"Um, really?" Danny is laughing.

"Yeah, it's about me making a deal with God, and in the story, it says, 'well, wait a minute, I know that ain't right. I know you don't make deals with Him. But He is very capable of making a deal with you."

Danny is laughing, "Yeah!"

"But it doesn't work the other way around."

"Un unh," Danny affirms.

"That is cool," I said.

"Against all odds, human odds, I was delivered from the lion's den. Literally, delivered from the lion' den, and I said, 'Okay Lord, ...'"

I cut him off, "Do you want to give me any details of that, a delivery from the lion's den? Or would you prefer that not to be a part of this story?" It dawned on me that I had already asked this question. I suppose I was going after the real nitty-gritty, but I was going to be disappointed.

"No, let's leave that part out."

"What about if I said something like, 'You had an encounter with some really bad people, and you made a deal with, uh ..., you begged God to get you out of the lion's den, and He did, and not go any further?"

"That'll work."

"So, that was somewhere around the neighborhood of thirty-seven years old, and you felt like forty or forty-one was more like the time you really came to Jesus?"

"Well, I started trying to serve the Lord then, but it was whenever ... in the aspect of driving a truck, with all the brawling and all the fighting, and that kind of stuff that a person does, from a kid, I was just a kid is all it was, uh, it's a hard habit, it's a hard habit. When somebody mouths off, I was always the person ... (a long pause), I didn't talk until after it was done. If it was one or half a dozen, I didn't talk 'til afterwards. I'd say, 'Now, why are you doing this? or why did you do this?' you know, and that was how it always was."

I said, "Have you ever thought about how you had that type of personality? I mean, that's an explosive personality, isn't it?"

Danny laughed, "Genetics."

I asked, "Mom, dad, grandmother?"

"Pretty much all of them, I guess. My great grandpa on my mother's side drove a getaway car for Pretty Boy Floyd, part time. Them two were buddies. They worked together for four or five years in Oklahoma before he started robbing banks and stuff. They were good friends. Anyway, his temperament was smooth and easy going, but when he'd check out, he was meaner than a two-headed copperhead. That was my great grandpa. My grandpa his side grew up in the depression and the WPA days, and he was champion for Arkansas state boxing, and that was fun to him. Now, my great grandpa, Bill, … I'm doing lineage, he was half Cherokee Indian."

"Did he come across in the Trail of Tears?"

"His grandpa did, on that side. On the other side, my grandpa Jim, he's my momma's dad, he was about half Cherokee also. Anyway, there's some Irish throwed in on top of some Cherokee, with some English."

"So, to make a long story short, you feel like some of your fighting personality was purely genetics. Was the one grandfather you said was a boxer, was he a big influence?"

"No, he really wasn't. He never really was."

"So, you just remember being that way. If somebody was going to act out and smart-off or something, you were getting involved."

"It was a done deal. I would be very nice sometimes, and sometimes not. Most of the time I didn't, … I'm not a very big person, not a very big guy. I never gave them a whole lot of opportunity for anything, so, that being said, through all the fights, knife fights, gun fights, bare knuckle brawls, I used to make a lot of money out back of the truck stop parking lots, fighting."

Danny had previously told me that he had won second place in a big underground fighting tournament in the eighties.

In a reflective tone, Danny said, "There's a lot to all of this. Through it all, it was building up. What I didn't see through all them years, through all that time, the Lord was with me every minute, even though I wasn't with Him, He was there with me, protecting me."

* * *

As he explained a little earlier, Danny eventually got his wish and began his life-long truck driving career at around the age of sixteen. Now, some thirty-five years later, the line he's in at the check-in window at the auto parts distributor in Little Rock is moving on up to the window. When Danny gets to the shipping clerk behind the window, he's told there would be no load for him because there was a screw- up with the broker's paperwork who assigned the load to the company Danny was leased onto. Another half a day wasted. Just add it to the list of problems he was having with the company: The money they owed him was hard to get, there were late settlements, there were incorrect settlements, legal hassles, you name it, oh yeah, and a few of those heated arguments with dispatchers – all truckers could tell *those* stories.

Driving back home to northern Arkansas, only a couple of hours away, Danny realized something was going to have to change. This arrangement just would not work out. And he more or less knew that the changes that were coming were going to be immediate and that they were being driven by God.

The next day at home there was a trip waiting for Danny. It had been sent to his on-board qual-com computer outside in the truck. But Danny's morning was going a different direction. He'd not even had the interest to go out and see what plans the company had for him. Normally, that would be the first thing any trucker would do at home in the morning. But today was not going to turn out to be a normal day.

His wife was at work, and his kids were in school. Danny's thinking was a clutter of mild anxiety and intense spiritual excitement. Something was about to happen. What?

The next thing Danny knew was that a friend of his pulled up outside and invited himself inside.

"Sure, come on in. What's up," Danny said.

After a few preliminaries, Danny's friend said, "Dan, I'm supposed to give you the money for a plane ticket. Don't ask me why, I just know I'm supposed to do it. So, if you are ready to go, pack your stuff, I'm gonna' put you on a plane, l believe, to Washington state. Does that sound right?"

Danny said, "You're exactly right."

Danny's mind was beginning to vibrate with a sure sense of some unseen mission that was welling up. A plane ticket to Seattle? Sure, he thought. Why not? Maybe this is supposed to be my wake-up call to get back to my mining claim near Chehalis, Washington, eighteen miles from Mt. Saint Helens. Hitting a good lick on my claim surely would alleviate some of the financial strain.

As Danny later told me, all that was happening and all that would play out in the next few days was, "The Lord had dwindled me down to put me to where He wanted me, financially, everything to where He wanted me, so I'd obey, I guess."

Yes, that was Danny's thinking. His unexpected trip to his mining claim was God's will, and Danny was a willing vessel to be used, and he was more than eager to get the trip started.

The flight to Seattle originated in Tulsa, Oklahoma. Danny's friend drove the less than three-hour trip and wished Danny smooth sailing as he deposited him at the departure gates of the airport. When Danny made his appearance at the check-in counter, he was told that the flight was cancelled and that the next flight to Seattle would be departing in six hours.

"Well Lord, You told me to go. I didn't expect this flight to be cancelled. I guess I'd better jump on the first bus going west."

Danny's next attempt to travel towards Washington was also nipped in the bud. There was no reason given as to why, except that as sure as the rain falls from the sky, the bus was "being delayed", and they didn't know if or when another would be available.

"You gotta' GO!" the Lord said again.

And that's what Danny did. He hitch-hiked to somewhere in northwestern Kansas. His resolve to please the Lord ever growing, Danny boarded, this time, an on-schedule Greyhound bus in Kansas and rode it to Seattle where, supposedly, he could make a transfer for the short trip to Chehalis.

Again, with no explanation, the powers that supposedly control the most dependable, most sophisticated public transportation system in the world ... those powers failed. The transfer bus didn't show up. There was no explanation other than there simply would be no transfer bus today.

With no other options, but with the voice of God ringing in his ears, "You gotta' go! You gotta' keep aiming south towards Chehalis," Danny did just that.

He boarded a city bus this time. Danny hoped it would get him a little further south. The bus was not supposed to leave its route and run any further than the southern city limits. But, it did. The driver told Danny, "I've got to meet someone down further south at a park-and-ride near Interstate 5."

By now, of course, Danny was just holding on tight. Nothing was going as planned, or, was it? He was still heading south. And, he knew that's where God wanted him!

When the bus driver put him off at the park-and-ride, Danny thanked the driver for his service and then he walked over to the on-ramp of Interstate 5. He intended to stick his thumb out and hitch on down southward. Before he could get his thumb out, a pick-up truck stopped and Danny jumped in. It didn't go very far, and it let him out, so, Danny walked up the next on-ramp and this time a car stopped and picked him up. "Mister, I never pick up hitch-hikers, never talk to strangers, but I just had to stop and give you a ride. I don't know why. I just had to. I'm not going far, just down here to the Pilot truck stop in Tacoma."

Danny's internal response was the same it had been on every other travel mishap, cancellation, and re-route, "Okay Lord, it's all in Your hands. Just show me where to go and what to do."

The "where to go" was going to be the Pilot truck stop on Interstate 5 in Tacoma. The "what to do", had not presented itself just yet, but it was very close to doing so.

Danny went inside the truck stop. He made a phone call to his cousin that lived down near the Washington-Oregon state line. Yes, his cousin would be glad to drive up to Tacoma and pick him up and then take him back down to his mining claim; be glad to do it. He was on his way.

After spending a little more time inside the truck stop, Danny stepped outside to smoke a cigarette. A late summer chill was in the air, not unusual this far north. It was now around 9:30 PM.

He looked out across the parking lot and saw two boys, maybe 16 and 19 pushing a broke-down car down the exit ramp of the interstate and heading for the truck stop parking lot. Danny went over and helped them push it in. There were two young, 17 and 18, innocent girls, sisters, inside the car, one behind the steering wheel.

As he told me this story, Danny continually reminded me that all four of these young people were just that – innocent lambs, thrust out into an evil world, untested, vulnerable, and Danny had the undeniable and growing feeling that they were about to be attacked. He told me, that at this point, his radar was one-hundred percent on guard-watch, like an eagle-eyed hawk, not knowing when …

It didn't take long. Danny and the two boys got the car into the parking lot and shortly thereafter a big car pulled in next to them. Four rough looking men got out and commenced to cussing, being ornery and acting mean. Danny told the two boys and the two girls to get inside the truck stop. The men said, "No, we're going to take them with us."

Danny pulled his watch off and said, "No boys, I'm the one you need to talk to here, you know, if you feel froggy or whatever. You won't bother these. You won't bother these kids."

They were still running their mouths, all four of them outside the car, Danny, alone, right in front of them. "Well boys, here we are. Just me and you."

The four got back in their car, cussing. They spun their tires out, and away they went. Danny recalled they were covered with "jailhouse tats", and they had a "far-away" look in their eyes and he suspected they were just high enough on drugs to make them brave.

A few minutes later the four kids came back outside. The girls were getting some things out of the trunk, some warmer clothes. They were two sisters and their brother and one of the girl's fiancée. They had been travelling to a church retreat on down further south, and they told

Danny they had called their dad to report the car break-down, and he was on his way.

Danny said that it was about this time that these four innocents began to realize what almost happened – that the boys would have been beat up and probably the girls would have been kidnapped and probably worse.

They were all outside now. It was about an hour later, Danny was looking under the hood again and the girls were going through the trunk again. Danny said, "The Holy Ghost "quickened" me, and I looked around and here comes another car. It slid to a stop, the doors flew open, two of them jumped out, and it looked like maybe a third one was still in the car. They were cussing and fixing to get the girls, and I said, 'Whoa boys, you got the wrong idea here.' It caught them off-guard that I spoke up. I told the girls, 'Go back inside. Here we go again'. Sure enough, they were running their mouth and were getting brave and were going to get the girls, and I said, 'Okay'. I took my watch off again, smiled, and said, 'Well, Okay, go get them.' They said they might shoot me. I said, 'Well Okay, jerk 'em.' They didn't pull any guns, it was just cuss, cuss, cuss, and they got back in the car and spun out and that was it."

Around about one or one-thirty in the morning the kid's father arrived at the truck stop and they were all talking about the earlier events. The younger boy who was the girl's brother told the father what happened when the first car-load of thugs showed up.

"Thank goodness it was over," said their dad.

"No, dad. It happened a second time."

* * *

As I've gone back through Danny's story many times, I've counted at least eleven particularly extraordinary occurrences that put him at a certain spot, at a certain time. They all, each one of them, had to happen, as if on some pre-ordained schedule, in order for him to have been right there at the moment those innocent kids needed him. Still, I have left out of my count two occurrences which makes the tale even more baffling (if you are *not* a believer), and even more spiritually charged (if you *are* a believer).

The first occurrence would be that exact moment Danny decided to step outside the truck stop and have a smoke. If he had done this two minutes before, or two minutes after he actually stepped out into that darkened truck stop parking lot, the two girls, the two boys, all four of them would probably be dead.

The second occurrence was the fact that Danny's cousin, whom Danny had called as soon as he got to the Pilot truck stop, well ... the cousin *did* jump in his car and start out to pick Danny up. If he had gotten there with no delays, he would have whisked Danny out of there, maybe before the bad guys showed up. What would have happened to the girls and the boys then?

And, you may ask, what happened to the cousin? Danny tells me the cousin drove right by the truck stop and ended up almost two hours later at the Canadian border. Danny and the cousin's son drove up there in the middle of the night to extricate him from a hospital. His cousin had "checked out" for a little while. They eventually got him back home early in the morning. Once again, there was no reasonable explanation for the man to have "checked out" when he did. He had no history of mental lapses, ever in his life. This was the first time. It just happened, that's all.

Later that afternoon Danny, nearly exhausted, he hadn't got much, if any sleep, was at his mining claim when the girls' dad drove up to his camp.

"I've got to thank you for saving my daughters and my son. I know they would be dead. The boys would have been beaten up and killed, and the girls raped and killed. I don't know how you did it. I came to thank you again."

"No sir. Thank the Lord," Danny said. "Give Him all the credit. I was just a willing vessel, that's it. I was just a willing vessel. There wasn't any, 'I don't know Lord,' not any, 'Maybe tomorrow Lord,' not any 'I ain't sure Lord.' He put me here for this very purpose, for your children. That tells me they got a great calling on their life."

And it tells me, Danny Nalley has had a great calling on his life as well!

The two men talked into the evening about God. The girls' father was a deacon in the church or maybe a pastor. Danny's high-caliber memory couldn't be sure which, but as the conversation continued, the father kept returning to the one essential question:

"How did you know you were to come halfway across the country to save my children?"

"I was a willing vessel. That's it. You hear that little steel voice in your ear, you hear it, and you know. You know. That's that, you know."

* * *

When Danny first told me this story about three weeks ago, I knew immediately that every word of it is as dependable as a baby's first breath surely is a gift of God. And I knew that telling this story might enable the door to open to the vault wherein lies someone's shackled heart. Danny and I both agree that if it could reach just one lost soul, just one human who maybe has never heard that "little steel voice" in their ear, it would be worth the risk.

What risk, you ask?

The risk that skeptics will surely attack with the very predictable speculation: So, just because a few circumstances puts somebody in the middle of an accident (in this case, a tragedy) about to happen, you're telling me a great spirit somewhere you call God manipulated events so the cowboy in the white hat shows up and saves the day?

Well, my dear skeptics, you tell me.

When was the last time you sat at your desk pondering over things, and you hesitated for a second, and you thought, "Is it really … can it really be?"

And then you thought, "Well maybe…"

No, you didn't think "Well maybe …"

You knew, you knew, that's that, you knew.

Gary H. Baker, Edgewood, Tennessee September 14, 2017

About The Author

GARY H. BAKER grew up in Louisville, Kentucky and is proud to claim his status as an "original baby boomer". The class of '46 was just that, and it marched off into the 60's as a force to be reckoned with. While some protested, and some sought peace and love, Gary did a four-year enlistment in the Navy and pulled a tour of duty off the coast of Vietnam. He later earned an undergraduate degree from the University of Hawaii and a master's degree in alternative education from Indiana University. Along the way Gary worked as a bouncer, bartender, teacher, coach, coffee salesman, insurance salesman, financial services broker, lawn care business owner, and truck driver, Gary currently calls himself a novelist.

In 1986, Gary ran and walked two thousand seven hundred miles in four months to promote the Just Say No clubs, the forerunner to DARE (Drug Abuse Resistance Education). Gary sees his writing as an attempt to follow God. Jesus is his Savior, and Gary will tell you quickly that he falls short most of the time, but that won't keep him from trying again.